Praise for Stephen Mertz

HANK & MUDDY

"A terrific novel! One of my favorite writers . . . a born
storyteller . . . Enjoy!"
—Max Allan Collins, author of *Road to Perdition*

THE KOREAN INTERCEPT

"An adrenaline rush!" —*Booklist*

NIGHTWIND

"Fast-paced...chills and thrills!" —*Booklist*

DEVIL CREEK

"A quality read! Excellent!" —BookReview.com

And more . . .

"Stephen Mertz writes a hard-edged, fast-paced thriller for those
who like their tales straight and sharp."
—Joe R. Lansdale, Edgar Award winning author
of *A Fine Dark Line*

"Stephen Mertz just keeps on getting better, each novel more
dazzling in story and style."
—Ed Gorman, author of *Save the Last Dance for Me*

Books *by* Stephen Mertz

HANK & MUDDY
THE KOREAN INTERCEPT
NIGHTWIND
DEVIL CREEK
DRAGON GAMES
FADE TO TOMORROW

HANK
&
MUDDY

a novel

Stephen Mertz

PERFECT CRIME BOOKS

Printed in the United States of America.

Perfect Crime Books™ is a registered Trademark.

Author Photograph: Sharon Holnback

This book is a work of fiction. The characters, entities and institutions are products of the Author's imagination and do not refer to actual persons, entities, or institutions.

Library of Congress Cataloging-in-Publication Data
Mertz, Stephen
Hank & Muddy / Stephen Mertz
ISBN: 978-1-935797-13-5

First Edition: August 2011

For
David "Kidd Squidd" Squires,
brother from another mother
&
musicologist extraordinaire

Prologue

It's two a.m., and we're rocking. Smoking. Tearing the place up. Ain't nobody in Chicago can throw it down like The Muddy Waters Band.

It's a Friday night and The Club Zanzibar is packed. Thirteenth and Ashland, on the West Side. There's a low ceiling with booths along one wall and a bar on the other, with a mess of tables between the stage and what they call a dance floor that's nothing more than a little space near the end of the bar where people can shake when the music moves them. And right now we're giving them something to shake it to.

The cigarette smoke is so thick you can't hardly see past the front tables, but that's all right because at those front tables ain't nothing but parties of pretty women, crazy chicks hanging on every word when I sing them deep blues and squealing like crazy on the up-tempo numbers like the one we're doing now, "Baby Please Don't Go."

I look over my shoulder and give Walter the nod, and he takes another ride. What us musicians call a ride, you call a solo. And man, there ain't nobody can blow a solo on that harp like Little Walter. And he's serving up some good stuff tonight. Walter throws everything he's got into every note he plays, cupping his harp—his harmonica--against the microphone, standing there with his elbows out, his heels together and his spine bowed back, making that Mississippi saxophone wail. Swooping. Whooping. Crying. Punchy tones pour from his amp, wailing over the drums and the electric guitars. Ain't nobody ever blowed the harp like Walter. The boy invented a whole new way of playing that fatback amplified harmonica.

We are burning.

They call me Muddy "Mississippi" Waters and I'm as restless, man, as the deep blue sea. I'm the mannish boy. The rollin' stone. I am the hootchie koochie man.

I was born McKinley Morganfield but my grandmother named me Muddy Waters and the name stuck. Fact of the business, I can't recall anybody ever addressing me as McKinley, or as Mr. Morganfield. Except for my doctors and them kind of people after I took sick. I'm through with them now. I told 'em. No more of that radiation stuff. They already took out one of my lungs. That's right. I've been under the knife even if no one knows about it. Haven't even told my own son, so you know I'm keeping this in my pocket.

Walter finishes his ride. His harp playing is driving the band like a hurricane.

My drummer, Elgin Evans, he's older than the rest of us. A portly guy. Looks like a judge, perched back there behind his kit. He'd rather be playing jazz. I know that. But he rocks solid when he's playing behind me. And there's Jimmy Rogers, holding it together there on the bandstand with his guitar playing right alongside mine. It was Jimmy taught me to keep time on guitar and more chords when I first come to Chicago. And he's been playing that guitar tonight until it's smokin'.

Sometimes these days my mind gets to rambling like the wild geese in the west. Didn't used to be that way. I reckon that's part of dying. After living on the road for forty years, it's peculiar waking up in my own bed every morning. I'm glad to be home. But in my mind, Lord in my mind I live in the past.

We're young and hungry like wolves on the prowl, playing our asses off in joints like the Zanzibar and hitting what they call the chitlin circuit, touring small towns in the deep south like Helena, Clarksdale, Shelby, Boyle, all them little delta towns.

Had me everything I needed. A family at home in a big old brick house on the South Side, where seemed like every bluesman in the world dropped by to swap licks and nip whiskey. Man, we had to work just to slow down long enough to catch a nap and grab a meal, and then we be off hitting it again. The music felt good as the loving. I was traveling and making money, playing for the people. And the ladies always did go for my line of jive.

Naturally enough, though, it was not always smooth sailing.

Chapter 1

Crowley, Louisiana
July, 1952

"Goddamn, there's a nigger in my house!"
Soon as I heard that, I knew I was in trouble.

It was hot. Hot and steamy. A sweaty night.

The sound of that man's voice thundered through the house, and shoe leather came pounding up the stairs outside the bedroom door.

This white woman and me, we were working up a sweat between the sheets. Reckon that tells you how much I love that stuff. I was risking my life for it. All of a sudden it sounded like I was about to *lose* my life.

It was a big bedroom, fancy, with soft lighting and pictures and such on the walls. Nice wallpaper, roses on vines that twisted from the high ceiling to a polished wood floor. A white folks' bedroom. A big moon was shining through the trees and the shadows from the branches made bars across the bed, like we were making love in a cage.

There wasn't nothing fancy about the way this white gal had her ankles locked together behind my back to keep me coming on strong while I did her, hard and fast. She was beating at my bare back with her little white fists. We'd been going at it heavy for close to an hour. She'd wanted to squall but she was risking her life too and she couldn't afford to make any noise, so her pearly teeth were chomping into my shoulder to keep herself quiet, biting me deep, breaking my skin and that almost made me shout out. But I kept my love sounds low, working my show, riding that woman like my back didn't have no bone.

Right now though, at the sound of a man running up the stairs, this gal and me parted like dogs splashed with cold water. She scampered across the bed away from me, grabbing the sheets up around her titties. I scrambled for my clothes, gauging the distance to the open window that overlooked the front porch.

She was a big-hipped blonde mama, about twenty-three with restless, wild eyes. She had something would make a preacher lay his Bible down. She'd been waiting for me out back in a two-year-old Ford coupe at 3:30 in the morning, parked near the stage door after everyone else had gone home.

Whites didn't go into the kinds of places I played in those days. I was working a tour with John Lee Hooker. One nighters. I wasn't too crazy on being down South in the summer, which is hot enough in Chicago. But I was getting records on the charts and heavy airplay on the colored stations, so a DJ named Groove Boy had booked us for a month around Louisiana.

This gal brought me home. Said her stepdaughter was gone visiting overnight and her husband was out of town. A lot of women in those clubs wanted a private performance from Muddy Waters.

I moved so fast, I was a chocolate blur. I tugged up my pants. My mind was racing like a squirrel up a tree. Did I have time to grab my shoes and socks and my shirt and jacket?

The pounding shoe leather came to a stop right outside the bedroom door and the man started twisting and turning the doorknob.

"Margie! Margie, I know what you're doing, goddammit!"

I decided, *No time for anything but that window.*

Margie was staring at me from over the sheets as if seeing me for the first time, as if I had seven heads. Her face was a mask of fear.

"It's my husband! I thought he was on duty!"

"On duty?" I said. "Oh, shit."

The hell with my threads and shoes. My best pair of alligators, too. But I was good as dead unless I made that window. I poked one leg through, pushed out and looked back at her.

"So long, sugar."

Then she started screaming. "In here, Jerry! Oh my God. He raped me! He raped me!"

The door burst in off its hinges from a kick and the doorway framed a big man in a khaki police officer's uniform. He had a narrow, pock-marked, mean face, wore a cap with a visor, and held a long-barreled .44 which he aimed straight at my head.

"Hold it right there, nigger."

That gun muzzle looked big enough to drive a truck into.

I couldn't run, and it wasn't in me to beg. I ain't built that way. The way I had it figured, he could have already shot me dead if he'd had a mind to. Since he hadn't, maybe I had a chance at finding a trick card to play, to get out of this alive. I eased back into the room and stood there in nothing but my slacks.

The rest of my clothes were scattered next to the bed. *His* bed.

Margie's face was red and she was stabbing a finger at me.

"Kill him, Jerry! The nigger raped me! You know I would never—"

He held his pistol on me but he spoke to her. "I don't know any such thing, you nigger-loving whore." He spat onto their nice carpet. "I know what's been going on. This buck ain't the first, damn your soul. You think you can hide something like what you've been up to in a town the size of Crowley, with me on the goddamn police force?"

Margie had forgotten all about covering her titties. She wasn't modest anymore, kneeling at the edge of the bed with her hands clasped and held up before her like a woman praying in church.

"Jerry, Jerry, it's not what you think. I swear. Don't do anything crazy!"

"You've been chasing dark meat while I've been working to support your worthless ass. I heard rumors, so I staked out my own house, by God. I followed you when you dropped Jen off at her friends. By God, I've been letting a nigger-loving slut raise my baby!"

"Jerry, please—"

"Killing ain't good enough for you. I ought to turn you over to my boys in the Klan, see how long it takes them to kill you and they'd have fun doing it, too."

While I listened to this, I was thinking, *This is good.* Long as this crazy cracker is raising sand with his woman, I'm buying time, looking for a way to play my trick card.

Tears streamed down Margie's face and she was jabbering like a crazy woman. "Jerry, don't hurt me. I swear to God this nigger broke in here. He raped me!"

"What about it, nigger?"

I'd been hoping that he wasn't going ask me any questions straight-out.

Best I could manage was, "Sir, I just want to get gone."

"I'll bet you do." He laughed and it sounded like a hiccup. "I'll deal with you when I'm done killing this cheating whore I married. As for you, nigger, I'm making a call to the Grand Wizard, and Crowley's going to have itself a lynching, yes sir. Ain't been a lynching in these parts in three years. Ain't that so, Margie?"

"Oh, Jerry. Please, kill him after what he did. Don't hurt *me*. I'm your wife!"

She commenced weeping into her hands. Her shoulders were shuddering like she had the chills and her titties swayed back and forth beneath her, looking round and firm.

Damn. I got my mind back on business.

But her husband had seen the direction my eyes were looking in.

"She's good, ain't she, boy?" A sneer slithered from him like a snake. "And you know what? I'm going to tell my captain and the newspaper fellas when they show up that you did rape her. I'll tell 'em that you took my gun from me and killed her with it before I wrestled you down and got my gun back and got the drop on you."

His wife shrieked louder than before. "Jerry, *no!*"

He swung the gun on her. "I'll see you in hell, whore."

That's when a new voice cried out from the doorway.

"Daddy, *don't!*"

We jerked our eyes in that direction.

A girl stood there. She was nineteen years old. She had natural blond hair, tied back into a ponytail. She wore dungarees. She was bare-shouldered and I remembered that her shoulders had freckles, though I could not see her freckles in this lighting and all the excitement. Her body was tense. She had drawn the back of one hand up to her mouth and her eyes were wide like saucers.

She dashed into the bedroom.

Jerry lowered his gun. His expression went from insane rage to confusion. "Jenny, what the hell? You're not supposed to be here."

"Daddy, please don't do this!"

The woman on the bed got a real strange expression on her face, not crying and pleading anymore like she had been but glaring, staring bullets at the girl.

I was holding my breath. I wasn't sure if things had just gotten better or worse.

Jerry looked from his wife to his daughter. He lowered the pistol so it was aimed at the floor. He looked like a man torn apart inside. His brow was all knitted up. He took a deep breath.

"All right, I'll spare your mama. There are things no child should see." Then he perked up some and started to shift his eyes and his gun in my direction. "But I'm killing me somebody for what happened tonight." His voice was climbing like a roller coaster hitting the top.

The window, I thought. I had to try again for the window. I'd never make it, but—

The girl threw herself at me with her arms flung open wide. She yelled at her father, "Kill that bitch you married if you want to! I don't care. But don't be killing Muddy. I *love* him!"

Little Jenny had a layer of baby fat but every ounce was right in place. She had a woman's figure. Rolling hips. A healthy bosom that heaved under her jumper.

I reached out and caught her by one wrist and I jerked her to me, not being gentle about it, twisting her around so she bumped against me hard and I held her against me with one of her hands held behind her back and my other arm under her chin.

She didn't fight me.

Jerry looked like his face wanted to tug in every direction at once. "Let her go, you coon son of a bitch." What was happening was slowly sinking into his peckerwood brain. His jaw hung slack. "Good God, daughter, do you mean to tell me that you served it up to this . . . *Muddy?*"

The girl gave her fanny a little push against my slacks.

"Your wife's jealous because Muddy slept with me first, *last* night. I was hanging outside that joint in colored town and she knows because she followed me. When Muddy came out and I talked to him, she liked what she saw and went down there tonight. At least I'm not married!"

Jerry was whiter than he had been. His eyes looked like he was dead drunk. "Huh?"

Margie started choking like she'd swallowed a chicken bone. "I was just keeping an eye on you, you lying little piece of garbage!"

Jenny laughed. She sounded high as a kite. "Jealous, jealous, jealous!"

"Stop it," Jerry yelled at them both. "How do you know this . . . this Muddy?" he asked his daughter.

Jenny gave my arm a squeeze.

"My friends and me, we have all Muddy's records. We listen to 'em when you parents ain't around. Muddy's got that . . . I don't know, that certain *something.*" She gave an extra twitch to her rear end, flush against the front of my slacks. "Ooh, Muddy."

Jerry's eyes looked at the floor. "I ought to kill y'all and myself too. My head hurts."

Then our attention was rattled again.

A car was approaching the house, coming fast.

I recognized the way the driver was downshifting, and the *ka-thump!* of a front tire bumping up over the curb out front told me I was right. That was Little Walter behind the wheel, showing up like the cavalry in a cowboy movie. I'd just been handed my trick card, so I played it.

I said, more to myself more than to them, "Man, I got to learn to leave this white stuff alone."

I let Jenny go and sent her away with a shove that bowled her into both her father and her stepmother before either of them could get out of the way. All three toppled like bowling pins to the bedroom floor, making a tangle of limbs and confused shouting.

I thought for half a second about taking the gun away from Jerry, but the best thing for a man of my race to do in the South— or likely anywhere else, I expect—is when you see a white man with a gun, move quick away from him, not at him.

You would have thought I was Jesse Owens, the way I hurled myself at the window. On my way I dipped low to scoop up my shoes. I was crazy about those alligator shoes. I went through the window without touching the frame and hit the slanting roof of the porch with a shoulder and rolled once, twice, across shingles that scraped at my skin. Then I was flying through the air, falling off the roof. It wasn't much of a drop, but enough for me to twist my body as I fell. I landed on both feet. A man has to stay in shape if he's working on stage every night. I do a lot of strutting and shouting when I entertain the people. My leg muscles are in good shape. So when I landed, my knees bent natural-like to cushion me.

I was in the middle of their front yard. Moonlight was touching everything, giving the world a silver glow. It was a neighborhood of white folks' homes, two-story brick houses and wooden-frame places. The houses on this residential street looked like they were asleep. Somewhere a dog was baying at the moon. But this house was the only one where anything was going on.

Jerry's cussing carried down to me. A woman screamed. I couldn't tell if it was Margie or Jenny.

My '51 fire-engine-red Cadillac was waiting, the engine idling, the headlights on, and a front tire over the curb.

Little Walter rolled down his window grinned out at me from behind the steering wheel. His eyes gleamed in the moonlight like there was a light bulb inside his head.

"Hope you ain't sore about me driving the boat, Muddy."

I leaned against the trunk just long enough to slip into my shoes, no socks. "How'd you know where I was?"

"That little blond girl I seen you with after the gig last night, she come by the hotel tonight looking for you and way she tore out fast after I told her about the gal you was with tonight, like she knew who I was talking about. I knew there was going to be trouble. I trailed her here"

"You alone?"

The rear door of the Cad opened and John Lee Hooker got out, holding the door for me like a doorman. Hooker was small-shouldered, a bantam-weight cat, which I always thought was funny when I heard that that big black snake moan of his, layin' down records like *Boogie Chillen*. Hooker liked to wear dark colors and I hardly saw him even with the Cad's dome light pouring out.

He said, "Y-y-you'd better get a m-move on, Muddy."

Ain't nobody growls the blues deeper than John Lee. Funny thing, he's got a real quiet speaking voice and you'd never know from listening to his records that he has a stutter. That's right. The stutter gets worse when he's excited, like now. But it's always there except when he's singing or pitching jive at a chick.

I tossed a look over my shoulder.

Jerry was leaning out of the bedroom window. It looked like he was waving goodbye at us until I saw that he was wrestling with Margie and Jenny, two to one. His gun arm was waving around because he was trying to aim at me and they were trying to stop him.

One of the women cried out, "Go, Muddy, go!" Again I couldn't tell which one.

Jerry was yelling too. He'd recovered from his shock of a few minutes ago. "Goddamn niggers! I'll track you down to the ends of the earth and kill every one of you!"

He fired. The gunshot sounded extra loud because the night was so quiet. The muzzle flash was orange-yellow. I heard the bullet whistle past above our heads and I know John Lee heard it too because he went from acting like a doorman to beating me into the car. I leaped into the backseat after him.

Another shot rang out and this time the bullet went *ker-plunk!* into the Cad's chassis.

Hooker and I crouched down low.

I shouted at Walter, "Go, man!"

Walter howled like a crazy mixed-up kid. Whiskey fumes were heavy inside the car, and I knew Hooker was a teetotaler. Then my eardrums were hammered by the thunder of three gunshots—one, two, three; *boom!-boom!-boom!*—that sounded like Walter was firing off his pistol inside my head.

Breaking glass from the house. No return fire.

I never saw John Lee so agitated. "Walter, you c-crazy!"

I stretched forward from the backseat and placed a hand on Walter's shoulder. I'm the only one can talk to him when he gets crazy. "Cool down, man. The cat has a wife and child in that house."

Walter had been firing from his left hand, without bothering to aim. He lowered the pistol and rested its grip on the doorframe. "Some child. I wouldn't mind babysitting that little girl."

He raised a silver flask to his lips for a long draw.

I nabbed the flask from his fingers and snapped the lid shut. "Drive, boy, or I'll kick your ass out of my car and drive my own damn self."

Hooker said, "D-d-do what Muddy say."

Walter brought the gun into the car and rested it across his lap. "Aw, all right."

The Cad tore away, leaving twin strips of burned rubber on the pavement, filling the night with a loud squeal and a white cloud.

I turned to look out through the rear windshield. Three people ran into the street in front of the house: Jerry and his daughter and his wife, who had thrown on a robe. Jerry was stamping about and waving his gun in the air, shouting after us. The females looked like they were shouting at him. Jerry looked like he wanted to fire some rounds at us and maybe at them too. Porch lights were flicking on up and down the street. Neighbors were being brought to their windows and porches.

Blind mad as he was, Jerry held his fire figuring, no doubt, that his life would be even more fucked up than it already was if he shot and killed an innocent bystander.

Walter took a corner so fast he almost rolled my Cad. After we rounded the corner, he slowed down some but not much.

Little Walter Jacobs was a compact-built fella with twenty-three years of nothing but hard living under his belt. Walter grew up living in the jukes, sleeping on pool tables, running errands for tips, sandwiches, or drinks. Seemed like the only two things Walter ever wanted was to get high and blow that harmonica.

He was laughing. "Shit, that was fun!" Gold in his teeth blinked in the passing streetlights. "Now can I have my whiskey?"

I tipped the flask to my lips and let the whiskey burn down my throat to warm me from the inside out. The night was hot, but now that we were clearing out, I had chills running through me. I emptied the flask before I handed it back to him.

"You can have some more when you're done driving my car."

Hooker was looking like a man who had just gotten sad news from home.

"That there was a police officer!" He was so shook up, he forgot to stutter. "He got the power to track us down!"

"We're cutting on out of this town tonight," I said, "soon as we get to the hotel, instead of tomorrow morning like we've been planning."

Hooker slumped back against the upholstery. "Won't do no good. How many red '51 Cadillacs with Illinois plates, full of spade musicians, you think be driving through Louisiana tomorrow? Damn!"

A moment of silence followed.

Walter went back to laughing like he was insane. He picked up his pistol while he kept driving. He gave the Cad some gas and started firing the gun off at the sky.

"Wahooo, y'all. They'll never take me alive!"

I put my head back and closed my eyes, and you know what?

I was laughing too.

Chapter 2

My name is Hiram. Hiram Williams. Course, everybody calls me Hank and that's most likely how you know me. That's right. I'm Hank Williams.

I'm the man who wrote and recorded "I'm So Lonesome I Could Cry," "Hey Good Lookin'," "Jambalaya," "Kaw-Liga" and a whole mess of songs I bet you know every word to. You and your friends sing along with them songs every time they come on the radio or the jukebox. They call me the Hillbilly Shakespeare. Pretty fancy for a feller can only read a comic book and that's if he puts his mind to it. They call me that because it's not just hillbillies like the way I sing. Seems like everybody in the world loves ol' Hank.

Except ol' Hank. Me, I've been doing some mighty hard traveling lately on that lonesome highway.

This story I'm fixing to tell you—well, my side of the

story, anyway—it really happened. The reason I'm writing it down is because, for all the mess I got into, now that's it's over and done, seems like it was real exciting in a way, like a cowboy movie with some cops and robbers tossed in. It got to be like the Wild West except it all happened right down home in and around Shreveport.

I don't want to spend too much time talking about me. If you haven't got wind of the state my career is in by reading the newspapers, by now I reckon you'll get the idea quick enough once I start writing down what happened. But I'll put it in a nutshell before I proceed. The newspapers call me a drunk and a no-show. Everybody and his country cousin knows that ol' Hank's been barely hanging on to the drop-edge of yonder for some time. But it's worse than they know.

I'm having considerable trouble these days getting new songs to come out of me, the way they used to like ripe pears falling off a tree. Oh, I still carry this notebook with me everywhere I go, just like a schoolboy. But the thing is, I haven't been able to finish off writing a complete song in quite a spell.

I aim to try something different by writing down what happened. I don't know as I'll ever show this to anybody and after I'm gone, should somebody find it, they most likely won't believe a word. But it's the gospel, every word I'm setting down. Maybe if I can get my words to come out right this way, the songs will start coming to me again. I aim to write down everything I remember. That ought to take my mind off the other troubles I'm having. Then I'll write new songs and polish up the ones I've started. That's how it will be. I'm not accustomed to taking pen in hand like this. This is sort of like writing a letter.

Anyhow, something crazy happened a few weeks back. Looking back on it now, I figure there's a damn sight more to it than I could ever put in one song or into a whole damn album. I'll try to write this down fast during every spare minute I can find, because that's the way it happened. White-hot fast and crazy, and there was violence too.

This colored fella, the blues singer you may have heard of named Muddy Waters and me we nearly lost our lives.

Here's how it happened.

For me, I reckon we ought to pick it up that afternoon when I first got off the train in Shreveport.

A pair of colored porters were assisting me from my compartment, holding and guiding me with my arms draped over their shoulders. My boots were dragging, and it was no cakewalk navigating me down the narrow corridor.

A portly conductor who was all red in the face, very solicitous of me, led us. He oversaw the porters like they were mules hauling valuable cargo.

"Snap it up, boys. Step aside, folks, if you please."

I heard someone say, "Why there's Hank Williams and he's drunk as a skunk," and folks commenced to twittering behind their hands.

We reached the steps at the rear of the car and I was mostly carried down to an upright position on the platform, still balanced between the porters.

One of them said, "Come on, Mister Hank. Everything going to be all right."

"Sure 'nuff," said the other. "You're back home with your people now, Mister Williams, suh."

There was considerable good cheer between the porters and the white conductor, as if I was the black sheep of their family and they held a long-suffering affection for me. That sort of put them in the same family, if they thought about it. Naturally, they didn't think about it.

I wasn't doing too good a job of thinking, either. I was wobbling half-in and half-out of consciousness. Truth is, unconscious was still holding the upper hand, although I was starting to come around from the hangover I'd been sleeping off on the train. My cross-country trip from Los Angeles—from Hollywood—had come to an end.

It was a hot, humid day. Thunderheads, black as lumps of coal, were gathering in a pale sky. I recognized smells and sounds drifting over from the port. That brought me around some more.

Audrey and Ma were there on the platform, waiting for me.

Ma looked stern and threatening like she always did. She reminded me of that wooden Indian I wrote the song about. Ma is fifty-three years old and you can tell from her face that those years were hard. She's a big, brawny, rough-hewn woman. She was wearing a plain lawn-green summer dress that draped from her like a tent. I've seen my mother whup ass good in many a bar room brawl and I'm talking full-growed men. Anyone who knows Lillie

Williams knows better than to get her peeved. Salty ain't the word. And she was looking right salty at that moment.

The sight of Ma standing there next to Audrey sobered me like a bucket of ice water thrown on me.

Audrey's green eyes looked like the shiny tips of arrows that wanted to pierce me. When I looked into those eyes, the surrounding commotion of the depot—the hissing of steam from trains, people hurrying, garbled announcements across the PA about departures and arrivals, redcaps and luggage wagons and the shouting of railroad men and the hawkers, folks saying hello or goodbye—everything got pushed into the background like it always did ever since the first day that I'd set my eyes on her. Her hair fell like a copper-red waterfall onto her bare shoulders. She wore heels and a bright, tight, thin yellow summer dress that was cut low at the top and high at the bottom. Audrey has gorgeous legs.

"Well well," she said. "The useless wandering son has returned."

With Ma and Miss Audrey, I don't rightly know who to be more scared of. I straightened myself and shook off the redcaps.

"All right, all right, let go of me. I ain't no cripple."

I'd tipped them each ten bucks. Or maybe it was more, judging by how merry they were. I don't recollect. They thanked me plenty and looked glad to get back on the train.

Ma said, "Hank, we've been worried to death about you. I even called Minnie Pearl because I know you and her are best friends, and even she didn't know what happened to you after you left that Hollywood producer's office."

"They were rascals, Ma, them slickers out west, just like everyone else lining up to steal a piece off of me."

Audrey said, "You make it sound like the hardest thing in the world, traveling with a honky tonk band and writing songs. They were going to put you in the movies, Hank. That's why you went out there."

"Shucks," I said. "I felt like going to California anyhow. Played me some club dates and a couple of fairs. Ol' Hank had him some fun in the sun, I guarantee you. Only reason I kept that appointment with that producer was because you wouldn't stop riding me about it. Shoot, I'm no movie star. And it *is* hard work doing what I do, Audrey." I gave her a little grin. "You ought to know."

I thought that jape might shush her up a spell.

Audrey wants to be a music star in her own right, not just as the wife of the famous Hank Williams. She wants to be the female Hank Williams. Well, she's got the looks all right, makes the boys whistle when she walks by, just like I put in that song. But as for personality, well, Audrey can make vinegar taste sweet when she's got a burr under her saddle. She can't find any serious musicians to work with her. She has trouble singing harmony, much less carrying a tune on her own. But that mule-headed woman honestly believes that she is the greatest female country singer in history.

If I was aiming to turn her damper down, I accomplished the opposite and only stoked the fires.

"What I *know*," she said, tart as grandma's lemon pie, "is that while your mama was talking to Minnie Pearl, I was having a conversation with Mister Fred Rose. I know exactly what happened in that movie producer's office because that man called Mister Rose, cussed him out, and then Mister Rose called me."

Fred Rose is my manager. Or he had been. We've been on the outs lately. That's part of the trouble I referred to, and I take responsibility for it. It's my fault. Fred Rose is the one man on Earth I'm closest to. He's the main cog in the whole Nashville music business. I call him Pappy. I'm ashamed to admit that I may have tried his patience beyond the point of endurance with my personal and professional troubles. These days Pappy tells everyone that he won't have anything more to do with Hank Williams.

Ma cast a cool glance Audrey's way. "Cut my boy some slack. Minnie Pearl is a fine Christian woman, and her and her husband love Hank. Don't be acting high and mighty, Missy, just because you've got the ear of some Yankee."

Audrey kept hammering on me. "You showed up at that producer's office acting drunk and surly and you wouldn't even speak civilized to him. All you did was mumble and grunt and act cocky while he tried to be polite and tell you about the screen test they had for you. But, no, not you, not Mister Bigshot Hank Williams." She turned on my mother. "I told you what he did, Lillie. Your son pulled his hat down over his eyes and put his boots up on that man's desk! They ordered him out."

I couldn't look either one of them in the eye. I felt knotted up inside. "I told you, Audrey. I didn't want to be in that fella's office in the first place."

She sniffed. "Seems like you don't want to be much of anywhere except in that dream world you live in. Look at you. Drunk in public and I'll bet you've got enough dope in you to kill a mule."

Ma growled like a woke-up mama lion. "Cut that talk, girl. There's people might overhear you and we've already got enough trouble. Let's get out of here."

Audrey drew her back straight. "Oh. So it's okay for your drunken son to fall down in public but it's not okay for me to talk about it?"

I reached around with one hand and gave my neck a good scratching while I looked at my feet. I didn't want these two scrapping. That always gets my nerves going. I do believe my wife and my mother enjoy the challenge of bucking each other over me. They've been doing it since Audrey and me got hitched in '44. They like quarreling between themselves every bit as much as they like picking on you know who.

I said, "I don't take nothing but medicine for my back pains."

Audrey sniffed again. She was looking down her nose at me.

"We sent you to up north to Pennsylvania for a week last year to that over-priced hospital so they could operate on you and fix that worthless spine of yours."

"Well, it didn't take. I still need my medicine. And what the dickens was I supposed to do," I said, "all on my lonesome on a long train ride? I drank to soothe my nerves, is all." I nodded in the direction taken by the conductor and the porters. "Them fellas was helping me over because I overslept and I was groggy."

Audrey said, "Hank, you're a fool."

Ma said, "Son, you need to pull yourself out of this hole you're in and get back to performing. There's Lycrecia and Hank Junior, your little Bocephus to consider. You should be writing songs and performing to provide for your children."

Audrey made a rude, unladylike sound. "He needs to check himself back into a hospital, this time to dry out." She spoke like I wasn't there. "Your son's an alcoholic and a drug addict, Lillie, and everything he touches turns to shit, including our marriage."

An angry rattlesnake lives curled up inside of me. It started to hiss and uncoiled to strike.

I said, "You ought to know about hospitals. Our two young ones at home and you out whoring around so much, you land in a hospital last month for an abortion, not because you was sick like everyone said."

Ma said something but all I could hear were the words spitting from Audrey's scarlet mouth, curled in a snarl.

"Those are filthy lies." Her fingers curled like claws. "I was a good wife to you."

"Ha."

Ma looked around. There didn't appear to be anyone within earshot. "Knock it off, you two."

Audrey kept right on snarling. "You're the one who's been whoring around, Hank, you tomcat, though what those chippies see in a broken down alky like you is beyond me."

I leered. "I reckon I'm still Hank Williams."

She made a face. "You can say that again. You've got that girl Bobbie up in Nashville two months pregnant, and you're shacked up right here in Shreveport with that little tramp Billie Jean. I know what's going on. You don't even try to keep secrets, damn you. Everyone in the music business knows what a fool you're making of yourself."

"Aw hon, you're just jealous is all because you know you're never going to warm ol' Hank's bed again but there's plenty others who are glad for the opportunity. That little tramp you're talking about just might be the next Mrs. Williams, so what do you think about that? Yeah, I'm doing all right for myself."

"Oh, you're doing great," said Audrey. "That's why your mother and your soon to be ex-wife are the only people left in the world who've got the stomach to meet you at a train station and be seen in public with you."

Several train cars along, the conductor shouted out, *"All aboard!"*

Most passengers were already onboard, and everyone who'd arrived on my train had already left by now, so we had the platform pretty much to ourselves.

The engineer tooted a couple of long blasts on the whistle. Funny thing about that train whistle. It sounded as lonesome there in the terminal as it would have going across a trestle under a full moon on the delta. A train whistle does something to me. There was more train noise and the train left the station, causing enough racket to buy me a few seconds of think time.

Audrey was right, naturally. Audrey is always right, and I'm not being sarcastic. It's why I let her run my business back when things were good between us in the '40's. Lord knows she tried to keep me sober. Audrey raised our children and was a good wife most of the time. She tried to make me act responsible. Lord, she tried. But I'm a wild horse that can't be rode and the more right she was, the more I went out of my way to show her how godawful bad I could be. Doesn't make a lick of sense to me, either. But that's what happened between us. And when I thought about it, I thought about how much this woman loved me. Dang if those old feelings for her didn't wash through me once again.

When the train had left the station, taking its noise with it, I took my hat in my hands.

"Audrey, I'm fixing to say something that might amaze you. But well, shoot girl, you're the mother of my children. I know I don't deserve one more chance with you, darling, but if you could find it in your heart to forgive me and give ol' Hank—I mean, give *us* — one more try, well, doggone it, you know I love you, Audrey."

"I know that, Hank. But forget it. That will never happen."

A powerful hurt welled up inside me, and I knew for sure that I wasn't drunk anymore.

"Audrey, you know you're the one."

"Yes, Hank, I know that. I am the one for you. You'll never find a woman to love you like I did."

Ma stepped forward. "I'll love Hank until my dying breath. And after that I'll love him from the hereafter. You'll never go unloved, son."

"He will as far as I'm concerned," said Audrey. She crossed her arms before her like she was protecting herself. "Hank, you know well as I do that way too much has happened between us for this to end in any way but in a divorce. I was scared for my life that day I came home to move out the children. When we were leaving I heard gunfire. Gunfire!"

"You heard no such thing."

"I surely did. I told it in my court deposition. Were you trying to work up nerve to kill yourself, or were you shooting at me and the kids?"

"Hon, that's plumb crazy. You know I'd never do a thing to harm our babies."

"All I know is that *you're* crazy, Hank. Our kids are going to have a proper upbringing, and you're going to pay to support us."

Anger welled up and washed away the old feelings.

"Am I going to pay for your stud service you too? You're supposed to be providing our young 'uns with a healthy environment but you can't because you're nothing but a born tramp."

Ma said, "Both of you, stop it! That's enough of that.   Son, Audrey's right about your duty as a man. You've got to get interested in your career again, son. The way you treated them movie people out in Hollywood, maybe they were slickers but they could have made you piles and piles of money. And you've been misbehaving onstage when you do bother to show up at all. That's what Mr. Rose said. You've been cussing out people from the stage."

"Only when they're booing me and heckling me."

Ma put a beefy hand on my shoulder. "Hank, it ain't right the way you're acting. You've got to straighten up."

I said, "I need me a vacation. Ma, this show business is eating me up alive. I need to go hunting and fishing."

Audrey sighed like she was in a stage play.

"Forget it, Lillie," and to me she said, "God help you, Hank, you poor, sad, twisted lovable fuck."

People were starting to meander onto the platform for the next train that was due in and shortly we would lose our privacy.

Ma said, "Damn it, Audrey, I said that's enough. Hank, get your bags. I've got a taxi waiting. We're getting the hell out of here."

I said, "I ain't riding nowhere with this she-lion. Damn you, Audrey."

"Goddamn you, Hank."

"Well, I've had enough of this," said Ma. "Y'all can stay here and squabble or come with me, but I'm through palaverin' in public."

She lumbered off like a burly bear in a summer dress, which I reckon is exactly what she was.

I looked at Audrey and she looked at me. It was one of those times when time sort of freezes in your mind. But I guess we'd said all we had to say. Enough damage had been done. I didn't know whether to beg her to take me back, or beg her to get out of my sight.

She made up her mind about something. She flounced off and stalked off after Ma. Her heels made an angry clacking sound on the platform. Audrey and Ma disappeared through an archway, into the depot.

There came the noise and commotion of another train chugging into the station.

I picked up my valise and ambled into the depot, where the humidity made you feel like you were in a steam bath.

There was no sign of Ma or Audrey. They must have been moving right smart and were already gone. People were sweating and moving about like they were half-asleep. The shuffle of shoe leather on the marble floor echoed from the ceiling, and you could hear random snatches of drowsy conversations.

I crossed to the line of phone booths, behind a half dozen rows of wooden benches, and squeezed into one of the cubicles, which was rank with the b.o. of its last occupant. I fed a nickel into the pay phone and dialed a number from memory. While it rang on the other end, my insides became knotted up and I realized that I was holding my breath.

"Hello?"

How can the sound of a woman's voice change while she's saying one word? I don't know. Billie Jean has a voice as pretty as she is and even across the telephone line, her voice sounded like she was harmonizing with herself. It was that sweet to my ears.

"It's me, hon. Your ol' Hank's back in town."

"Hank!" She sounded fresh and breezy. "Sweetie, if you'd only called and told me what train you were due in on, I'd have been down to meet you."

My stomach muscles relaxed and my breath came out in a long, wheezing sigh.

"Had me some things to take care of," I said. The closeness of the booth and the stink of b.o. were getting worse, and my skin was starting to itch. "Get your sweet self into one of the Cads and drive on down here to pick up poppa."

"You have been taking care of yourself and eating right, haven't you, hon? How did it go in California?" She was chirping like a cute chipmunk.

"We'll talk about that when you get here, bright eyes. Get moving now, will you, sugar? I got me a pair of arms that are lonesome as all get out and I'm wanting to hug you real close."

"Hank honey, I'm on my way. I'll look for you out front of the depot."

"Uh, you know, Billie Jean, I do believe I'll find myself a stool at the bar and grill inside here. Come on in and have one with me."

"No, Hank. Wait. Don't—"

I knew what she was going to say and I didn't want to hear it. I hung up on her just like that. I unfolded my frame from that smelly booth. My skin was getting itchier by the minute. I needed me a tall cold glass a beer and a shot of whiskey.

Chapter 3

Hank

I woke up in bed in a puddle of my own piss.

It was just turning from warm to cold. I found myself in that in-between world 'twixt sleep and being awake. I didn't know where the hell I was. I heard highway sounds. Nearby vehicles were whooshing past at a fair rate of speed.

The piss was still warm under me but was starting to chill at the edges. I sat up, cursing a blue streak. I swung my feet to the floor and stayed on the bed. I scooted away from what I had done. My cussing was interrupted by a hacking cough that made me feel like my lungs were going to explode. I coughed up phlegm and spat it on the floor.

I looked around. First thing I saw was my pack of Chesterfields next to an overflowing ashtray on a burn-scarred wooden nightstand. A pack of matches was under the cellophane of the cigarettes. I shook loose a coffin nail and the matches, stuck the butt in my mouth and fired her up. I inhaled deeply. The smoke caressed my lungs. I took a few more puffs and looked around some more.

No sign of Billie Jean. No sign of anyone. I was completely alone.

It was a shabby little cabin and right away I tumbled to the notion that I was in a motor court. They were starting to call them motels. The walls were off-brown. A picture of a horse in a field hung on the wall over the bed. A ratty rug was crooked on an unvarnished floor. A paint-chipped bureau with a cracked mirror was next to a love seat with mismatched cushions. A reading lamp was turned on. An archway showed a small kitchenette with a drop table opposite a sink where the faucet made a steady *drip-drip-drip*. The bathroom door was half-open, opposite the foot of the bed. The smell of piss hung heavy in the humid air.

Damn.

Damn damn *damn*.

When it happens, I don't know what to think. It's embarrassing, to put it mildly. Billie Jean knows about it because it happened once when I stayed overnight with her brother and his wife. It was brand new bedding and man, they were peeved at ol' Hank. "A goddamn alcoholic" was the least offensive thing they called me. Billie Jean pretends it doesn't happen, like it couldn't possibly happen to the great Hank Williams. But I can't help it. It never used to happen.

My clothes were on the floor in a heap on top of my boots, between the bed and a wall. My Western hat rested on its crown in a corner.

I fetched up my jacket and reached into the inside pocket. There was my flask. I uncorked it and took a quick eye-opener of white lightning. That brought on another coughing jag when that lightning struck. I coughed up black phlegm, looked around for something to spit at and sent a gob directed at a wastebasket full of beer cans. I missed and the gob struck the wall near the baseboard and clung there like a smoky pearl.

I corked the flask and set it on the nightstand. Bile rose in my throat. My guts started to churn. I sprang off the bed. I busted open the door to the head, fell onto my knees and grabbed both sides of a dirty commode. I started heaving involuntarily but nothing would come up, so I fell onto that nasty floor, curled up in a ball until the dry heaves went away.

When at last I could, I drew myself up by steadying myself using the sink. I turned on the cold water and bent my knees, stuck my face into the sink and I used both hands to splash myself again and again while the water got colder and colder. I turned off the water and raised my eyes to take a look in the mirror.

The eyes looking back at me weren't those of the dapper Hank Williams everybody knows from the publicity pictures. I'm only twenty-nine but the face staring back at me looked twenty years older; gaunt and pasty. Sunken, bloodshot eyes with purple bags underneath that could have belonged to some poor shell-shocked soldier just home from Korea. I blinked and the cobwebs started to clear inside my head but that face didn't change, so I looked away.

All right, Hank, I told myself. *You're in a cabin out on the highway somewhere and Billie Jean is nowhere to be found.*

I couldn't remember a thing after talking to her on the telephone from the station, after that scene with Ma and Audrey. After that . . . nothing.

These blackouts of mine are like the bed-wetting. I hate to admit it even to myself, but incidents of both increased ever since they canned my ass from the Opry. They said I was showing up drunk. Well, what if I was? I can sing my songs standing on my head, much less with a snootful. There are thousands—millions!—millions, of folks who tuned in to that show to hear Hank Williams sing them "Lovesick Blues." I'm a big star, and I was pulling the Grand Ole Opry up with me. Course, they didn't see it quite that way. I'd show up and except for a few of them like Minnie Pearl and Faron Young, that so-called "family" of country singers avoided speaking to me. They turned their backs when they saw me coming, and they weren't subtle about it. Jealous, those Nashville folks, that's what they are. And if they thought I'd been hitting the bottle before they fired me off the Opry, well, that's when I really took off. And that's when the blackouts started happening, maybe once or twice a month. I hadn't had one in more than a month, until this one. . . .

Looking around the dingy cabin, I put one foot in front of the other and crossed over to a window with a faded curtain. I eased the curtain aside and looked out.

It was dark. A gray trace of dusk was low to the west beneath coal-black clouds. It wasn't raining but a pink neon sign, blinking the word *Motel* with the *t* missing, was reflected on the rain-swept pavement. The lights of a liquor store shone from cross the street.

Ten or twelve cabins bordered three sides of a parking lot, which was about half-full of older model cars. Most of the cabins looked unoccupied. I didn't see either of my Cadillacs.

A couple was just getting situated in the cabin two down from mine. A middle-aged woman stood in the lighted doorway waiting for the man, a balding, heavyset guy in suspenders and shirtsleeves, as he went about locking his car door. They didn't have luggage. This place didn't feel like a family place; more like an out-of-town nest for lovebirds.

There was a telephone booth near the motel office.

I spent a short time cleansing myself, using the dirty wash cloth and towel at the bathroom sink. Then I put on my slacks, shirt and boots and took another slug from the flask. I thought about Billie Jean. I wondered how long it had been since I'd made that phone call to her from the station.

I walked over to the phone booth by the office and fed it a nickel and dialed Billie Jean.

There was a crack of lightning that briefly illuminated the parking lot. I didn't see anybody but I had the strangest sensation that someone was watching me.

Billie Jean answered on the second ring.

I said, "It's me, hon," and I barely recognized the croak of my own voice. I cleared my throat and spat phlegm.

"Hank, are you all right?" Her concern reached across the line like a warm embrace. "I've been worried sick about you. Where have you been?"

"Uh, before I get into that, sweetheart, uh, do you mind telling me what day it is?" My temples started pounding. "Was it this afternoon that I called you to come pick me up?" There was a long pause. I thought maybe we'd been disconnected. "Billie Jean, are you there, honey?"

"I'm here." The warmth in her voice was gone and the temperature had lowered by several thousand degrees. "Hank Williams, you've been off on a drunk." She sounded serious as a cop accusing a suspect in a triple homicide.

"Now listen, darling . . ." I wasn't sure what to say, so I tried again. "Uh, I reckon I'm a mite confused. Billie Jean, was it today that you came down to the station?"

A longer hesitation than before.

"Hank, you *have* been out honky-tonkin'." She sounded like she was collapsing inside, resigning herself to fate. "I kept telling myself that maybe you came up with a new song and you'd high-tailed it to Nashville to record it hot like you told me you do, and you were just too carried away to call me." She laughed at nothing funny. "Sounds stupid just hearing myself say it aloud. But that's what I was hoping. Dang me for a lovesick fool."

"Baby, I'm sorry."

"I don't want to hear that," she said. "Since you ask, it was yesterday afternoon when you called me. I drove down there like you asked me to. I couldn't wait to see you. I was so excited. I looked all over for you, Hank."

Things were starting to come back to me.

I said, "I called you, then I headed over to the bar and grill."

The gulp of her swallowing hard came across the wire. She was holding back tears. "I described you to the bartender but he said he never saw you. I . . . I even checked in the alley out behind the station."

"The alley?"

"I know how you like to make friends with bad people, Hank, lowlifes that take advantage of you because you're good and generous. You letting them get away with that is your downfall."

"Now don't start on me, Billie Jean."

"*Me* start on you? Well, that's rich. You started this by going off on a bender instead of coming home to a woman who loves you. Those hangers-on who want to chum with you, they're parasites, Hank."

"Now, now, that's no way to talk. My friends are my business." I broke into the title line of one of my songs. *"Why don't you mind your own business?"* I followed that with a chuckle to let her know I was just teasing.

"You promised me that you'd turned over a new leaf." She spoke quietly. I had to press the telephone receiver against my ear to hear through the noise of the passing traffic. She said, "You promised me that you were going to turn your problems around."

"Well, I am."

"So where have you been for the last day-and-a-half?"

"I told you, Billie Jean, right now I ain't sure. But it'll come back to me. I remember calling you from the station. That's a start, ain't it?"

"Yeah, that's terrific, Hank. That's a great start. So now that that's out of the way, why don't you explain to me why you're not touring. Oh, don't bother, I know the reason! Every promoter in the South is afraid to book you because you might not show up and if you do, you'll show up drunk. And now you're having blackouts again."

"Girl, you're starting to sound like Audrey and my Ma."

She said, "I've got no use for Audrey, and your ma looks like she could skin the hide off a mountain lion with her bare hands. But us three women do have one thing in common. We all love you, Hank, and we want what's best for you. But you've got to *want* to change, mister. I've given you my heart and soul and provided you with all of the encouragement you'd ever need. I even put meat on your bones with my cooking. But you know what? It looks to me like you don't want to change."

She hung up on me. The buzz of the dial tone stabbed at my brain like a dentist's drill. I replaced the receiver and told myself, *Well the hell with her.*

A bolt of lightning leaped across the night sky and rumbled like a big bass drum as if God Himself was saying, *No, Hank. The hell with you. . . .*

I shivered and stepped from the telephone booth. I noticed movement at the main entrance of the motel office.

A woman stood there, leaning against the glass door, propping it open. She was in her early twenties. A brunette, slim-figured in a cotton dress. Slim she may have been, but her breasts were nice to look at—perky, I guess you'd call them—and her hips were curvy and firm. In the light of the office I could see that her gaze was direct and her chin was prominent and lightly cleft.

She said, "Excuse me."

The condition I was in, I didn't much want to talk to anyone. But what could I do?

"Yes, ma'am?"

She was smoking a cigarette, scrutinizing me across a distance of about fifteen feet. I heard country music from a radio or a record player.

She said, "Don't I know you?"

"No ma'am, I don't believe so." I started to turn away.

"Ever register here before?"

"Not that I recollect." As long as we were talking, I added, "Uh, by the way, this may sound foolish but, uh, would you mind telling me where I am?"

She nodded to indicate the passing traffic. "We're just across the Shreveport line." She drew on her cigarette and kept right on scrutinizing me through the cloud of smoke that she exhaled. "Matter of fact you weren't paying too much attention when your friend checked you in last night."

"My friend?"

"Squirrelly little feller. A Yankee. You stayed out in the car. Looked like you were asleep."

I gave her a small smile. "Reckon I was in a manner of speaking."

"You boys ain't queer, are you? We don't cotton to that sort of going-on here."

"You know, ma'am, honest to God I sometimes wonder if my life wouldn't be less complicated if I *was* a dern flute player. Uh, say, this friend of mine. Where is he now?"

"I wouldn't know. He drove off this morning." She studied my face. "You look like you just got up. You must have been real sleepy."

"Reckon I was. Well, thank you kindly." I started to turn away again.

She flipped her cigarette into the darkness.

"Listen you, I'm a miss, not a ma'am. My name's Ava and I get to feeling lonesome when the weather turns like this. Rain depresses me."

"I'm sorry to hear that."

"I'm feeling lonesome and you seem like a nice fella. I've got beer in the icebox. We can listen to some music, and get you back to feeling right. What do you say?"

From the office I could hear Ernest Tubb waltzing across Texas.

"Much obliged, ma'am. I mean, miss. I mean, Ava. But, uh, I'm afraid I'm feeling a mite under the weather. Is there a restaurant in the neighborhood?"

"I'll cook something for you." She wouldn't take her eyes off me. "Dang, you look familiar. Are you a singer or something?"

And that tells you how just bad off I was looking. This gal was a country music lover so I'm willing to bet she had my records or some of them. She'd seen my picture plenty of times. And I only looked "familiar" to her.

Another bolt of lightning snaked across the night sky, making the gloom of the parking lot crackle with silver brightness for a few seconds. Then the rain started. It can rain hurricane-strength in that country, but this was more of a gentle, steady mist rolling in off the Gulf.

I told myself that I was in enough trouble.

"Thank you kindly, Ava, but I believe I'll keep to myself tonight," and with a neighborly nod I left her there and hot-footed it back toward the cabin.

I felt her eyes on me every step of the way.

Chapter 4

Hank

Someone was waiting for me in the cabin. He must have slipped in while I was talking to Ava.

He was a squirrelly little fella, just like the girl said; short and small-boned. He sat on the ratty couch, comfortable as you please with his legs crossed like a gentleman. He was drinking a beer and idly paging through my song notebook like it was an old issue of *The Saturday Evening Post* and he was waiting in a doctor's office. He wore a cheap brown summer suit, matching wingtip shoes and a white shirt that was badly wrinkled from the heat and humidity. He had sandy hair and round-rimmed glasses.

He looked up with what I think he meant to be a smile but it was nothing more than a crinkle of his thin lips.

"Hi there, Hank. How's the boy?"

He spoke with a Yankee accent, sure enough.

I let the screen door slam shut and crossed the room to rip my notebook out of his hands. I quickly flipped through it to make sure none of the pages had been torn out, that none of my songs were missing.

"What the hell do you think you're doing?" I waved the notebook over my head like a preacher waving his Bible. "This here's private property. This here's sacred. Who the hell are you?"

He didn't get riled or even shift his crossed legs. He sipped from his can of beer. "Hank, slow down." He addressed me like we were old pals. "You know who I am."

"I do?" I lowered my arm, losing some steam but none of my salt. "Well why don't you tell me again because I disremember."

He chuckled. "Damn, man, when you get blind drunk you just leave the world, don't you?" It occurred to him that his beer can was empty. He gave it a little shake to make sure, then rose from the couch and tossed the can. It clinked against the cans in the overfull wastebasket and fell to the floor. He ignored it and went to the refrigerator. When he reached in I saw a fresh six-pack, which he must have brought with him. "Want one?"

I said, "What the hell. It'll take the edge off." I reached over and slid the songbook into my valise.

"Good man." He made an underhanded toss to me with one can. "So how much *do* you remember?"

I caught the beer and popped the top.

"I'd be obliged if you'd start with how we met in the first place and why you're here."

"Okay. We met in the bar and grill at the train station yesterday. You were down and out. Real blue. I introduced myself and bought you a beer and we started to talk." He watched me with eyes that were trying to gauge my reaction, to see whether I believed him or not. His words came lawyer-smooth. "Even with you not looking so good," he said, "I knew who you were, of course."

His sharpie manner had me on guard. He had a city way about him. The closest he'd ever gotten to hogs was eating a ham sandwich.

I said, "Of course. Ever since Perry Como had that hit with my song, everybody knows ol' Hank . . . even up there in Yankee land."

"My name is T. J. Cantwell," he said. "I work for Fatty Hewitt."

I said, "Is that so?" and kept right on listening.

I'd met Fatty a couple of times. He was the biggest music promoter in Shreveport. He was the biggest noise in Shreveport, period. He ran the town.

Cantwell said, "I'm no Southerner, I know that's obvious, but that doesn't mean I can't recognize great music when I hear it."

He had me there. He knew just how to win over a hillbilly singer.

"Well that's nice of you to say, Mr. Cantwell. But it doesn't tell me what I need to know, does it? Now I know *who* you are. So now tell me *what* you are and why we're having this here conversation."

"We can help you, Hank."

I narrowed my eyes. "Help me how?"

"May I be candid?"

"Please do."

"Hank, we know all about the condition your career is in. You've got your audience across the country conned into thinking you're a healthy, happy country boy with a song in your heart. The first international star in the history of country music." His eyes shifted to indicate the soiled sheets on the bed. The stink of piss hung in the humid air between us. His thin lips crinkled again. "Trouble is, you're not a happy country boy, are you, Hank? Happy country boys don't get blackout drunk and piss all over themselves. A song in your heart? None of the songs I was looking at in that notebook have been completed."

"They will be."

"I know people in Nashville. The word up there is that you feed a good lyric to Fred Rose every now and then and *he* writes the songs that you record."

"Bullshit," I said. "You didn't see anyone else's handwriting in that notebook of mine, did you? Now I admit that performing has gotten to be tough for me, but when I finish those new songs, they'll be hits for anyone lucky enough to record 'em."

"Maybe. But in the meantime, you've got a situation. None of the booking agents in the South will handle you. What are you going to do about that?"

I took another swig of beer and wiped my mouth with the back of my hand. I belched.

"Look here, man, I don't need to be told what I already know. You and me got drunk and I know that I talk plenty when I'm stewed. Audrey says so, anyway. So what have you and me been talking about?"

He nailed me with a direct stare that looked honest and frank enough to get a man elected to office.

"We can get you working again, Hank."

"So Fatty Hewitt sent you to meet me at the train? That ol' boy's personable enough but he's just about as crooked as a crawlin' snake."

He chuckled as if appreciating a confidence between friends. "He figures you came back to Shreveport to try and get yourself onto the Louisiana Hayride."

There are three national network radio hookups for what a lot of folks are still calling hillbilly music. In order of prominence, there's the Grand Ole Opry in Nashville; a hallowed institution. Right after that, some would say right along with it, you've got the Hayride, which broadcasts out of Shreveport on KWKH once a week with an hour of country music. Then there's the WLS Barn Dance up out of Chicago, which is mostly for Yankees with a hillbilly heart or Southern folks that had to relocate up there to find work. Anyway, the Hayride is big noise. There'll never be another Nashville but Shreveport was a jumping town full of music and musicians.

I said, "How much of this did we discuss yesterday while we were getting hammered?"

"All of it," he said. "You're booked into Fatty's club starting tonight. It sounded good to you. Don't worry, I'll see to it that Fatty stays honest."

I said, "That old boy's got his fingers in a lot of pies here in Shreveport." I gave the back of my neck a scratch. "And every one of them pies was stolen out of somebody's kitchen."

"I said I'd keep him honest, Hank, and I will."

He set down his beer and reached into an inside jacket pocket for a pack of cigarettes. He offered me one and fired us both up. He returned the cigarette pack to his inside pocket. The jacket lapel fell away just so this time and I saw something I hadn't noticed before: the belt-strap of a shoulder holster peaked at me from behind his tie.

I scratched the back of my neck some more.

"Here's my question," I said. "Given the troubles I'm in, and you got most of that right, well, why would I want to tie up with a sidewinder like Hewitt? Why should I lie down with a snake?"

His eyes locked with mine and wouldn't let go. "Fatty's got the money to stake you and he's got connections good enough to get you back on track, performing in the area. He's willing to take a chance on you, Hank. He's offering to pitch you to promoters at a lowball figure and initially he's barely going to break even. He'll start raising your asking price when word gets around that you're back on the ball to being dependable."

"Yeah well, what if I ain't?"

"Hank, answer me straight. Do you want a career or not?"

"Reckon I do. Reckon this hillbilly Shakespeare gig is the only real thing I've got in this world after my children."

"That's what you said yesterday at the station and again last night when we were doing the town. Here's how it is." He spoke with the sincerity of a salesman. "Fatty wants you to play a three-night engagement at his place in Shreveport. He wants to make sure that you *can* play a show."

"I can do anything if I set my mind to it."

"Now you're talking. You make that fat boy happy and he'll play those connections to see that you start working steady."

"And what do you and Fatty get out of it?"

He winced the way a used car salesman would if you brought up that the transmission needed replacing. "Fatty wants fifty percent. I know that's stiff."

"Stiff? Hell man, that's highway robbery."

"Hank, right now he's the only game in town and it will be a stepping stone to better things. What do you say?"

I finished my beer with another belch. "Sounds interesting."

"I was hoping you'd think so. I, uh, took the liberty of setting things up for tonight."

I pitched the can at the pile by the wastebasket and missed. "Work kind of fast, don't you, mister?"

"Call me T. J. Where I come from, moving fast is how things get done. Besides, you told me last night to go ahead and set it up."

"Shoot. I damn sure need to cut back on my drinking, don't I?"

He sent another glance at the piss stains. "That wouldn't be such a bad idea."

"So what about tonight?"

"Fatty's already put together a backup band for you," he said. "Local boys who know all your songs. They're all set up on stage, waiting on you. The club's about ten minutes from here. That's why I checked you into this place. So, do we proceed?"

I went to the screen door and looked out, buying some time to think.

The mist had let up but hadn't cooled things off. The hot night air was so thick, I could have sliced off a piece and mailed it home to Montgomery. The hissing of tires on the highway sounded like ghostly voices whispering low.

Lights were on in the office but I didn't see Ava. I thought, *Maybe later tonight when I get back*. With Billie Jean not speaking to me, wasn't any need for me to be lonesome. . . .

Lightning crackled and lit up the shadows of the parking lot with more shimmering silver and for an instant my eyes picked out what I thought was a man standing against the wall of a cabin kitty-corner from mine, perhaps two hundred feet away. I saw a tan trench coat and a fedora, and he stood there with his hands in the pockets of his coat, giving the impression that he'd been there for a while and had weathered the rolling mist. Then blackness reclaimed the night.

Cantwell stepped next to me and looked out, following the line of my vision. "What is it? Did you see something?"

"I ain't sure."

"Did you see someone?"

"I think so."

He raised his right hand to his mid-chest and his fingertips danced near the front of his cheap jacket. He was thinking about drawing his gun.

"Man or woman?"

"A man, standing there like he was watching this cabin."

"Shit. Maybe he was."

He toed open the screen door just wide enough to ease on through, out into the gloom, catching the frame of the door and easing it shut behind him without a sound. Then he disappeared into the darkness.

I stood there, not sure what to think.

Me, I always carry one gun. Hell, I collect guns and cars. I had a .38 Smith & Wesson in my suitcase. Of course, Cantwell would know this since he had searched my valise when he found my songbook. Should I get my gun out? Would it still be loaded, with the box of spare shells nestled in the scabbard? I wondered, *What the hell.*

I had a good chance of getting on the Hayride on my own with no help from Fatty Hewitt or a slick Yankee wearing a shoulder holster. I had already spoken with Mr. Clay at the Hayride and they claimed that the paperwork would be drawn up. That's where things stood with the Hayride to the best of my knowledge. On the other hand, there are people around in the business who don't like ol' Hank and even more that are jealous of me. Who knows what mischief they could do to sabotage me since I'd been kicked off the Opry? And of course there was my own knack for getting myself in a pickle at the worst possible time, just about every time. In other words, the Hayride would not be solid until I was on that stage, singing into that microphone to the world, with my paycheck safely in my bank account. And that hadn't happened yet. So here's this fella, T. J., with a Plan B that looked pretty good even if Fatty Hewitt was involved.

Another snake of lightning whipped across the night. Not as bright or long as previous flashes.

The only reason I saw anything was because I was staring straight at the spot where I'd seen the man. Cantwell and the man in the trench coat were speaking to each other. I couldn't tell what they were saying, whether it was an argument or a polite conversation. Then they were swallowed by the gloom. The thunder rumbled away.

Less than a minute later, Cantwell stepped back inside the cabin.

I was watching over his shoulder, across the parking lot. There was no more lightning. I couldn't see any trace of the other man in the darkness.

"Trouble?" I asked.

He shook his head and gestured like it wasn't worth discussing. "Naw. He's a private detective and you were right, he is on stakeout. But we're not the ones he's got under surveillance."

"I saw a couple checking in a while ago."

"They're the ones. Says he's retained by her husband's lawyer. That's a dirty business. But how about us, Hank? What'll it be? Have you considered my proposal?"

I felt like scratching the back of my neck but I resisted. I didn't want him to think that *I* was the squirrelly one. But I sure was feeling squirrelly.

I said, "I'll wear my white suit with the sequined music notes. That gets the fans to whoopin' even before I start to singing."

His tight mouth crinkled and he gave me a pat on the arm. "Hank, my friend, you're making the right decision. Let's get moving. People are waiting to hear you play."

Chapter 5

Muddy

We had the night off between playing Crowley and the gig in Shreveport, and that was just as well.

Little Walter is part Creole. He was raised down there in Louisiana, out in the country near Marksville in Avoyelles Parish. That's why Walter's harp playing is so different from the older cats that came before him. Walter would tell folks that when he was a kid, he kept running away until one time they just said the hell with it and let him go. He ended up playing his harmonica on the streets in New Orleans for tips and sometimes sneaking in to blow some in the club for tips when the featured band was on break. As a young man, when he blew he was always hearing those Cajun squeezebox players he'd heard as a child. He still had people in that county, so that's where we went to ground.

It was a homestead well off the main road, surrounded by lush, dense countryside that was so bright green it hurt your eyes. We caused quite a stir when my driver pulled the red Cad into their farmyard with the boys behind in the station wagon, pulling a three-wheel trailer with the amps and the drums.

Walter's people were right glad to see us. They were fond of Walter, and everyone there knew my music. We stashed the vehicles in the barn, and that's where we slept during the heat of the day while everybody else worked. And that night we sat up with them farm folks, playing music in the parlor, getting tall and having a good old time. Wasn't no cops in sight. I figured laying low would throw that Crowley policeman off our scent.

There was one little gal at the party, plump and sweet and old enough for marryin'. She worked in a white folks' kitchen across town and had nicked her some of their Chivas Regal. While the party was going strong and everybody was nice and high, sometime in the wee hours me and her slipped off to one of the bedrooms and Muddy got himself some of that baby-fat little country girl.

Laying low wasn't all that bad.

Only one who didn't get right that night was John Lee. Hooker slept curled up like a pretzel in a big armchair off in the corner with his guitar case in his arms and his suitcase on the floor next to the chair.

Come dawn, the lady of the house fixed up a big country breakfast, grits and biscuits and gravy and flapjacks and slabs of ham an inch thick with no gristle.

Hooker ate in silence. That cat had a way of drawing into himself. When he was done with eating, he looked up at the rest of us seated around the kitchen table. He finished his coffee and stood up.

"G-g-got me a week of gigs and some recording down in N-new Orleans," he said.

The twin billing we'd been working had only been booked for the first half of that tour.

I set down my knife and fork, stood up and embraced his wiry frame. It was like hugging iron and concrete. "Thanks for what you did in Crowley, man. You and Walter saved my ass. You tell the girls down on Bourbon Street that Muddy says hello."

I could always get a grin out of that hard-set ebony face.

"Mud, that woman-lovin' stuff's going to p-put you six feet in the ground, man, you d-don't watch out." John Lee glanced around at the guys in the band. "Y'all keep an eye on this crazy mother—"

He remembered that there were ladies present, and everyone had a good laugh at my expense.

"Don't you worry none about Muddy," said Jimmy Rogers. "We're watching his back."

Walter had been spiking his coffee with shots from his flask, and he'd been drinking a lot of coffee. "That's right, we got to keep Muddy alive. He's our paycheck!" He threw his head back and let loose a Cajun yowl.

Elgin the drummer didn't speak; just kept wearing his down-in-the-mouth face, looking down at the food he was eating like this sort of foolishness was beneath him. He looks even more like a judge when he's hung over.

I didn't mind the boys kidding around. I live the life I love and I love the life I live. I don't do nothing I ain't proud of.

Running a band isn't the easiest thing in the world. We were a roughneck crew, I'll say that. Wasn't a man in my band had ever been given a damn thing. A man has to work and scrape for what he's got and then he's got to fight to hold onto it, whether it's your job or your business on the street or your woman. When a band's on the road together, the other guys become like your family. You talk about home with them. You talk about the woman they had last night. You've got to talk about your troubles. You keep them straight on who's boss. They can't forget who they're working for. But sometimes a bandleader has to ease up. They know you're the main man, but you've got to be a regular fellow too. That's why I was letting everybody laugh it up some at my expense. It was good for me too, having a laugh with the fellas.

Way it was in '52, we worked all night and slept all day. Course, work was nothing but a party going on, playing music for people who had been busting their hump on a job five or six days a week. They drive themselves ragged fifty, sixty hours a week or more, trying to make ends meet. Sunday morning they're in church getting right with God and Sunday afternoon is for family. That leaves Friday and Saturday night to cut it loose and let the good times roll. I always knew I'd grow up to become a preacher or bluesman. There's something in me that moves the people. I never could see getting up early no matter what day of the week it was, particularly on Sunday, so I took the blues road.

We laid low that next day with Walter's friends before saying our goodbyes and heading out in late afternoon. The sky was overcast. Thunder thumped in the distance, sounding like cannon fire far off somewhere. We stayed to the back roads.

We'd be arriving at the joint later than the owner would be expecting us. They like for musicians to be all set up with their amplifiers and drum kit in place so it looks more professional when the customers start filing in. The Muddy Waters Band always arrives at a gig two hours before show time.

But not tonight.

There was no way of knowing if that policeman from Crowley wasn't trying to track me down. I was hoping he'd sobered up the next morning and gotten a good talking to from his Chief and been told to stop making a fool of himself in public. It reflected poorly on the Department. But it could have gone different. Jerry the cop said he had friends in the Klan, so I was going to stay on my toes. We had another week to go on the tour before heading back up North.

Like most of the Gulf Coast cities in those days, Shreveport was wide-open. Gambling and prostitution, bootleg liquor and extortion on the docks. The politicians and the cops had a good old boy Dixie Mafia and they were running the town. The citizens of Shreveport didn't much mind because the cash was flowing in. From the waitresses and cab drivers to the pawnbrokers and the property owners, everybody black and white was getting a piece of the action by just being there. A wide-open town is always good for musicians. The working people want to let off steam and the high rollers want to have music playing while they spend their dough.

At one point Bo, my driver, just inside the city limits, saw a police car in the same lane we were traveling in, four or five cars ahead, so I had him pull sharp on the wheel before John Law could spot us, so fast that the guys in the station wagon behind us almost missed the play. We cut over to a cross street and took the back streets into the colored section.

We were booked at a place called The Boogie Woogie Inn. They had flashing neon lights above the entrance that splashed the front of the building with electric reds and blues. It was a one-story brick building with a tin roof. The night was filled with the noisy rattling of its air conditioner.

The manager was a narrow-faced mulatto cat with kinky hair so greased you could see lines of blinking neon lights reflected off his process like wiggling red worms attached to his scalp. His face was sweaty and pockmarked, with a pencil-thin moustache that lined his upper lip.

"You're supposed to be on time," were the first words out of his mouth. "Guitar Slim played here last week, and those boys had their shoes shined and their music stands set up before I even got the doors open." His eyes checked me out. I was wearing a white cotton shirt and tan slacks that weren't new. He shook his head and spat. "Damn country coons."

The guys were uncurling from inside the station wagon. Walter heard him and whipped around in our direction so fast, his checkered hat flew off his head.

"We're from Chicago, you jive shit." His small fists came up and he started shifting balance from one foot to another like a bantamweight fighter. "Southside Chicago's bigger than this whole piss-ant town you call a city."

The manager backpedaled and looked at me. I stepped between them. Jimmy Rogers ambled over, looking easy-going like always. Elgin was hanging back.

"Walter," I said, "mellow down. Easy, man." I turned to the rest of the band. "I want you boys to look sharp. Set up with no messing around."

Jimmy said, "We're on it, Muddy." He draped an arm across Walter's shoulder. "Come on, Joe Louis, let's get to work."

Walter lowered his fists like nothing had happened, and the three of them and Bo got to work unloading the equipment.

I looked back at the club man. His name was Lyle. He wore a gray plaid jacket, dark slacks and a white shirt with a clip-on black bow tie.

I said, "Had us some cracker trouble a few towns back."

"I don't want no trouble in my place. You niggers want to get paid, you do things right."

I didn't like the sound of that.

One of the problems playing on the road is club owners and promoters who skip out without paying you. They disappear while you're performing your last set. You can't make trouble because you're a thousand miles from home. You're on that man's turf and he's got every wheel greased; the cops and anyone else he needs to butter. It happens. That's one reason I've always got some guns close at hand. Cats are less likely to fuck with you when they know you're packing. Bo keeps a .38 under the front seat. I've got a .32 in my back pocket and a .22 in an ankle holster. Yeah, it could get rough in those days playing the chitlin circuit.

Lyle saw a look in my eye that made him stay clear of me from then on. The guys carried in the amps and drums and our little PA system past the crowd and up to the stage.

The Boogie Woogie Inn was halfway between a country joint and a big city club. The tables were packed with working class people. They were lined up two deep at a bar that ran the length of the place. Three bartenders were keeping busy. Waitresses worked the tables. It was smoky and loud. A jukebox was shaking the walls with an Amos Milburn piano number.

The patrons were good-natured and friendly as my guys carried our equipment through the club.

I stayed to the back of the club while the boys made quick work of setting up, placing the amps and guitars and drums while bantering with some girls at the front tables.

Then we stepped into the men's room and changed into our stage outfits. The band wore dark stage suits that set off my striped lime green jacket and a gold silk shirt buttoned to the neck with a kerchief in the breast pocket. Creased slacks and two-tone shoes and man, I was sharp.

Walter stepped into one of the stalls and tried to be discrete but the sound of him sniffing up cocaine off the back of his hand was amplified by the tile walls. He left the stall like a colt bolting from its pen, slapping his hands.

"Well all reet. Let's play some blues!" He strutted out into the club.

Jimmy and Elgin looked at me.

Elgin said, "That punk's going to cause you a whole lot of trouble, Muddy, you wait and see."

Jimmy nodded. "You're like a daddy to him, Mud. Can't you say something to straighten him out?"

I said, "Hell man, you knew him before I did. You're the one brought him into the band. I don't mess with a cat's private life, you know that. Walter's doing his job. Now get out there and do yours."

The band stepped onto the stage right on the dot of starting time and played three opening numbers without me. They always start and close with a bouncy instrumental built around Walter's harp playing, a tune where he works the whole range of that little ten-hole Hohner Marine Band harp. That fat horn sound pours from his amp and fills the club and makes people laugh and dance.

I held back in the shadows at the end of the bar and ordered a Seven-and-Seven. It's good to let the sidemen shine on their own, before they announce me and I come up to join them. That way, they get a chance to get the people whooping and hollering and it builds suspense for the star of the show. Plus, I like to wet my whistle while I get a feel for the way the acoustics and the sound plays in a place. Then Jimmy calls me up and I make my way through the tables, onto the stage. The crowd has been warmed up. They're applauding and whistling.

I strapped on my Les Paul model electric guitar, made sure I was in tune with Jimmy and the harp, then counted off "Goin' to Main Street."

The band plays three sets. The first one we play with the amps turned down low. I go for that warming-up swing with medium tempo shuffles. I save my deep blues for the second set after folks have been loosened up some. That's when I slip in the deep ones like "Sad Letter" and "Long Distance Call." By the time we take the stage at midnight for the last set, man, everyone in the house is primed. Then we crank up the volume on the amps and lay the rockers on them, "Rollin' and Tumbling" and a couple of grind groovers like "Rock Me" and by the time I'm done, we've peeled the paint off the walls we're so hot, and we send them out of there laughing and singing and wanting to get home and make some love. But you've got to build for that. You play an audience the way you play a woman; break the ice with that sweet charm and warm them up before you get to hitting heavy.

On this first set, after "Main Street" I eased into another instrumental. Joe Liggins recorded it as "The Honeydripper" but we strip it down and call it "Muddy Jumps One." After that I slipped the metal slide onto the pinky finger of my left hand and I nailed them with a couple of slow blues, "Honey Bee" and one that I'm writing on the road and haven't got a title for yet.

The people there knew my music. The chicks in front went crazy when I brought up the tempo and dedicated "Goin' Down Louisiana" to all the ladies in the house. They squealed and clapped their hands and hid their smiles when they laughed and the men folk laughed too and cheered me on because they all knew I was singing about more than just going down a highway.

That seemed a good place to cool it for a spell while it was hot, so I gave Jimmy the nod and he started calling out my name for applause and I got plenty as I set my guitar down, switched my amp to Standby and came down off the stage.

There's always people waiting around to congratulate me and say how they like my music. They want to tell their children someday that they met Muddy Waters. So it took me some time get to a table back in the corner. I took a seat, ordered a shot of whiskey and a bottle of Schlitz and fired up a cigarette while onstage Jimmy took a vocal on one of his better known records, "That's All Right."

Next number they played was the same bouncy instrumental they'd played at the top of the set. Most bands have what we call a band instrumental or a break song and this was ours. Walter sort of borrowed it from one of the old harp playing boys, but it became something else with Walter's chops and the way he amplified that harp through those booming speakers, making it sound like a jumping saxophone. At our last studio session, Mr. Chess—who owns the record label I'm on, Chess Records—heard us warm up with that number and went ahead and cut it. He dug it a whole lot but we never did get to giving it a name. It was just a crazy little thing. We were on the road promoting my latest release, which was recorded at that same session.

The band finished playing and there was a nice round of applause. The people were digging us. Then the guys walked over and joined me at the table, each of them reaching for his cigarettes and lighting up. A waitress came over and took their orders. Walter ordered a gin and tonic. Jimmy ordered a glass of wine. Old Elgin just mumbled for coffee. Our waitress was a petite thing in a white hostess gown with hair that fell onto bare bronze shoulders.

Walter watched her sashay away. He kept shifting his weight from side to side in his chair like he heard music inside his head.

"Oyo-wee. Didn't I tell y'all that there was fine foxy mamas in Louisiana?"

Jimmy pretended not to hear. He and Walter were running buddies but they lived different lives. Jimmy had a wife and baby children at home. He minded his *P*'s and *Q*'s when we were on the road and he stayed faithful to his woman. I admired him for that.

Jimmy looked around and said, "This place got a right clean sound to it. We got the balance just right first time out."

Elgin muttered. "I need my coffee."

Walter cackled like a hyena. His gold tooth reflected the stage lights. "Old man, you need you some pussy to wake you up. And man, you've got to start drumming harder behind me, man. I want me some beat behind that harp thing I'm doing. If you fuck like you drum, I pity your old lady."

Elgin growled. "Don't be telling me how to drum, fool. I was laying down a solid backbeat while you were still at your mama's tit."

I'd heard enough and I was going to say something. Running a band is like being a referee. It's only natural for guys to get on each other's nerves from time to time when they're traveling and living in close quarters. But before I could say anything, something happened that I'll remember until my dying day.

A selection started playing from the jukebox, and it took a couple of beats for every man at our table to stop what he was doing or saying and look in the direction of the jukebox where people were dancing. It was like an echo of the break instrumental the band had just finished playing before stepping down, the number we opened and closed every set with. It was note-for-note the same arrangement.

It was *us.*

Jimmy said, "Must be the B-side of your next single, Uncle Mud."

Elgin grumbled like an unhappy judge. "That ain't right. How can it be a Muddy Waters record if Muddy ain't singing?"

I said, "Chess ain't set to put out a new single yet. He's still working the last one. Chess don't release my records that close together."

Walter leaped to his feet. "I'm going to check this out." He almost knocked over the waitress as he started off.

She served the drinks and waited while Jimmy and Elgin ponied up.

Jimmy mused, "Been almost two days now. I reckon we can stop worrying about that cop in Crowley."

Elgin sipped his coffee with a dissatisfied expression. "I won't stop looking over my shoulder until we're back in Chicago."

I said, "Hey, look here. What's this?"

They craned their necks around to spy what had caught my attention.

There was some sort of low-keyed disturbance at the back of the club where the door was. Someone was being ushered in. The disturbance rippled through the crowded club, coming our way. Folks around our table started to chatter and I thought, *Could be a local celebrity, maybe a prize fighter who held a title.* In those days fighters were about the only kind of celebrity you'd find in a blues joint.

A tough-looking guy emerged from the haze of cigarette smoke into the green, yellow and purple lights cast from the stage. This guy had to be a gangster, wearing a snappy pinstriped suit with key chains and a diamond stickpin, and an expensive snap-brimmed fedora. He eased on up to a table with a *Reserved* card on it and positioned himself with his back against the wall and a hand near his jacket lapel. There was no doubt this hood was packing heavy.

Then a glimmering, shimmering mirage materialized from the shadowy smoke.

Chapter 6

Muddy

She was a big woman and she strode with the arrogance of an African Congo queen through the opening made by her bodyguard. She stood five-eleven, big in a foxy, large-boned sassy way. The glimmering and shimmering were stage lights reflecting off rubies in the tiara, earrings and necklace she wore and from the countless rubies that had been stitched into her floor-length peach gown. A burst of dyed feathers fanned out from behind her head, which she held high. She was smoking from a long cigarette holder. Her features could have been Chinese; high cheekbones and cat-like eyes and lush lips. Her gown was elegant with a V-front and her bosom was trying to overflow; ripe brown melons that jiggled as she walked. She wore heels and the gown was pasted to her rolling hips and muscular legs and a high, tight, round ass.

There was a muscular young stud in a tuxedo accompanying her on one arm and on her other, a thin blond white girl in a low-cut burgundy gown. Maybe twenty-two, her cheeks were flushed and her eyes were wild.

The bodyguard held out a chair and the woman sat with the young buck and the crazy blonde to either side of her. That hood never stopped watching the patrons at the surrounding tables. His eyes moved over me and Jimmy and Elgin, then moved on.

Lyle scurried over to their table like a waiter, dry-washing his hands and doing everything but bowing down and kissing the black woman's feet. The sharp young stud ordered for the table. The woman exchanged a few words with Lyle. Her eyebrows lifted like she was amused. While her young man placed their orders, she fixed a rolled cigarette into a long cigarette holder. The white girl leaned over with a match and lit her up, whispering something eager. The big woman turned with a haughty expression and looked even more like an African queen than before. She narrowed her eyes and blew smoke in the girl's face.

I said to our waitress, "Hey sister, who's that over yonder? She acts like she owns this place?"

"That's Delilah Buie," she told me. "No, she don't own the joint. She don't have to. She gets a cut of the action."

I studied the woman, Delilah. The smell of hashish drifted across from their table. Delilah and her stud were sharing a deep kiss with their arms around each other. The girl was lighting her own cigarette with her fingers shaking while she watched.

I grinned at the waitress. "Big noise."

"I'll say. She runs the rackets in darktown. She was married to Big Gyp."

"Don't recollect the name."

The waitress leaned in closer. "You would if you lived in Shreveport. Big Gyp ran all the rackets until some punks put him on the spot. Delilah tracked down the ones that did it and gunned them down like dogs in the street in broad daylight. One of them almost survived but she walked into his hospital room the next day and finished the job with a tommy-gun. She took over Gyp's business and ain't no one has tried to stop her since."

"What about them good old white boys running this town?"

She leaned down even closer and made a point of not looking in the direction of the woman we were talking about. "Delilah's running the colored rackets for them. They don't want to dirty their hands with us, even if it's to make a buck. She pays them a big cut."

I brought out my billfold and took five and slipped the money down the front of her hostess gown.

"Here's something for you to spread around, sugar. I like to know whose turf I'm on, and you just hipped me solid."

She stroked the back of my neck with the fingertips of her hand that wasn't holding the tray. "Muddy, you don't have to spend your money on me. You can have me for free, baby. I've got all of your records. I paid off another girl so I could work this shift and meet you. I just love the way your music sounds."

It felt good the way she was touching me so I started to ease an arm around her, forgetting about Delilah Buie, when Walter came running over from the jukebox.

It's not easy to run through a crowded club but Walter managed it. His face was shiny with excitement.

"Muddy! Muddy! You won't believe it, man."

I gave the waitress a slap on her ass. She made a happy sound and batted her eyes at me and I swear she gave that backside of hers an extra twitch as she walked away.

I looked back at Walter. "What is it, man?"

He was like he had an electrical current shooting through him. "That song they just finished playing. It is us, man. But you know what? They're calling it *Juke* and the jukebox says it's by Little Walter! Damn!"

Jimmy said, "Well that's good for you, little brother. Congratulations."

The record on the jukebox had finished but someone slipped in some coin and the same number started booming again, rattling the walls. More people were dancing to it around the juke box.

Elgin snorted. "So three of you boys got records out. Reckon I'm drumming in a goddamn all-star band."

I could never tell when Elgin was being sarcastic.

Walter grabbed my arm with both of his hands. His small hands held me tight like a pair of claws. "Damn, Muddy. I'm a *star*. A fucking *star*! Got my own record on the jukebox, Chess label and everything. Damn! I got me a record, man! I'm a star just like you and the Howlin' Wolf and B. B. King."

I yanked my arm free. "Don't go fathead on me, boy." I spoke it like a slap to his face.

Jimmy said, "Don't let it go to your head, Walter. I got me some records out too but only one man can be the star. This here's Muddy's band. He's the star."

Elgin grunted. "That's right."

Walter snarled at the three of us. "Y'all are just jealous 'cause that's *my* record they're playing on that jukebox and dancing to. I'm a *star*, goddamn it. Man, I'm a recording artist. I could get bigger than you, Muddy."

I snapped at him, "One record don't make you no star. Don't forget who brought you to that studio so you *could* play that number, boy. Shit, Chess didn't even tell you he was putting the damn thing out. You still ain't nothing but my harp player."

Elgin was looking over my shoulder, at something behind me.

He said, "Uh oh. Here come trouble."

Lyle walked up to our table. He had a white police officer with him.

The cop was built big and solid as a tree trunk and he stood there in the middle of that crowded colored joint knowing he was safe because he was white and he was John Law. He held his billy club and was slapping it into the palm of one hand.

Things had quieted down. I saw a few customers ease out of the nearest exits.

I said, "Can I help you, officer?"

The cop's eyes swept the table. "Which one of you is Muddy Waters?"

Lyle pointed to me.

"That's him, officer. That one right there. He's Muddy Waters. I don't want no trouble in my place."

Walter said, "Lyle, you a prick-ass weasel, I'm going to take my razor and cut you when this copper ain't around."

The cop lifted his club and pointed it at Walter. "You shut up, boy, or I'll run your black ass in just for the hell of it. The boys at the jailhouse can have a go at you. You want that?"

Jimmy made a friendly gesture to the cop. Jimmy is friendly no matter who he's talking to. "He don't mean no harm, officer. Walter, he's just a hothead."

The cop sneered. "Hophead is more like it."

Lyle said, "Goddamn country coons."

Elgin sipped his coffee and set the cup down like he was contemplating something deep, and said nothing.

I said, "Officer, we haven't done nothing. We're law-abiding boys."

The cop snickered. "That ain't what Deputy Jerry Smith says over Crowley way."

Humor was in his eyes but the rest of him was hard-ass. He went back to striking the club against his palm. Our number on the jukebox ended and the *thwap!-thwap!-thwap!* of wood against flesh was clear, what with conversations tapering off to nothing at the tables near us. Everybody was watching.

Best way to survive in a situation like that is to let the man hear what he wants to hear.

"I never heard of no Deputy Smith," I said slowly. "Boss, we ain't broke no laws in Crowley." I was ready to dodge that billy and make a run for it, if I had to. The boys would block him from chasing me, and then they'd fade into the crowd. Things had gotten bad, real fast. That's how it happens.

The cop said, "You played in Crowley night before last."

"Yas, suh."

"Deputy Smith done called my chief. Nigger, I've got two of my boys in a patrol car outside. Told 'em I didn't need no backup in a goddamn dinge joint." He said to Lyle, "If I don't walk out of here with this man in my custody within the next four minutes, the law's going to shut this joint down so hard it'll bounce."

Lyle said, "This ain't none of my business."

The cop again stopped slapping his palm with the billy. He held it like he'd prefer taking it to my head.

"Let's go, boy. Move your ass outside. You're under arrest."

"No, he ain't."

It was a woman's voice. Time froze for a few seconds. Everyone turned in the direction of that voice.

Delilah Buie had pushed her chair back and stood, towering at her full height and scowling. Even the young stud and the white girl at her table looked scared.

The cop hesitated. He swallowed hard, twice, before he could speak. "I, uh, didn't see you there, Miss Buie." He said it in a funny voice. He lowered the billy so it dangled against his leg like a limp dick.

Delilah sashayed from behind the table with her hips rolling fine beneath the clinging fabric of that ruby-studded gown. Her bodyguard flanked her, one step behind, his hand buried beneath his lapel, ready to draw.

She stepped up to confront the law. "Well you see me now, don't you?"

I thought, *the hell with sitting* and stood up from my chair. The officer's face said he didn't like that much but he didn't say a thing because his attention was on Miss Buie. When I stood up, the three of us were facing each other in a triangle. Me, the cop and the jungle queen.

The cop threw his shoulders back. "Miss Buie, this ain't none of your business. I'm here to enforce the law and make an arrest. You can't interfere with that."

She took a long draw on her cigarette holder. When she exhaled, I smelled hash again.

"I do any damn thing I want to in this section of town, Mister Man. What you're doing here *is* my business. I came down here tonight to hear Muddy Waters play and sing and that's what I'm going to do."

"But, ma'am—"

"Don't interrupt. I know why they sent you and your boys down to pick him up. I got contacts at your station house and in Crowley, too." She looked at me then and her eyes glowed like the rubies she wore. She licked her full, lush lips. "This here's Muddy Waters. Don't you know his records? He's the Mojo Man. You tell Deputy Smith in Crowley that a man got to watch his woman when Muddy Waters in town."

Someone in the place said softly, "Amen."

The cop looked at Delilah. He turned to me. He looked at the expectant faces of the onlookers. He was a man wishing he was somewhere else.

"Uh, Miss Buie," he said, "you're, ahem, putting me in a difficult position. I know what you're saying. Believe me I do. But I was sent down from headquarters to pick this boy up," and he pointed at me with his club.

I was watching that club. I had my knees bent and my hands at waist level, looking casual-like in the excitement but I was ready to leap and make a play if I had to.

Delilah raised her free hand and snapped her fingers one time. The atmosphere was so tense, it sounded like a cracking tree branch. She held her hand over her shoulder with the palm up and spoke to the hood at her side, never taking her eyes off the cop.

She said, "Give me three hundred."

The hood grunted and dug out a roll of cabbage big enough to choke an elephant. Everyone's eyes bugged at the sight of all that money. It was hundred dollar bills. The tough guy peeled off three of them and placed them in Delilah's palm. He returned the roll to his hip pocket and his hand returned to beneath his jacket and his concealed weapon.

Delilah extended the bills to the cop.

He wiped the back of his hand across his mouth. His eyes were bugging like everyone else's. "That . . . that there's a bribe, Miss Buie."

She nodded. "And a damned good one. A yard for each of you cop boys. Unless of course you want to tell your buddies out in the car that I only paid two. Won't be no one to call you a liar."

The bills dangled less than eighteen inches from his face.

"But what'll I tell the Chief? He knows Muddy Waters was playing here tonight."

She sneered. "Nobody who's white knows anything about darktown after the sun goes down. You tell the Chief that someone hipped Muddy that you were coming and he lit out."

The cop licked his lips. He was just about drooling, looking at that money. "But . . . what if someone comes down to check it out?"

She made a crude snort sound. "There's a joint full of people in this club who want to hear Muddy play tonight as much as I do. They'll say Muddy split if anybody checks, which they won't." She looked around the club. "Am I right?"

A noisy cheer broke out and bounced off the walls.

The cop looked at me. He eyed the money. He snatched the money from her fingers like a kid stealing an apple off a tree. He spun about like a soldier doing an about-face and double-timed it out of there without looking back.

Another cheer went up, louder than the first.

I smiled at the jungle queen. "Thank you, baby. That was slick."

Her cat eyes sized me up—my shoulders, my waist, what was below that—like she was measuring me for a suit. "My pleasure, Muddy Waters." She held out her hand to me.

And I'll be damned but if I didn't lean over and plant a kiss on the back of her hand like an actor in some movie about old-time kings and queens. I never did that before.

I said, "Hello, girl. Pleasure to make your acquaintance."

She reached her hand back over her shoulder again and snapped her fingers. "Card."

The hood brought out a leather packet this time and took a business card from it. He handed it to her, and she passed it to me.

A flowery scent wafted up to me and I raised the card to my nostrils. It was faintly scented with gardenia. There was a telephone number. A pen and ink drawing of a gardenia blossom contained the words:

Delilah Buie
Entrepreneur

She arched an eyebrow. "Like I told the cop, I'm a big fan of yours, Muddy." She took her time looking me over again from my alligator shoes to my processed hair. "And I like what I see even better in person."

I gave her my lady-killer smile. My mojo smile.

"You're easy on the eyes your ownself, woman. And I'd sure enough like to keep on talking to you. But right now break's over." I looked at the nervous cat hovering close by. "Ain't that right, Lyle?"

Lyle looked like the scared rat that he was. "Now look here Muddy, don't you go getting hot under the collar at me. I got to stay on everybody's good side, you know. I got a business to run."

I said, "Just so you know that I'll run a .38 slug up your ass if I don't have my money at the end of the night."

He dabbed at his sweaty forehead with the hanky from his jacket pocket. "I'll have the money for you, don't you worry none about that."

Delilah chuckled. It sounded like water burbling across stones in a creek. "Lyle, Muddy ain't the one needs to worry. You best worry about keeping your ass from being shot off. Now run along and play with your boys."

"Yes, ma'am." Lyle scurried off and disappeared into the heavy smoke of the club.

Things were getting back to normal. The club patrons were laughing again and clinking their glasses and talking about what had just happened.

Delilah said to me, "I like your style, Muddy, in case you haven't noticed."

"I read you, darling. You're a real gone gal."

"Anything you need while you're in Shreveport, you look me up, hear? Delilah Buie. I will set you up right." She lowered her voice and reached out and curled her fingers lightly around the back of my neck. Her touch was hot. She licked her lips slowly and they glistened and there was a bedroom look in her eyes. "*Anything* you need, Muddy, anything you want, you come to *me*, daddy. You got me?"

I said, "To my soul. But right now I'm on the job and there's music to make." I looked at the guys in the band, who were seated there at the table with their jaws dropped. "Come on fellas, break's over. Get to work."

Delilah gave me another bedroom look and returned to her table, flanked by her bodyguard.

When the bartender flicked the switch that shut off the jukebox so the band could play, he cut off the third straight play of *Juke*.

As Walter walked to the bandstand, I could hear him muttering to himself.

He was saying, "I'm a star, man. Goddamn, I be Little Walter. I'm a goddamn *star!*"

Chapter 7

Hank

Fatty Hewitt was all smiles. He shook my hand vigorously, like it was a broken pump handle.

"Well hey there, ol' pard. Good to have you back in the fold, Hank. Welcome to Fatty's Corral."

Cantwell had driven us the short distance here from the motel. He guided me in through the club's front entrance, to where Fatty stood at the bar.

Everybody called him Fatty, but he wasn't.

Fatty Hewitt was over six feet tall. I'd guess him to be around six-two or -three. And he wasn't just tall. There wasn't an ounce of fat on that towering frame of his. He possessed a head of curly hair and a wide, dimpled smile full of teeth that were too white. His broad shoulders were encased in a pressed white suit with a red carnation, a red silk shirt and a garish tie featuring scantily-clad cowgirls with lassos, riding horses. A diamond stickpin shone almost as bright as his smile.

I recalled meeting him some years ago when he'd booked me to headline a show with Faron Young and Wanda Jackson at the fairgrounds. I hadn't seen him since. But he was acting like I was his long lost brother just back from the war.

I lied some and smoothed on the butter. "Nice to see you again, Fatty. Thanks for inviting me to play here."

I recalled Ma and Audrey being so mad about the way I'd treated that movie slicker in Hollywood and I reckon they were right. Fatty was handing me a fresh start doing the only thing I know how to do, singing for the people, so I wasn't inclined to mess this up. But I couldn't make myself act overjoyed as he was, either.

He didn't let go of my hand but stepped up close and draped one meaty arm across my shoulders. It felt like I was shouldering a sack of grain. He gestured expansively with both over-sized hands, which reminded me of ham hocks.

"Hank, this here is the flashiest country palace in ol' Louisian' and as such I believe it's the perfect showcase to display to your public that you still have what it takes. Yes sireee, this here's just the beginning for you and me, ol' hoss."

I didn't like having his arm over my shoulder and I didn't much care for him.

Fatty's Corral was spacious, with an L-shaped mahogany bar with every stool held down and a half-dozen waitresses working the room. The lighting was good so the patrons crowding the tables could show off to one another. Most of them were dressed Western-style, lots of cowboy hats, and cowgirls too with pleated skirts and snazzy boots. The stage was by the curve in the L of the bar. Four musicians stood there waiting. They wore matching rhinestone stage outfits with black string ties. There was a guitar player, a drummer, a fiddle man and a guy seated behind a steel guitar.

Someone in the audience called out, "Hey everybody, here's Hank!"

The place came alive. Applause broke out and folks started calling out stuff like, *"Hey, Hank!"*

Fatty and Cantwell each took me by an elbow and guided me through the tables toward the stage. People were patting me on the back as I passed. Someone shoved an arm across my path to offer me a bottle of beer. I brushed it aside, friendly as I could, and kept moving.

When we reached the stage, Fatty introduced me to the band. I disremember their names but I could see by their manner that I didn't need an introduction. The guitar player mumbled something about how proud they were to be playing behind me, but his words were drowned out by the audience who were still clapping and cheering me on. Some were whistling like they were at a ballgame.

I unpacked my guitar from its case, a nice Gibson acoustic. I strapped her on, strummed a few chords to get in tune with the boy on guitar, then I called out "Lovesick Blues," counted it off and turned, wearing my best stage smile for the audience. I wrapped my skinny frame around that microphone stand and began to sing.

The women shouted with glee and the fellows howled and whistled some more. Something about "Lovesick Blues" just gets to people whenever I open with it. The band speeded up the beat some but not so much that folks noticed. On the part where the band breaks to a stop and I yodel, I always wobble my knees together and stretch both arms out and let them shake when the music comes back in, and that drove these folks plumb crazy just like it always did.

It had been awhile since I'd played a club engagement. Before things started slowing down for me, I only played theaters and fairs where I'd share the bill with other entertainers and they expected me to do one show. But Cantwell had told me on the drive over from the motel that I was expected to play from 9:30 until 12:30. The way I handled that was to play two hour-and-fifteen-minutes sets with a half-hour break in between.

I was used to playing with pickup bands. The fellas I'd started with had gone their separate ways long ago. I still called whoever was backing me The Drifting Cowboys, the name of my original band when I cut my first records, but anymore The Cowboys consisted of whomever the promoter found to play behind me. Sometimes I got salty onstage and got hard to deal with because the musicians backing me on a particular night might not be up to snuff, be missing cues, playing songs in the wrong key or, worse, not even knowing the songs of mine that I wanted to sing. I'd stomped off-stage for that reason. But tonight was smooth sailing after the bumpy start with "Lovesick."

I decided to pace each set like I was playing a theater concert or a fairground. I like the folks to be swinging and up for at least the first half of my set, let them get their laughing and dancing out of their systems before I hit them with the listen-to songs.

So I gave them "Jambalaya" and "Hey, Good Lookin'" and "Rootie Tootie" for starters. I had the whole place singing along and the big polished dance floor was packed with people doing that old Cajun two-step. I spoke some between songs, letting folks know how glad I was to be there. I got a round of applause for the boys in the band, who were putting on a good show. Then I started laying on the heavies: "I'm So Lonesome I Could Cry" and "My Son Calls Another Man Daddy." I moved folks to tears with a recitation I had recorded as Luke the Drifter, "Too Many Parties and Too Many Pals." But naturally you can't leave folks all depressed and down in the mouth. Toward the end of a set, you've got to offer them hope and lift them up before you let them go the way a preacher does, so I ended that first set with "Wealth Won't Save Your Soul."

When I left the stage, folks congregated around to let me know that they were my biggest fans and they were enjoying the show. I shook hands all around and made friendly small talk, but the truth is that I get all knotted up inside when strangers get that close to me.

The fellas in the band stepped outside through a stage door behind the bar. I excused myself and eased out after them. They were taking a breather in the parking lot, smoking cigarettes and laughing and passing around a bottle of moonshine.

I shouldn't have taken a swig, but I only took one. Well, maybe a few. These were nice country boys and we passed the time with good-natured palaver.

At one point I glanced over toward the stage door and there was Cantwell, leaning against the back wall of the place. He was smoking a cigarette. He was hard to make out there in the dark, even with the parking lot lights, because of his dark suit and because he was in the shadows, content to smoke on his own. I saw the red dot of his cigarette tip as he puffed.

I felt a chill. He wasn't just by chance catching a breath of night air at the same time as us. He was keeping an eye on me. I thought about his concealed weapon. I remembered him going out and talking with the man I thought had been spying on my cabin. Something was wrong.

Then it was time for the next show. When I stepped onstage this time I was feeling spry thanks to that moonshine. And I was proud of myself. I hadn't taken more than a few nips. The young fellas in the band had seemed almighty pleased that they were getting high with Hank Williams, but I wasn't high. I did have that warm glow, though, going that made the stage lights softer and warmer and made the audience chatter less strident.

I did trip on the last step leading up to the stage, but that could have happened to anybody and no one seemed to notice. Or at least they pretended not to.

Now the truth is, I don't recall exactly which songs I sang in that second set but I was right *there* dead on it while it was happening, I guarantee you. The lyrics poured from me as if they weren't songs at all but me talking with these folks about my life, about the things that happen in all of our lives sooner or later. I started out with "Kaw-Liga," and a few more snappy sing-alongs and then the cheating songs and a honky-tonk song or two.

What I mostly remember is the dream. . . .

It came to me right smack dab in the middle of the set, even as I was warbling my songs and the band played and the audience laughed and danced. I was somehow transported to another time and place. It was so real that I could feel, smell and hear it, and it lived, a world of its own alive in my brain.

I was nine years old.

Me and my sister Irene were straddling a board fence out back of our house in Georgiana, listening to a colored congregation sing gospel songs in the Negro church across a big field and through the trees.

Irene is a year older than me and in those days, when I was growing up with Daddy gone and Mama working all the time, she I were inseparable. She wasn't just my sister. She was my best friend. Perched on that fence, hearing the music drift over every Wednesday night, was something we rarely missed.

I was born to be a musician. Mama bought me my first guitar for my eighth birthday, a second-hand guitar that cost her $3.50. This at a time when she was making only a quarter a day nursing and sewing. I would hear songs on the radio and right off start trying to sing and play like them.

But my dream, this dream I was having onstage that night at Fatty's Corral, wasn't about any of that. I just wanted to set you straight so you can understand the world in my mind that carried me away while I was halfway into my second set.

In the dream, a breeze from the south had picked up the joyful sounds of those colored folks singing, and it was unusual the way the music was carried to the little boy and girl sitting on that fence, cloaked in the final sunlight of day when the world is sort of a smoky place. Crickets and traffic noise from far off were pushed aside by the sweet music of those people lifting their voices to God. The trees across the field and the distance combined to orchestrate the singing so that one minute it was soft, then it would pick up.

I was holding my guitar, but hearing their music only made me feel restless because I couldn't figure out the chords that would allow me to play along.

I said, "Irene, one day I'm going to write songs like that."

Irene was a chunky dark-haired child, with Mama's square jaw. Her uneven soup-bowl haircut matched mine. We'd been straddling that fence for a while, side by side.

"I know you will, Harm," she said, smiling. "Oh look, yonder comes old Tee-tot!"

Tee-tot had a sort of shambling gait that wasn't exactly a shuffle but was clearly the pace of a man used to taking his time. He ambled up along the dirt path that ran by the fence, past our house.

Was this a dream I was having? Or was it a memory of things gone by, a real incident that really occurred, drifting back to my mind while I stood onstage in that nightclub?

He was a colored man, was old Tee-tot, and I mean to say he was black as the Ace of Spades. He wasn't a big fellow but he loomed large in my eyes. His guitar was slung across his back and his wide, yellow-toothed smile shone from beneath the brim of a battered gray derby. He wore mismatched jacket, shirt, vest and trousers, and he could have been thirty years old or sixty. His nappy hair had more salt than pepper, but a colored man could age before his time in Alabama in 1932. I heard people call him a "shiftless nigger" many a time, often to his face. An old razor-cut scar ran down one side of his face from the corner of his eye to the corner of his mouth. But when he smiled, which was often, that scar went away.

Tee-tot was a man amongst men. He was my hero.

"Hello there, young 'uns."

Irene said, "Hello, Tee-tot. You heading home?"

"I am, child, after a long and profitable day on the street corners of our fair town." He leaned against the fence and looked across

the field to where the church steeple poked above the treetops.
"You kids getting some religion, eh? That's good." He stretched out
the last word to indicate his pleasure.

I returned my attention to the guitar balanced on my knee, and
continued trying to match the rhythm of my strum to that of the
music from across the field.

Everybody in our neighborhood knew Tee-tot. Us poor whites
didn't live "across the tracks" from the colored. We lived on the
same side of the tracks, just maybe a bump further up the road.
There was a colored hobo jungle under the trestle a half-mile from
our house and that's where Tee-top had made his camp. His days
were spent strolling the streets and at the train station, playing and
singing for tips.

I first heard him play at the station when I was shining shoes.

In the beginning he didn't know what to think about a little
white boy following him everywhere, but I couldn't help myself. I
was too young to think about it then but I see now that I was
latching onto a kindred spirit for dear life. An old black street
musician and a skinny, sickly cracker kid looked on the surface like
they couldn't be more different. But in important ways that
mattered, that old man and me were cut from the same cloth.

We were both outsiders. I knew even at that tender age that I
was different from most folks; that I would never fit into their idea
of what a normal life was. Tee-tot was outside of "normal" society
because he was a black man in a white world. The other way we
were alike was that music made our hearts beat. I was always
singing and practicing on my guitar. And every time I saw Tee-tot
just about, he was standing where the most folks could be found,
playing music for their coins and the rare paper money that a
passer-by might toss into his derby, which was placed at his feet.

He played blues and country and waltzes and what they used to
call hokum blues, which means they were dirty songs, songs about
sex, sung with clever lyrics that were amusing. These different
musical styles sounded like no one but Tee-tot when he played and
sang. His voice had a thick gargle to it, but he could pitch it sweet
on the high notes when he sang about careless love.

His performance on the street was always punctuated with
"Thank you, suh!" or *"Thank you kindly, ma'am, God bless,"* as people
dropped money into his hat. He would keep his eyes downcast and
his voice was respectful, servile. Tee-tot had some living under his

belt. He was wise in knowing how to survive in his world. He must have figured that invoking the Almighty was added insurance against incurring the wrath of a passing white man who might find him addressing a white woman to be offensive regardless of the circumstance.

As a boy I did not understand these things but Tee-tot must have seen it, and I wore him down with my childish nagging. One afternoon we sat on a bench in the shade of a willow tree in the town park, with the scent of flowers heavy in the air, and he started teaching me how to really play the guitar. He taught me how to strum. He taught me my chords. He showed me what he called "natural" tunings and what he called "boogie runs" on the top strings of the guitar neck.

For two years I made a pest of myself to that man, so much so that folks in town would laugh and point at the scrawny white boy tagging along at the heel of the salty old street minstrel with the heart of gold. Tee-tot got used to it and his nickname for me became "Li'l white boss" in public and in private.

I never saw anything of the drinking or woman-chasing or the cutting that went on in the songs he sang. (I taught myself those vices later.) Tee-tot taught me most of what he knew on the guitar, and everything that I know.

Mama didn't mind. As a matter of fact, she would often slide him a sandwich if she came home from work and found us sitting on the front step, Tee-tot playing his guitar and me trying to accompany him. Ma must have figured that if she had to listen to me sit around the house playing that guitar every day and night, she could at least expect me to play something tolerable to the ears.

Tee-tot was nice to Irene. Most girls her age would be trying to ditch their little brother, and most boys would be trying to figure how to best sabotage their big sister with another prank. Tee-tot accepted Irene as my best friend.

In my dream, she was beaming at him. She jumped down off the fence. "Tee-tot, Mama made a sandwich for you. I'll go get it."

He patted her on the head. "You tell your mama I said thank you kindly."

"I'll be right back!"

His eyes were merry. "Child, I ain't going nowhere without that sandwich."

Irene ran off. Tee-tot returned his attention to me an my guitar.

"Looks like the li'l white boss done stumbled onto something new. You like that music them folks are making, do you?"

I quit trying to strum and looked up. "Sure do. It ain't like the blues you play, Tee-Tot, but it moves me deep, you know?"

He brought his guitar around so that he was holding it in a playing position.

"Then it is like the blues, ain't it? But you right. Them folks over yonder, they Christian folks. They call my kind of blues the Devil's music."

I blinked. "I didn't know that."

He played a few practice licks on his guitar.

"You got a lot to learn, boy, but you're on the right track. Listen to every kind of music there is. Get hep to what makes it the same, not different. Do the same with people and that will serve you well."

I couldn't take my eyes off those fingers of his, gliding across the frets.

He went on, "Now, if a white boy was to learn himself how to play the blues *and* the Lord's music, well, I reckon he could set the woods on fire with the music that would come out of him."

"But I don't see how they're the same," I said. "Seems like the chords and the rhythms are different."

"The *feeling*, son. Blues and gospel both them kinds of music don't come from no songwriter's pen. They come from the *soul*. Always have, always will. You can't play them low down blues or sing praise to your Lord and expect other people to believe what you're singing unless *you* believe it, and that's got to come from your soul."

"I think I understand."

"You do. Your mama done give you children a good Christian raising. Oh, you're going to know what heartache feels like soon enough, once you grow yourself a few more years, believe that. I can tell, Hiram. You got feelings down deep. You're the hurting kind, boy."

Across the field, the congregation stopped its singing. The preacher most likely was delivering a prayer or sermonizing, but that didn't carry the way the music had.

"Tee-tot," I said, "will you teach me how to play gospel music?"

He stopped his idle picking, and his eyes grew dead serious the way they always did when he was about to show me something new. "I believe it's past time for that, young 'un." He chuckled.

"And won't it surprise your mama to hear you singing 'Amazing Grace' instead of some song about a wrong-doing rounder that I done taught you."

I couldn't help but laugh. I sure did love that old man.

"Reckon it would make her happy," I said. "And she might make you bigger sandwiches."

It was his turn to laugh. A throaty laugh that was comfortable to a person's ears.

"There is that. Lordy lord. Okay, li'l boss. One thing that separates the blues from gospel is the way you strum that guitar, and some of the chords. Lookee here, now, and pay attention."

And that's where my dream, or my fond old memories, started to fade.

Me and Tee-tot and the music.

Sometimes I wish I had stayed a kid.

I returned to the present. I was on stage at Fatty's Corral, fixing to bring my second show to a close. Yes, I had lost track of what songs I was singing but the audience didn't seem to notice. When my brain came back to fix on the present, I saw nothing but smiling folks clapping their hands and carrying on and calling for more. I must be giving them a good show!

I nodded to the band that they could step down. I would sing my encore *a cappella*. That means without accompaniment.

After my thoughts of Irene and me sitting on that fence, of Tee-tot and the colored congregation across the field singing hymns, there was something extra in my singing when I gave them "I Saw the Light" and, hand on the Bible, by the time I'd finished there were some who had fallen to their knees right there on that barroom floor and held their hands clasped in prayer. Others were raising their hands to testify. Tee-tot would have been proud.

Someone in the audience shouted, "God bless you, Hank Williams."

I said, "I hope He does," in a humble voice that I hardly recognized as my own.

I gave them a farewell wave, and left the stage.

The place burst wide apart with applause.

There were folks waiting for me in front of the stage, like after the first set, but the house lights had been turned up. People were beginning to file out. They looked exhausted and satisfied, which is a good way to leave an audience, I always say.

I shook some hands and exchanged a few rounds of "Good night," then I started looking around for Cantwell, my ride back to the motel.

There was no sign of him.

I spotted Fatty Hewitt standing about where he'd been when Cantwell had first shown me in two hours earlier. I sauntered over. His face lightened up with a smile and he extended one of his ham hocks. We shook hands.

"That was a mighty fine show, Hank. Yes siree, mighty fine. Everybody thought you were just marvelous."

I thought, *marvelous?*

I said, "Glad to hear it. So are we on for tomorrow night?"

"You better believe it. Uh, one thing though, Hank, and I trust you will receive my counsel in the spirit in which I intend, namely as constructive criticism."

This boy sure did have a way with words.

I said, "I reckon." My eyes kept looking over his shoulder for Cantwell.

"Well, uh," he said, "I'm a God-fearing believer and all of that, Hank, but uh, maybe you ought to ease up on that gospel stuff. You know, the way some folks was kneeling and praying just, uh, well, I don't know if everybody wants to see that in a honky tonk."

"They come to see me," I said, "and that's what I give them. Fatty, they want to laugh, they want to cry and they want to be reminded that their souls have been saved from eternal damnation."

His big smile stayed in place but you could tell he wasn't used to being disagreed with. "Well now, that's all fine and good, Hank, I suppose, but uh, isn't that the preacher's job Sunday morning?"

I stopped looking over his shoulder and looked straight at him. "These folks like what I gave them, as you said. You're going to have to trust me on this, Fatty. I know what I'm doing."

He eyed me up and down like he was thinking of dropping his smile and saying what was on his mind. Then he said, "Of course, Hank, of course. You're Hank Williams, after all. If you don't know what your fans go for, who does, right?"

"That's right."

He gave a good-natured chortle but that didn't fool me. Most of these good ol' boys with their expansive nature and their slapping everybody on the back, they're the ones you've got to watch. You could look into Fatty's eyes and see that he was a beast of prey, if you were paying attention.

He said, "Main thing, Hank, is that this here association of ours is off to a flying start. I look forward to it with anticipation."

"You ain't seen Mr. Cantwell around, have you?"

"Matter of fact, Hank, T. J. was called away on business."

That feeling in my craw that said something wasn't right started acting up again. I looked at the clock over the bar.

"It's half past midnight. Sort of a peculiar time for taking care of business, ain't it?"

"Not if you're working for me. You know that, Hank. This is the time of day or night when our sort of business gets done."

"Reckon so, but uh—"

"How are you getting back to the motel? Dog, man, we ain't going to leave you high and dry. We'll be taking good care of you from here on out. There's a cab waiting outside for you, Hank. Come on, I'll walk you to it. T. J. said for you to get a good night's sleep and he'd be by to pick you up from the motel at noon tomorrow. He'll bring you here and the three of us can sit down and develop a strategy for booking you all over the great state of Louisiana. Now, how does that sound?"

Chapter 8

Hank

The rain had started again while I was playing my second show. Wavering gray sheets of falling water reflected the neon of Fatty's Corral so that the sheets of rain looked dyed with shimmering strands of yellow, red and green. Fat raindrops pelted the pavement like buckshot.

Women and some men stood clustered under the canopy, and at intervals would dash for cars arriving at the curb, driven from the lot by husbands and boyfriends. The ladies delicately lifted nyloned legs over the gutter that ran like a small coursing river, but they got plastered wet just the same in the brief seconds between canopy and car.

A Yellow cab was waiting for me.

Fatty grabbed a closed umbrella from the hand of a

startled man who stood waiting with some women. The man started to protest but then thought better of it when he saw that it was Fatty. Fatty was already opening the umbrella, holding it up to shield us from the rain slashing down. Moving with considerable speed for a man of his size, he extended his free hand to open the cab door for me.

"You get yourself a good night's sleep, Hank." He had to raise his voice for me to hear him over the racket of the falling rain. "I'll see you and T. J. tomorrow."

I slid into the taxi. "See you, Fatty." I closed the door after me.

Without hesitation the driver eased the taxicab into gear and drove off before I had even settled in. All I could see of the driver was the back of his head; a cap worn at a jaunty angle, a cigarette lodged behind his ear.

"Howdy, Mr. Williams." His attention was on merging us with the traffic in the rain but in the light of a passing street lamp he caught my eye in his rear view mirror. "I'm right pleased to have you as a passenger in my cab, sir. I've got every one of your records."

"Then drop the 'sir'," I told him. "Call me Hank. You wouldn't happen to have a sip up there with you by any chance? I could use one."

"Why sure, Mr. Williams. I mean, Hank."

A flask encased in a stitched leather pouch was passed to me.

I took a swig. I turned and looked out the rear window. Through the rain I saw Fatty returning the umbrella to the man without speaking to him. Fatty watched us drive off. Then he disappeared from my view beyond the curtain of rain. I took another pull from the flask.

Seemed to me that Fatty wasn't the kind to be glad-handing and playing doorman to just anyone including the great Hank Williams. And yet he was working hard to create the impression that he was my newfound best friend. He was helping me out by giving me an opportunity, but why was he so palsy-walsy about it? And I wondered again where T. J. Cantwell had gone off to.

The 'shine in the flask burned down my throat and raced through my veins, firing me up. I thought about that gal, Ava, at the motel office.

I handed the flask back to the driver. "Much obliged, amigo."

"My pleasure. My girl is crazy about you too, Hank, but I ain't jealous." He took a swig from the flask before putting it away. "They call me Driveabout."

"Hey, Driveabout," I said for something to say.

"How'd the show go tonight, Hank?"

For some reason I always get bashful talking about myself. I can sing about myself right enough, but that's when I have a guitar to hide behind.

"Aw well, you know," I said, "they seemed to go for it."

As he drove, we continued to talk, just two amiable guys whom circumstance had placed together for a short spell. He told me about the time he drove Gene Autry from the Shreveport station. Gene was all duded up in his fancy rhinestone singing cowboy duds and a ten gallon hat, but he was drunk as a skunk and kept changing his mind about which hotel he wanted to be taken to, and then forgetting that he'd changed his mind. It was an amusing tale.

The return trip to the motel took a little longer because traffic barely inched along. Rainwater flooded every gutter to overflowing. We saw a few minor accidents. Raindrops tattooed on the taxi's roof like BB-gun pellets.

As we wheeled into the motel parking lot, I noticed a light from a curtained window to the rear of the office. Through the darkness and rain I thought I saw the curtain shift slightly in that window but I couldn't be sure.

The office was dark. A *Closed* sign hung in the window. I looked some more as we passed the office. No Ava. That made sense. It was raining like hell. A Louisiana soaker. She was most likely all curled away in her warm bed with nothing on but the radio, listening to a Hank Williams song.

Driveabout braked to a stop directly in front of my cabin. He turned around and offered me the flask. "Pleasure to have met you, Hank. Have another nip?"

He was a button-eyed, freckled, friendly-faced lad, chewing gum while a toothpick wagged from the corner of his mouth. A thatch of red hair defied the grease he had applied to hold it in place.

I took a nip. "Thank you much. How much do I owe you, hoss?"

He took the flask and had another swig.

"Ixnay. This one's on the house. How's about if you need a taxicab again while you're in Shreveport, you call the dispatcher and tell her that you want Driveabout."

I thought about Cantwell and his car.

"Don't reckon as I'll have the need, but thanks, I'll keep that in mind. You watch out for yourself in this rain, hear?"

I slipped a twenty into his hand and let myself out before he could say anything else.

The taxi circled around in the close quarters of the parking lot and returned to the highway and disappeared from sight.

I stood there for a moment under the porch overhang, listening to the relentless pounding of rain on the blacktop and the roofs of cars parked in front of some of the cabins. My cabin was dark.

I looked through the veil of rain toward the darkened office. I thought about running across there, to knock on the glass door. Ava would take in a rain-soaked stray like me, especially after I told her who I was. I think she already half-guessed. But that rain was growing fiercer, hammering in from the Gulf. It wouldn't do me any good to catch a cold and lose my voice. I'd wander on over there when the rain let up.

I got my key out and unlocked the cabin door. I stepped inside. Pocketing the key, I reached over and flicked on the light switch, and stepped directly into the bathroom to take a long overdue piss. I stepped out from the bathroom and that was when I caught the first whiff of burned gunpowder.

I had started for the refrigerator and a beer when I saw my open suitcase on the floor. My socks, undergarments and pajamas were strewn about. My .38 with the pearl grip with the HW monogram was on the floor between the suitcase and the bed.

I cursed, and fell to my knees next to the suitcase, which was at an angle indicating that someone had idly tossed it down for a search. My hands darted through my folded clothes, knowing already that what I was looking for was gone.

My song notebook was gone!

My heart was pounding against my ribcage the way it does after I wash down bennies with Jack Daniels. It was obvious what had happened, but with the reflex of an animal, I scrambled around on all fours, searching through my scattered garments.

My songbook! I've kept one, carrying it with me everywhere I go, ever since I was that kid in Georgiana following ol' Tee-tot. I would fill up one after another, scribbling down my rhymes and song ideas that come to me at oddest times of the day or night, sometimes when I'm at home but more often when I'm out on the road, up late at night in a lonely room five hundred miles from the people I love. Some of those lyrics become songs, or I'll take one verse into a recording session and Mr. Rose will help me finish up the writing there on the spot. Some lyrics never get used. But that's the process I've use to come up with every song I ever recorded. All of the hits started in my songbooks. Those dime store ring binders are worth their weight in gold when you consider how much money those songs make. In the current book, there were a dozen or more fragments of ideas and rhymes that I had written down. And now . . .

The songbook was gone.

My attention shifted to the gun and I picked it up. My index finger automatically curled around the trigger. That .38 was one of my favorites from my collection, which is why I kept it as my traveling gun. I raised the muzzle to my nostrils and nearly sneezed at the bite of burnt cordite. My gun had been fired!

Something else caught my eye over at the corner closet near the foot of the bed. A widening stain of something dark like motor oil was spreading out upon the wooden floor from beneath the door.

I thought, *What the hell* and I crossed to the closet with the gun in my hand. My heart was hammering. My tongue got so thick, I couldn't swallow. I reached down and dabbed an index finger into the spreading pool. I brought my fingertip up for inspection. It was blood. Something told me to get out of there quick as I could. But I couldn't stop myself. I opened the closet door.

At first glance I thought the man in the closet was hiding there to spy on me. He wore a trench coat that matched the one worn by the man who'd been spying on the cabin earlier. The front of his coat looked like he had been rolling around in red mud. And there was a bullet hole in the middle of his forehead. A round purple hole that was bleeding a single red tear. He had been propped upright inside the closet, leaning against the door.

When I opened that door, the dead man toppled forward onto the floor, sprawling with a heavy *thump!* that sounded like a dropped sack of grain.

I let out a squawk and reared back as if I'd been given an electric jolt. I was still holding the gun in my hand. I didn't know what to do.

Two men stormed into the cabin, not caring how much ruckus they made. Big, broad-shouldered guys with hard, chiseled features. Each wore a fedora and a raincoat dripping with moisture, and each held a .45 automatic in his hand. They fanned out just inside the door and stood side by side with their guns aiming at me.

"Hold it right there," said one.

"Lose the piece," said the other, "and step away. Hands in plain view. Go on, do it or you're dead."

I did as I was told.

I said, "Whoever you fellas are, I want you to know that I didn't do that," and I nodded to the body on the floor.

The one to my left made a sniffing sound. The scent of burnt gunpowder lingered in the air.

"Sure looks and smells like you did it," he said. "You were holding the gun when we came in."

My heart wasn't rattling against my chest anymore. I felt frozen like a statue. My gut was a block of ice.

I said, "Uh, would you fellas mind if I asked who you are?"

The one to my right snickered. "We've got the guns, bub. We ask the questions."

His partner said, "Hell, Mack, maybe it'll scare something out of him."

The other considered this, then nodded. He produced a leather packet and held it up for me to see. It was too far across the room for me to make out the writing or the face on the ID, but I saw the badge plain enough.

He said, "We're FBI. I'm Agent Macklin. This is Agent Wiley." He indicated the dead man. "That's Agent Sallis." He spoke with a Yankee accent.

From behind his gun, Wiley said, "Why'd you do it, asshole?"

Even with everything that was happening—a dead man at my feet, me holding that gun when they broke in—well, the very notion of what he was saying made my jaw drop.

I said, "Wait a minute. I didn't do nothing. I swear I didn't! I just walked in and—"

Wiley's eyes glittered like polished stones. "Pete Sallis was my friend. He was my daughter's godfather. We go fishing together. He has a wife and three kids. Asshole." He started at me, drawing his arm back, intending to swipe the .45's barrel across my face.

Macklin moved fast and caught his partner's arm. "Hold it. We want that mouth of his to work."

But Wiley tried to get around him. "Goddamn. He killed Pete and I'm going to kill him, the little punk."

Macklin held his ground, both of his hands on Wiley's chest, and held him back.

"He could know something, and maybe he didn't kill Pete." Macklin turned to me, still blocking Wiley. "Well, say something, punk. If you didn't kill Agent Sallis, who did?"

My back was against the wall.

I said, "I don't know, mister, and that's God's truth. I walked in just now and found him. Swear to God, I ain't no killer. I'm a singer!"

Wiley let his arm drop so that he was holding his pistol against his leg. "Let's see some identification from you."

Their slit eyes watched my every move. I reached around to my ass pocket and pulled out my wallet. Wiley snatched it from my fingers and flipped it open so they could both see my driver's license. Their eyes swept over my white Western suit with the stitched design and my white hat.

Macklin said, "Hiram Williams. You look like Hank Williams to me."

Wiley said, "Well I'll be goddamned."

"I am Hank Williams," I said, "and I've got an alibi for where I was all night if I need one. I tell you I never killed nobody."

Wiley tossed me my wallet. I caught it and returned it to my pocket.

He said, "Hank Williams. I'll be damned. A goddamn hillbilly singer."

"I didn't kill him," I said. "Shoot, I never saw him before."

Macklin was watching me like a guy trying to form an opinion. "We spoke to the young lady who works in the office. She says a man checked you in here last night, went away and then came back after dark to pick you up."

"That's right. His name is Cantwell. T. J. Cantwell."

Wiley said, "That's what he signed on the register. His real name is Leopold Lentz."

"Mr. Williams," said Macklin, "you'd better tell us everything you know."

And so I did. It didn't take long. I told them about meeting Cantwell at the train depot the day before and about his proposition and him taking me to perform at Fatty Hewitt's Corral. They traded glances at my mention of Fatty.

I said, "A taxi brought me here. I walked in and found that

man's body and before I knew it, here you fellas come scaring the bejaspers out of me."

Wiley still held his gun against his trouser leg. "We haven't even started on you."

Macklin said, "Now hold on. He could be telling the truth." He shook off his raincoat and draped it across the body on the floor while he asked me, "You sure you never saw this man before?"

Wiley was staring holes through me. I concentrated on Macklin.

"I ain't sure," and I told about what happened before Cantwell and I left tonight. I told about me seeing someone out in the rain and how Cantwell went out to confront the man, and how he told me the man in the rain was a private detective keeping an eye on some other cabin.

Wiley said, "You think it was Sallis you saw in the rain?"

Before I could respond to that, Macklin broke in. "It makes sense. Fucking Lentz was just ballsy enough to stage a play like that, going out to confront Sallis face to face."

"So why didn't Sallis take him down when he had the chance?"

"He was waiting on us to show up."

Wiley said, "Damn," and anger heated up his eyes.

I said, "Pardon me, gents, but I don't understand a thing that's going on here. What kind of mess am I in?"

Wiley said, "A commie mess, and the murder of a Federal agent."

I blinked. "Commies?"

Macklin looked like he'd made up his mind. He reached into his jacket and produced a deck of Luckies.

"Cigarette, Mr. Williams?"

I said, "Much obliged," and helped myself to a coffin nail and fired up.

Wiley said, "Now wait a damn minute."

Macklin told his partner, "No. You wait." There was steel in his voice. "I think we ought to give Mr. Williams the benefit of the doubt. He may have information that can help, and I know he'll cooperate."

I liked the sound of that. I drew on the cigarette and said through the smoke, "I'll be glad to help you fellas any way I can."

Macklin reached into his coat and brought out a five-by-ten glossy photograph, which he handed to me. "Is this the man you're talking about, who's calling himself T. J. Cantwell?"

I didn't need more than a glance. It was a police mug shot. I handed it back.

"That's him."

Macklin shook a cigarette loose from his pack and stuck it into the corner of his mouth. He fired up. "Mr. Williams, what do you know about the Communist menace?"

My brain tripped for a second like a stumble over that last step. These boys were bubbling with the unexpected.

"Well," I said, "I ain't proud to say but I reckon like most folks I don't pay much attention to the news."

Wiley hadn't holstered his .45. "Then you don't know what the fuck we're talking about, do you, asshole?"

"I know what's going on," I said. "My neighbor lady's got two sons over there in Korea and I know President Truman is doing a right fine job, if you ask me. I know what Senator Joe McCarthy's been saying about Russian spies inside our government and living among us."

"Well, what do you think about that?" It sounded like Wiley was challenging me to a fight.

I scratched the back of my neck. "I reckon like most folks, I'm inclined to believe him. I mean, we was allies with the Russkies back in the war but ever since then it's been a mighty rocky road with ol' Joe Stalin and them rascals behind what they call the Iron Curtain. Seems like they're against everything we stand for and they want to take over the world with their way of thinking. But ain't nothing down here in the swamps of Louisian' or the cotton fields of Mississippi for them Commies to have much interest in."

Macklin gestured with the mug shot. "Leopold Lentz is a Russian spy. He emigrated at the end of the war. We've recently learned that his real name is General Andrei Strahkov of the Soviet intelligence apparatus."

"Dang, how many names does he have?"

"More than we know. He was working in Washington for the State Department."

Wiley glanced at the corpse at our feet. A puddle of blood was beginning to spread from under the edge of the raincoat that draped it. His stony eyes lifted to me.

"Lentz stole a complete list of every American agent in Europe and their European contacts. He killed his supervisor to get the list."

Macklin nodded. "We're entering what's being calling a Cold War, Mr. Williams. If that master list gets to Moscow and the Soviets act on it, it will have a devastating effect on this country's intelligence networks."

I put out the cigarette in an ashtray. "Reckon I'm not sure what that all means."

"There won't be any big battles in this Cold War," said Macklin. "It's going to be a war between the U.S. and the Soviet Union, but it's going to be fought by diplomats and spies and by small, poor surrogate countries. Mr. Williams, we *must* stop Strahkov and retrieve that list before he can leave the country with it."

I said, "Could you do me a favor and call him Cantwell? That's the name I know him by. This here's confusing me something fierce. Commie spies, huh?"

Macklin said, "Call him whatever you want. His name isn't important. That list is. We have to locate him and stop him by whatever means possible."

"What's he doing way down here in Shreveport?"

Wiley sneered. "Put it together, hillbilly. My partner just told you our boy's trying to get out of the country."

Macklin said, "We have the Northeast sealed up tight. We'd be on him the second he showed his face in an airport and he knows it. That leaves the South as his best escape route. He could catch a freighter for South America or Europe from any number of ports down here, including Shreveport. We trailed him here and he lost us."

I said, "But what's he doing messing around with me? What's he doing booking country music acts into a honky tonk if he's running for his life? I would have never in a million years guessed that fella was a Russian spy."

"The point is," said Wiley, "he did contact you. What did you talk about?"

"We didn't talk about nothing but music. Worst I thought about him was that he was a Yankee."

Wiley growled. "Smartass." His arm came up in a blur too fast for Macklin to stop him or for me to see it coming.

The barrel of his .45 caught me alongside the head and my knees buckled as my head was slammed into the wall. My eyes teared up and pain coursed through me. The wall was the only reason I didn't tumble over. That's how hard he clocked me.

Macklin said, "Goddamn it, go easy on him." Then I felt his hand on my upper arm, steadying me. "Hank, listen to me. I can't stop Wiley. He's pissed off because his friend is dead. If you know where Cantwell is or if you know anything about him, spill it."

Wiley said, "Look at those stains on the bed. Big star's a bed-wetter."

I shook my head to clear my vision. My hat had been knocked off my head. Wiley looked like wanted to take another swing at me. Don't ask me why but I was more riled than scared.

I said, "Jesus H. Christ! I'm an American citizen. I ain't no Communist. If you fellas knew anything about Hank Williams, you'd sure as hell know that. What are you doing, roughing me up? I'm a victim here too! I'm sorry that man is dead, but that son of a bitch Cantwell stole my songbook and here I am, getting beat up."

Macklin's mouth grew tight. "Songbook?"

"The notebook I keep my songs in. It's missing. Cantwell took it. He stole it. It's worth a fortune to me and maybe to him too."

Wiley said, "That don't help us. Tell us what we want to know."

I said, "I can't tell you what I don't know." I pointed at the opened suitcase and the clothes strewn about the floor near the body. "Cantwell went through my junk and run off with my songbook. I want to find him just as bad as you do. I was supposed to meet him after I finished my show tonight, but he was gone when I got through. I tell you, I don't know where he is."

Wiley lowered his stony eyes and studied the gun in his hand. "Know what I think, bed wetter? I think you're making stuff up so you won't have to tell us where he went to."

Macklin stood shoulder to shoulder with Wiley. "Is that true, Hank?"

"Hell no." I tried not to sound as shaky as I felt but I sounded pretty scared. "I didn't know Cantwell was a gol-dang spy and I sure as hell don't know where he took off to."

Wiley sneered. "You're more afraid of Cantwell than you are of us. We've got to change that. Mack."

Macklin said, "Sorry, Hank," and slipped fast around behind me and before I knew it he was holding me by each arm with a vise-like grip.

Wiley raised his .45, not to shoot me but to heft the gun, gauging its weight because he intended to work me over enough to break bones and cause pain, but he didn't want to kill me.

I said, "You ain't no G-men."

Macklin chuckled, though there was little humor in it. "I should have known you wouldn't buckle under, but I had to try." He said to Wiley, "All right, do it."

Wiley sneered a mean laugh. "With pleasure." He drew his arm back. The barrel of the automatic glinted dully in the overhead light.

I braced myself, wishing I could figure some way out of this. But I had run plumb out of ideas.

A car engine accelerated and the front wall of the cabin exploded inward like a bomb going off. Masonry and splintered wood and shards of flying glass and thrown-aside furniture exploded into swirling dust and debris as the front end of a car plowed right in through the wall, the front right tire coming to a stop atop of the sprawled dead man.

Macklin shoved me away and pawed for his shoulder holster. Wiley yelled something and tracked his gun around at the onslaught. The force of Macklin's shove sent me hurtling against the car's right fender. I know something about cars. I recognized the grill of a '49 Chevy. A cloud of dust shrouded the car. I tripped over the dead man's arm and almost fell.

A figure emerged from the swirling dust. A mighty nice figure. Big around the hips, but in a nice way.

It was Ava, the brunette from the office. She held a pistol, a long-barreled .38 revolver. It looked big in her hands, but she was doing just fine holding it with both hands, looking sure of herself and very dangerous. Her expression was a mask of feminine fury. Wiley and Macklin saw her but she had the advantage of surprise, to put it mildly. The dust hadn't settled yet.

She raised the pistol and fired a round into the ceiling. The report was real loud inside the cabin even with the new hole that had just been busted through the front wall.

Wiley and Macklin froze with their pistols just short of drawing a bead on her. Ava faced them squarely with her feet solidly planted, her knees bent and both arms extended. The barrel of the .38 shifted between them.

"Drop your guns." Her voice was cold as a slashing knife. "I know I'm outnumbered. You'll drop me but I'll take one of you down for damn sure. I'm not worth it, boys. Drop 'em."

Wiley said, "Lady, you are fucking with the United States government."

She said, "Mister, my government is fucking with me. Last chance. Drop 'em."

Macklin and Wiley exchanged a glance. Macklin dropped his gun first, then Wiley did the same.

I heard people outside the cabin shouting questions to each other.

Ava said to me, "Get in the car."

I sidestepped the body on the floor and the jagged masonry around the busted-in window, and by the time I scrambled into the passenger side of the Chevy, she was coolly sliding in behind the steering wheel. The biggest black purse I'd ever seen rested in the middle of the seat. I slammed shut my door as she rammed the heap into reverse and backed away from the mess she'd made. The Chevy's rear tires bounced onto the blacktop of the parking lot, which was slick with moisture. It had stopped raining. Lights were on in the other cabins and people stood in open doorways.

Ava wheeled the heap around, up-shifting like a racecar driver. She floored the gas pedal and we rocketed off.

Gunfire opened up from behind us. Bystanders were diving for cover. A slug whistled through the Chevy, shattering the back windshield and leaving a clean matching hole through the front right between the two of us.

I was hanging on for dear life. I couldn't think of anything to say. Squealing tires, skidding across wet pavement, filled my ears.

Ava drove with her jaw set and her knuckles snow-white on the steering wheel.

We tore off down the highway, into the night.

Chapter 9

Muddy

The Jefferson Hotel, where the band was staying in Shreveport, was the top two floors of a three-story red brick building on a busy street corner in the heart of darktown. It wasn't prime real estate, naturally, but was close enough to the water to hear the sea gulls. The rooms had Salvation Army furnishings and threadbare rugs. Each man paid his share out of his own pocket.

The hotel was three blocks from the Boogie Woogie Inn, where we were booked through the weekend. I planned for us to layover Sunday and Monday, then head out for New Orleans where Groove Boy had us booked for two more weeks.

Walter and me shared a room. Elgin and Jimmy had the adjoining room. It was a good setup for hanging out during the day, when musicians laze about and pass the time playing cards and watching the television.

Rooming with Little Walter let me keep an eye on him. Thing about Walter, when he was blue he was liable to drink until he got crazy and then get his mouth working, trying to goad you. Or he'd flip out and get one of his nosebleeds so bad it would look like someone had punched him the face. If he was feeling good, well, he wouldn't think about nothing but scoring him dope and pussy. That's a fact. Walter was a crazy mixed-up kid but you know, this here's a crazy mixed-up world. So I let Walter blow his harmonica and I tried to keep him out of trouble.

The morning after our first night at The Boogie Woogie, I herded the guys downtown to a men's clothing store where we got outfitted in new threads. We'd been sweating our asses off in the clothes we brought down with us from Chicago. Even our casual summer clothes were too heavy for the swamp heat of Louisiana in July. We got measured for new stage uniforms. I picked us out seersucker suits and little yellow eggshell colored short-sleeve shirts, and beige slacks. We could rinse off the shirts after work, hang them for the next morning and they'd be ready for the next gig.

The complication was that Walter was so damn thin. We found a shirt that fit him but they had to do some alterations to the slacks. The tailor told us to come back in a few hours. When it was time to go back that afternoon, Walter acted like he didn't want to get off the couch. He was watching a ball game on TV.

I said, "Come on man, they're your pants. Walk on down to the store with me. You ain't drunk."

I figured it was better during daylight hours for us to walk, instead of being seen in my red Cad. I hadn't forgotten the cop from Crowley or what almost went down last night when that other cop had showed up at the club looking to haul me in. Delilah Buie had snatched my bacon from that fire.

Maybe that's why I woke up with wood, thinking about her that morning. . . .

Walter rested the back of one arm across his eyes. "Aw, Muddy, I ain't feeling myself, man. I gots to rest up."

"You got one of your nosebleeds?"

"Naw man, not yet. Maybe it's what I ate. I need to rest up."

I fired a cigarette and watched him through the smoke.

"You've got something on your mind, Walter. You've been real quiet all day, even down at that men's store. You most often get to smart-mouthing at times like that."

"Muddy, don't mess with me, man."

"You're tied on about that new record Chess put out on you."

He brought his arm away from his eyes and propped himself on one elbow. "When I went downstairs for them cigarettes a while ago, I put in a collect call to Mr. Leonard up in Chicago."

I felt myself grow tight.

"Don't be talking like some plantation nigger. His family call him Leonard. You and me, we call him Mr. Chess."

"I know that. You know what he told me?"

I wanted to bend over and cuff him behind the ear. My temper has got a short fuse. My blood was starting to run hot. "What did Chess say, you uppity nigger?"

He pretended not to hear that. Walter was small and wiry, but he was a scrapper. But he wasn't about to scrap me.

"Chess told me my record is getting heavy play in Chicago and Detroit and Memphis and Dallas, maybe more places by now. And *Billboard* done give me a good review, Muddy. Man, that record is going to the top."

"What are you saying, nigger?"

"I'm saying that here I am getting jackshit sideman pay when it's *my* record on the jukebox what the folks are dancing to. That ain't right. I should be getting more."

I said, "You're talking out your ass, little brother. Look at Jimmy. Chess done put out records with Jimmy singing and us playing and Jimmy, he's still in my band."

"That's because Jimmy's got something to lose," said Walter, "with his wife and family and shit. Me, I ain't got nothing to lose. I aim to make things happen."

I said, "Come on, Walter. Stop mumbling and talk straight."

He sat up on the couch and avoided looking at me. He reached into a pocket and withdrew a handkerchief, which he pressed to his nose.

"I said what I wanted to say." He drew the handkerchief from his nostrils and looked down at the red specks that stained it. He said, "Damn now, you see? Muddy, you done started my nose to bleeding." He stretched back out on his side, facing away from me.

I said, "Fuck you, Walter," and I went into the adjoining room.

Elgin was seated at a table by the window, reading a newspaper through wire-rimmed glasses perched on the end of his nose. He was filling the room with cigar smoke. Jimmy sat next to an open guitar case on his bed, and he had just finishing restringing his guitar.

I said, "Jimmy, let's you and me head downtown to pick up those threads."

He set the guitar in its case and snapped the case shut.

"Sure 'nuff, but don't Walter want to try on his pants before he takes them?"

Walter would be listening from the couch, through the adjoining doorway, so I ignored the question.

"Elgin, keep an eye on Walter. Come on, Jimmy."

Elgin didn't look up from reading his newspaper. "Uhm," he said, and took another puff on his cigar.

So me and Jimmy took a cab down to the men's clothing store. It's always smart for a black man to partner up when he's out on a new town even if it's in the colored section.

The day had started cool and clear after last night's rain but the thermometer had climbed steadily throughout the day and by late afternoon, clouds were creeping in again to blot out the blue and there was no breeze. People walked and talked slow. It was humid as hell. Thunder rumbled way out over the Gulf.

The shop had our orders boxed up and ready to go, including the alterations to Walter's trousers. Jimmy and me didn't talk much on the way down or back. Jimmy's an easygoing cat. He doesn't have to be working his mouth all the time.

The hotel rooms were empty when we returned. Walter and Elgin were gone. We stashed the packages and went downstairs. Jimmy and I stood on the sidewalk and looked around.

A Walgreen's took up the ground floor of the hotel, with a restaurant next door. The entrance to the hotel was between these.

I led the way into the restaurant. It was nice in there, with checkered tablecloths and leather upholstery.

Elgin sat in a booth. At this time of day he had the place to himself except for a pair of lovebirds holding hands at a corner table. They didn't pay attention to us. Elgin was sipping coffee and working on a newspaper crossword puzzle. A cigar rested on the rim of an ashtray, a curl of gray smoke rising from it.

Jimmy and me slid into the booth across from him.

He looked up, looking more than ever like a judge when he

pushed his reading glasses from the tip of his nose up to the bridge. He took some puffs off his cigar. He looked satisfied.

I said, "You seen Walter?"

"He headed out five minutes after you split. Said something about buying some cigarettes."

Jimmy glanced at his watch. "We've been gone close to forty-five minutes. That's a long time to be buying cigarettes. There's a theater around the corner. Maybe he went to a movie."

I said, "He ain't at no movie. Fellas, I've got a feeling. Elgin, I told you to keep an eye on him."

Elgin frowned. "I ain't no babysitter. I told you what he said and when he split, didn't I?"

Jimmy said, "Muddy, don't be hard on Walter. You know how he is."

Elgin replaced his cigar on the rim of the ashtray and took another sip of coffee. "We're professional musicians. That punkass boy never carried himself like a professional, always smarting off and acting the fool and playing so damn loud. We're better off without him."

"Like hell," I said. "I'm going to see what I can find out at the desk."

Elgin returned his reading glasses to the tip of his nose and went back to his crossword puzzle. Jimmy and me went out to the street and next door, upstairs to the lobby.

The girl working the desk was a lanky twenty-year-old chocolate drop, wearing white bobby sox with saddle shoes and a tight dark skirt and white blouse. I'd gotten to know her some since checking in, just to talk to . . . so far.

When I asked her about Walter, she said, "That little guy with the checkered hat on?"

"That's him."

"He told me to call him a cab, then he went down to the street to wait on it. He said for you to take care of his amplifier. He's sick. He had a terrific nose bleed."

Jimmy was frowning. "Maybe he's gone to the hospital. I've been thinking for a while that them nosebleeds could be serious."

The girl shook her head. "He's going back to Chicago."

I said, "How do you know that, sister?"

"He told me. Told me he was a recording artist. Is that true, Muddy? Said the name of his latest record is *Juke*."

I caught myself cussing a blue streak. "Latest record. It's that boy's *only* record if I get hold to him. Come on, Jimmy. I'm calling Chicago."

Jimmy tagged after me. "But I don't understand. Muddy, Walter ain't no punk. He's just got him a restless soul."

"He's a punk to me." I sat in the phone booth. "He ain't shit, running out like he done right in the middle of a tour. And after all I've done for him."

I got the long-distance operator and gave her the number in Chicago that I knew by heart. The girl who answered the phone at Chess Records put me on hold and in my mind I could see Leonard Chess in his office, rushing to finish a project before taking my call. Scratching his balding head. Chain-smoking cigarettes the way he does.

Chess Records was a family operation. Leonard and his brother Phil had started it years before, first running a club on the South Side, then recording the musicians that played there and releasing the records in Chicago. By 1952, Chess Records was the national boss independent label for the blues. Weren't no white folks buying blues records in those days. They called the records that black folks listened to, Race Records. Most radio stations were aimed at white folks. It was a hustle. Leonard ran the company on South Michigan Avenue and produced the recording sessions. Phil traveled through the South, talking their artists up to black radio stations and supplying record stores with the newest Chess releases from the trunk of his car.

Leonard tried to make the people working for Chess feel like part of his family. They treated me and Howlin' Wolf right because we were stars. Leonard gave me a Cadillac for a present one Christmas, same for Wolf. Everyone got a yearly Christmas bonus and they remembered your birthday. Trouble was, even though he *felt* black music better than any white man I ever knew, Leonard was a stone cold ghetto Jew businessman. I don't mean disrespect. It was a *good* thing, because he carried us black boys with him. A white man's got to be hard as nails and ruthless and tight-fisted if he wants to succeed in a racket like the record business. That was Mr. Leonard Chess.

"Muddy, it's good to hear from you."

I thought, *Like hell it is, you backstabbing son of a bitch.*

I said, "Mr. Chess, I've got myself a situation."

"I understand, Muddy."

"I know you do, sir. Walter told me he called you this morning. I wish you'd told him to stay on with me until we finished this here tour."

"I appreciate that, Muddy, I really do. About the tour, I mean. But there are dictates of commerce, you understand? We've got the pressing plant working overtime to keep up with the orders on *Juke* and I may have to hire extra help for the shipping room. The people love that harp sound Walter's playing on that record. They've never heard anything like it and they're grooving, baby."

Chess could pull off talking like a black cat. Reckon that's because he worked with us all day long.

I said, "Walter got that sound playing behind me. You know how he is, Mr. Chess. You've seen him in the studio and around the office. He ain't ready to front his own band."

"Well, he doesn't have much choice. I've got him booked at the Apollo in New York next month and you know what a showcase that is. Muddy, I know Walter's a wild child. But Chess Records has released *Juke* and now it's time to recoup our investment and make a profit. Don't take it personally. This is a business decision."

"Well," I said, "I reckon that boy deserves whatever comes his way after the way he done me. But that still leaves me behind the eight ball. I'm playing Shreveport two more nights, then New Orleans. I need someone to replace him."

He sighed in my ear across the long distance.

"As I say, Muddy, I appreciate your predicament. There are other fine harp players in Chicago. Junior Wells. Not as good as Walter but—"

"They're in Chicago," I said. "I need somebody this afternoon who can play my songs tonight."

"Now Muddy, this is what the responsibility of leadership is all about. You're in charge down there, aren't you? I'm doing my job. I'm sorry if it's caused you inconvenience, but you must endeavor to persevere."

We mumbled a few more things to each other and that was the end of our conversation. He broke the connection, the son of a bitch.

Jimmy was leaning against the doorframe of the phone booth. He'd followed my end of the conversation.

He said, "Sounds like we're on our own."

"You got that right. I've got to figure this one out, man. People come to hear us, they're going to expect that fat horn sound Walter puts on my records with his damn harp."

Jimmy stroked his chin. "Well you know, Muddy, we do call that harmonica a Mississippi saxophone."

I dug where he was going.

"A tenor sax," I said. "Yeah, that could work. A harp would be best, but people will dig it if they hear a sax man blowing Walter's lines behind me. That's a good idea, man. I'll get me a tenor player to finish off this tour, and we'll get us a new harp man when we get back to Chicago."

Jimmy was nodding. "It'll be easier to find a saxophone player down here than a good harp man. There's jazz men everywhere and most horn blowers can play the blues."

"Long as he don't have himself a fucked attitude," I said, "like Elgin."

"Question I've got is, where we going to find a cat like that on such short notice? We don't know nobody in Shreveport who can help us."

I took out my wallet and found the card with Delilah Buie's address and telephone number.

"Yes we do," I said.

"Damn, Muddy," Jimmy said, "that there's a cathouse."

We stood in a small park across the street from the address on Delilah's card. It was a colored residential neighborhood. People were strolling through the park, and there was light traffic passing on the street.

The address was a two-story wooden frame house with a peaked roof, a front porch with a swing that was not in use and a white picket fence around a well-kept lawn. The curtains were drawn in every window. An old oak tree stood in the front yard, tall as the house, and provided shade. Flowers bordered the walkway from the front porch to a gate in the fence.

A steady flow of men, mostly working men in their twenties and thirties but a couple of cats who had looked like they could have been doctors or professors, filed in and out through the front door.

An alley cut the block along one property line. There was a side entrance to the house.

I said, "Reckon I'll have to check out the merchandise if I get the time."

Jimmy said, "I ain't going in no whorehouse."

I felt my blood starting to run hot. "Jimmy, don't be throwing no curve ball at me. I've got enough on my mind."

"I ain't doing that, Mud. But shoot, you don't need me to talk to that lady, Delilah. I'm respectable, Muddy, even if I do pick guitar in a blues band for a living. Be just my luck that place would get raided while I was in there with you. That would be a hell of a note for my wife and children now, wouldn't it?"

"Aw, man, you talk like an old woman. Maybe we're wrong about what she's got going on there."

"You know we ain't."

Three boys in Little League baseball uniforms came along the sidewalk. They had gloves and bats over their shoulders.

I called out to them. "Hey young 'uns, what do you know about that house over yonder?"

One of them piped right up. "That there's Miss Delilah's whorehouse."

"Yas suh," chimed in another. "Best looking gals in Shreveport!"

And they all busted up laughing.

Jimmy snapped his fingers a couple times and pointed down the street. "You all are too young to know about that sort of stuff. Go on now, scat. Get on home and do like your mamas and daddies tell you to."

They trotted off, laughing at us.

Jimmy said to me, "I ain't going in no whorehouse. I'm going back to the hotel."

"Suit yourself," I said, and I started across the street toward the alley.

Chapter 10

Hank

"Hey, Slim, wake up."

This blackout business is strange, I've come to find out. What I mean is, you never know when it's going to hit. Damnedest thing is, sometimes you're out as if you were in a deep sleep without dreams and there's nothing in your mind when you come to but an empty black cloud. Other times, it's like waking up from a sleep filled with dreams.

Think of some time when you were sleeping and dreaming, and a telephone call or someone talking woke you up for a short time, then you fell back asleep and dreamt some more and when you woke up in the morning, your memory of those hours of sleep is messed up. You start bringing things around you into focus but you're not sure what you've dreamed and what was real because it's all woven into itself like a quilt sewn by a colorblind crazy woman. That's what it's like, coming out of one of these blackouts.

"Slim, can you hear me? Oh God, you didn't stop a bullet back there, did you? Please don't be dead."

I felt the motion of the car. I was sitting in front, leaned against my door. The window was rolled down halfway. Sun was shining and a breeze stirred my hair. It felt good.

My brain struggled like a deep-sea diver trying to make the surface before his air runs out and he drowns. Sometimes when I'm coming around, I think that sometime I may not make it to the surface; that I'll die in those dark deep waters. But so far I always do break to the surface and the warmth of sunshine. . . .

So, okay, I told myself. I'm rattling along in a car. It's got to be the '49 Chevy because Ava is driving. She's shaking me on the shoulder.

"Come on, Slim. I don't see no blood. Wake up, damn you. We're almost there. You've *got* to wake up."

I heard myself snore and it startled me. *That's it*, I tell myself. *You're coming around.* . . . But that black void won't let go and tries to suck me back down into the dark waters of my dreams.

No, I told myself. Not dreams. Things that really happened. Words that were spoken.

But it's dream-like, the way everything was blending together.

Our getaway. Squealing tires. Men who claimed to be G-men firing after us. A man lying dead in the cabin. Ava driving like a hotrod racer for a couple blocks before slowing to obey the speed limit, properly signaling her lane changes like she's Little Miss Driver of the Year. We don't talk at first except for "That was close!" and "Are you okay?" as we catch our breath. I'm looking over my shoulder. Traffic is light. Near as I can tell, no one is following.

I find my bottle of pills and throw back two. They don't take long if you're drinking. I try to light a cigarette, but my fingers are shaking.

"I want to thank you, Ava, for, uh, coming to my rescue. That was, uh, quite a stunt, the way you plowed through the front wall of that cabin. Jesus, that was something!"

She says, "Goddamn shoddy construction is what it was."

"Uh, I hope you didn't mess up your car too bad."

"Drives all right. Grill's messed up some. Dents to the hood and the paint's scratched. But she'll look fine after a little body work."

"Well, thanks. My name is Hank Williams."

"Dang!" she says. "I knew it. I knew, yes sir I knew it." She extends a hand. "It's time for proper introductions. My name is Ava Proudfoot. I aim to be a country music star just like you, Mr. Williams."

Her handshake is firm for a woman, sort of vibrating with something like electricity.

"You can call me Hank, darlin', especially after what we've been through . . . I mean, through . . . I mean—" I laugh. The pills are kicking in. The sounds and the blackness of night start to soften. I say, "Ol' Hank, he's got himself a real eye for talent." I laugh. Yeah, I was high. I remembered something I wanted to know. "Uh, Ava . . . how'd you come to, uh, show up on the scene to rescue me the way you did?"

She says, "I was in my apartment behind the office before you rolled in. I heard a couple of shots. It could've been a backfire but even through the rain I know gunshots when I hear them and they sounded like they came from one of the cabins. I was born curious."

"You were born brave."

She laughs. "You're damn right. Well, it was about 1:30 and the only light I saw was in your cabin. Everyone must have thought it was a car backfiring, or that's what they told themselves. I snuck up and spied through the blinds. Those two fellas were standing there in your cabin, talking on each other. I couldn't hear what they were saying, but they had guns and they looked mad."

"Told me they were G-men."

She made a face. "Like hell. I know cops and I do mean fed, state and local. Those guys weren't cops. Anyway, I went back to the office and watched. They turned off the lights in the cabin and stepped out and walked across the parking lot right near where I was, under an overhang, out of the rain. I had on my black raincoat, so they didn't see me. They were waiting for you, Hank. I went back to my apartment until you showed up."

"I saw a curtain move when the cab brought me back."

"That was me. I wanted to see what was going on so. Those tough guys followed you into the cabin. I eased up on the window again and I watched them talking to you."

"You worried about your motel?"

"Shoot," she said, "it ain't my motel. I'm slave labor. I've only been there for a week and I'll bet that after tonight my position will be terminated."

"You saw the body that fell out of that closet?"

"I sure did."

"Well," I said, "ain't you tough as nails."

"I've seen dead people before."

"Do you think those men killed him?"

"Could be. I don't know."

"So, uh, what made you come to my rescue?" The words sounded slurred, like I was listening to someone else. Darkness was at the edge of things.

She was saying, "I couldn't hear what y'all were saying in that cabin but I could see they were interrogating you. When they started to roughhouse, well," she pats the Chevy's steering wheel affectionately, "this heap of mine was the only implement at hand." She laughed and sparkling smile-eyes beam on me. "You gotta admit, Hank, that was some fun."

I start to reply, but those deep dark waters claim me. . . .

And then I'm back in the here and now like a disembodied spirit trying to ground itself in reality. I shift into a sitting position in the front seat. The Chevy is stopping and waiting and going and I can hear other vehicles. We're in traffic. Hank Williams, master detective.

I gulp in surprise when a cigarette is placed between my lips.

"Here, let me light this for you," says Ava. "You've got to get right, baby. The address you got from Fatty is just around the corner. Come on, Hank. Get right."

Fatty. Fatty Hewitt. Fatty Hewitt's Corral.

And I slipped back into the sweep of nothingness. . . .

"It's me, Fatty."

"Hank?" His voice over the phone wasn't surprised like I thought it would be, and it wasn't expansive as was his style. His voice was tight and the words, clipped. "Damn boy, where the hell you calling from?"

Ava sits in the Chevy, the engine idling like a big contented kitten. She's smoking a cigarette. We're at a phone booth at a closed filling station outside Shreveport, a state road that isn't much traveled since they put in the new highway. It's an hour before dawn.

We'd talked it through, Ava and me. And I'd thought it through. The pills have my brain bobbing in and out. After I'd passed out the first time, she drove us out of town. I awoke once in the car, at the edge of a pasture, slumped in the front seat. Stars winked at me through breaks in the clouds. A cow mooed and further off, a dog barked. Then more darkness.

And now this phone call.

"I don't want to tell you where I am, Fatty. I'm doing you a favor."

"I know. See, I just had me a couple of visitors here at the club. They left not five minutes ago."

"Tarnation." I describe Wiley and Macklin.

"Yeah, that's them. They're G-men. But then you know that."

"I ain't so sure, Fatty."

"About them? One of them showed me a badge. 'Course, I didn't see it up close but, well son, I reckon anything's possible."

"What did they say?"

"They're out to nail you, hoss. One of their own is dead. They wouldn't tell me much but I know how they found me."

I said, "Cantwell. They're after him more than me."

"If you say so. Now you listen to me, Hank, because what I'm a-telling you is life or death. Son, you're hot. I mean h-o-t like lit dynamite. Them FBI boys told me they're not going to let you get out of Louisiana. They want you real bad."

"What did you tell them?"

"Fatty Hewitt don't rat out his friends. But you've got to appreciate the volatile situation I find myself in. You do appreciate my status in this community?"

"You run the show, is what I've heard."

He chuckled. "Crudely but accurately put. Well, amigo, needless to say those G-men possess that same knowledge. That's why they came to me. Hank, they told me that you killed a man."

"I didn't kill no one. God's truth, Fatty."

"I want to believe that, son, I truly do. But, hoss, these are Federal agents we're talking about. I had to cooperate to a certain extent. You do understand? Them Yankees didn't need to remind me that they can make my life a living hell if they start investigating my, uh, my business concerns."

"Well, what did tell them?"

Another throaty chuckle oozed across the line. "I didn't tell them squat they could use, I guarantee you that. I told them that you performed here tonight but that was all I knew."

"Did they know about you and Cantwell?"

"Seemed not to."

"How much did you tell them?"

"Wasn't nothing I could tell. I ain't seen T. J. since he headed out from here tonight while you were playing."

"He stole my songbook, Fatty."

"Your what?"

"My songbook. The notebook I write my songs in. That book's worth a fortune. Cantwell knew where it was. He saw me stash it in my suitcase."

"Hmm," said Fatty. "Sort of looks like Cantwell killed that man while he was in the process of lifting your songbook. That's what it sounds like."

"I don't know what to think," I tell him. "I wonder where Wiley and Macklin are right now."

"Sitting outside my club," he says with displeasure. "A stakeout, waiting for you to show. This sort of thing is bad for business, Hank."

"Fatty, I'm in a pickle and no damn mistake. I need some help."

There was a long pause before he said, "And I'm wishing that I could help you, son."

"Meaning you won't?"

"Whoa now, hear me out. The FBI has this town trip-wired for you. Those fellas told me there are agents scrambling to cover the bus depot and the train station. Best thing going for you is they ain't putting it out to the newspapers and radio and TV. Folks in these parts know what Hank Williams looks like. They'd have you in custody right quick. But they're keeping a lid on it. National security, they told me." He chuckles again. "You sure as hell made a dramatic getaway, son, having a girl bust through the front of your cabin with a car. I am impressed."

"It wasn't my idea."

"All the more impressive. By the way, the Feds are looking for her too. You do know who she is, don't you, Hank?"

"Tell me, would you?"

"She's old Jud Proudfoot's daughter. You remember Jud?"

"The John Dillinger of the South, they called him."

"You might want to ditch the girl, Hank. They say she drove her daddy's getaway car for half the bank robberies he pulled when she was just a teenager and her mama drove rest of the times. A family of outlaws. She was cleared in a court of law thanks in no small part to her tender years at the time. The Feds sure as blazes know what she looks like. She's an albatross around your neck. It would be safer for you if you were on your own."

I look over to where Ava sits behind the wheel of the Chevy. She tossed away the cigarette butt she'd been smoking and looked up and down the road. She sent an antsy look in my direction.

I say into the phone, "Fatty, I don't know. She seems all right to me. I owe her, y'know. She's part of the package now. But I don't know what to do. I'll be all right if I can just get out of Shreveport."

"The FBI, Hank. That stands for Federal Bureau of Investigation. Federal. It means they don't give a damn about state lines."

"Maybe not, but I ain't staying alive for long in this town. And I told you, I'm not so sure those guys are G-men. That's what Ava thinks too, and she ought to know."

"Don't be listening to her, Hank. She's bad blood."

"I've got friends up in Nashville," I said. "Powerful friends like Mr. Rose. They'll get me out of this. But I've got to get there first. I've got to get out of Shreveport."

"Does the girl have any ideas on where you could lay low? Her mama shot it out with the cops alongside Ava's pa. They got Ava to scram. Her mother caught a bullet and died. Old Jud died in prison. That child was raised knowing where and how to hide out."

"She says she don't know no one in these parts she can trust. I was hoping you'd have an idea."

"Well, maybe I do. All right, let me think. They've got Shreveport sewed up and they're on the street looking for you. Okay, I've got me an idea. They've got white Shreveport covered. But they ain't got their people in darktown."

"Shoot, man," I said. "I can't go there. I'd stand out like salt on a pepper farm."

"Uh-uh," he said, "not if you go to an address where white fellas are known to frequent. Neighbors and folks on that street won't think nothing of seeing one more cracker show up and once you're inside, you'll have yourself a place to lay low until I figure a way to get you out. Those Feds will never find you."

"I don't know if I like the sound of this."

"Maybe you don't want my help."

"No, Fatty, no. I do. I want your help. That's why I'm calling. Wait a minute. How much should we be saying over the phone?"

"Nothing, after this conversation. Those G-men haven't had time to put a tap on this phone, but they will."

"What about Ava? Me and her stay together on this. She wants to be a country western singer."

"Terrific. I'll tell you what. You and my friend can talk that over. That is, if Miss Delilah wants a piece of this."

And I was easing back again into the here and now, this time to stay. . . .

I was riding in the front seat of the Chevy, tooling down a city street with Ava at the wheel. I took a few more hits on my cigarette. The smoke itched my lungs and made me cough. But Ava was right. Smoking that coffin nail was bringing me the rest of the way into consciousness. The sun shining through the windshield felt warm on my face.

I struggled to open my eyes and they stayed open. I focused on my surroundings.

Ava was turning from an avenue of storefronts, onto a less-traveled side street, into a residential neighborhood. Her bulky black purse, on the seat between us, no doubt held her gun.

Ava was observing my recovery from the corner of her eye while she drove. "Welcome back. It's about time."

I took a last drag on the cigarette and flipped it out the window. "I need a drink."

She steered us to the curb. "Here we are. Why don't you ask Miss Delilah for a drink? I'm sure that's the least she'll want to offer you when you go into that place."

I smiled and said, "Aw, hon. Don't be sore."

"Sore? Why should I be sore? I risk my neck, not to mention this fine automobile—at least the only one I have!—to save you from Lord knows what. I chauffeur you around all night and half the day to keep you out of harm's way. I get myself put back on the Feds' wanted list, according to your friend Fatty. And now I'm told to sit on my duff in broad daylight while you go into a whorehouse to find out if the madam of the place will allow me in. Now why should I be sore? That's a fine way to be treated. It's nice to be trusted."

"Aw, sugar, don't be that way. She don't know either one of us. I'll clear it up with her first thing. Don't be mad with me."

She sighed and the tartness melted away. "You're right, Hank. I'm sorry." She looked past me at the two-story frame house we were parked in front of. It had a peaked roof and a white picket fence. She said, "I'll wait out here like a good girl. But you keep your eyes to yourself and your mind on your business, Hank Williams."

I grinned, knowing that I'd won her over. "I sure wish I knew what is it about me that makes a woman want to nag."

She reached over with both hands and straightened my hat.

"We think of it as taking care of you, darling, and you love it. So okay, we spent time driving around like Fatty told us and here we are, right on schedule. You go on in there and you see that woman. If you hear me lean on the horn, there's trouble showing up. Good luck. I'll be waiting for you."

She drew close and closed her eyes and puckered her red lips and laid a humdinger of a kiss on me. Her lips were pliant and moist and I felt her tongue dart into my mouth and flick my tongue like a hot, moist little serpent. There was a fresh soapy scent to her even after everything we'd been through.

Women.

I eased out of the Chevy with her kiss tingling on my lips and her scent in my nostrils.

Folks walking by--just your everyday folks--were all colored. But as I stood there, a white man emerged from the house. He stood on the front porch, basking in the sunshine. He cocked his fedora at a jaunty angle and took his time lighting a cigarette. He walked past me without meeting my eyes. He was whistling a merry tune.

I crossed to the alley and entered it, as I'd been instructed. I paused for a look around.

A delivery truck drove past. A mother pushed a baby carriage by. No one was interested in me.

I went down the alley, to the side entrance of the house.

Chapter 11

Hank

From somewhere inside the house, a saxophone was playing. A man laughed. A full-bodied, throaty laugh. Rich, I'd call it.

I knocked on a screen door and waited.

There were no lights on just inside, so with the sunlight glaring down, baking me on the outside, I couldn't see a thing through the screen door. A trace of air seeped out from inside, telling me that they did have air conditioning. I waited for close to a minute, which is plenty long when you're standing waiting for someone to answer your knock. I knocked again, a mite harder than before.

That saxophone kept moaning. They were having a time in there. They couldn't hear me because of the saxophone.

I glanced up the alley, across the street to where Ava watched me from the Chevy. From this distance, you couldn't much tell that the car had recently driven through the front wall of a cabin. She smoked a cigarette. I made a shrug gesture to her. She returned the shrug as if to say, *Don't ask me!*

I tried the screen door handle. The door was unlatched. I sent another look to Ava, holding the screen door half-open, wondering what to do. Fatty had said that this was my ticket out of Shreveport, so I stepped inside.

Wooden steps led up to where I saw the bottom half of a pantry and part of a kitchen table. I was nervous. I'd rather someone had heard my knock and come to let me in. The saxophone playing stopped. I heard the murmur of conversation, not from the kitchen but beyond it, close by. I went up those steps and into the kitchen, wishing I had a gun.

The kitchen was bathed in cool shadow. A man sat at the opposite side of the table where I'd been unable to see him until I found myself facing him.

He was a hefty colored lad. I suppose some gals could have found him handsome in a rough sort of way. He wore a natty double-breasted gray suit with a pearl stickpin. His polished shoes were on the table, his legs crossed at the ankles. He was leaning back in his chair on its hind legs. He held a snub-nosed .38 revolver, aimed at me.

I tried to ignore the gun. "Uh, pardon me. Didn't you hear me knock?"

"I heard you."

I said, "You've been sitting in here the whole time? Well why in tarnation didn't you—"

"I don't get paid to wait on peckerwoods. You'll find the girls up front in the parlor. Use the front door like you're supposed to, jackoff."

In the next room, the saxophone player resumed playing and a man began singing a medium tempo blues, though I couldn't make out the words. That singing voice had a familiar quality to it. I'd heard that voice singing on the race radio, but I couldn't recollect the name since this man was pointing a gun at me. Maybe they were playing a radio.

I said, "You've got me wrong, mister. My name is . . ." I caught myself, not sure how much I should divulge until I knew more about this. I said, "Anyway, I'm expected."

"Do tell." His legs came off the table and he sat the chair down onto its four legs, his every movement cool and deliberate. He studied me and I felt like a bug pinned to a board. He said, "Let me tell you something, you chalk son of a bitch. You're talking to Straight Johnson who don't like rednecks who don't do what I tell them to do. Now get gone."

I gestured with both hands to show that I meant no harm. Harm? That was a laugh. Hell, this boy could tear my arms off and use one to pick his pearly teeth while he used the other one to scratch his ass.

I said, "Hold on, feller. I was told to come here. I'm supposed to meet someone. Delilah Buie."

"Who sent you?"

"Fatty Hewitt. Told me he'd call ahead and set it up. Man, I've been driving around half the day, dodging beneath the dash every time I saw a cop, because Fatty told me I had to show up at this precise time."

The tenor sax player finished playing with a flourish and the other man stopped singing. A woman laughed and clapped her hands.

The gunman frisked me in a professional manner, searching for concealed weapons.

I said, "I remember that voice now. That's Muddy Waters."

He stepped away from me, satisfied that I wasn't heeled. "Ain't a whole lot of white boys would know that."

I mustered up what was left of the Williams braggadocio. "I ain't most white boys, partner. I'm a musician. I love the blues. Been listening to 'em and playing 'em since I was a shaver." I regarded an archway on the other side of the kitchen, through which the music had drifted. "I wish more folks was hip to Muddy."

His face shifted into a quick grin that was here and gone. "You're all right, chalk." He turned his back to me and led the way through the archway, into a hallway that bisected the house.

The floors were polished wood. There were nice etchings and such on the walls. Further down, the hallway opened up to a large room, which would be the parlor. I could hear voices conversing from the front of the house. I heard what sounded like a player piano. A woman and a man walked arm in arm from the parlor to a wide staircase. The woman was a high yellow in heels and a wrap of lace and not much else except for bottle-red hair and lots of makeup. The fella wore a suit and carried his hat in his hands. He followed her upstairs like a puppy.

Straight Johnson knocked at a door midway between the kitchen and the parlor.

A woman's voice called, "What you got, Straight?"

He opened the door and nodded for me to enter. I did and he followed me in.

It was a woman's bedroom, but that doesn't do it justice. I'd walked into a *boudoir* that looked like something out of the Arabian nights. A four-poster bed dominated a room that was full of Eastern statuary and Persian throw pillows and plush armchairs.

In one of the armchairs sat a colored man in shirtsleeves, holding a bottle of Blatz beer in one hand. He was a dapper cat, with Cherokee features, high cheekbones and eyes that were sort of slanted. This would be Muddy Waters. There was an elegant, lazy grace about him like a panther in repose, there being no doubt of the feral power living within him, ready to be set off.

The woman seated on his lap was lush, large, beautiful, and black. A wrap embroidered with brightly colored dragons molded her curves.

A tan fellow—he could have been Mexican or Cuban but I knew he was black—stood facing them, holding a saxophone. He wore a porkpie hat, a loud Hawaiian shirt and tan slacks. He stood expectantly, and had obviously been playing the music I'd heard.

Straight said, "Miss D, this is the cat you've been expecting."

Delilah Buie's left arm was curled around Muddy's neck. She wore ruby earrings that shone in candlelight. She smoked a rolled cigarette from a long cigarette holder and damned if I didn't catch a whiff of hashish. When she'd got a good look at me, her face beamed.

"Well I'll be damned as I live and breathe. Fatty told me he was sending over some dude on the run named Hiram."

I said, "That's my name."

"Yeah, but the world knows you as someone else. Muddy," she said, "this here is Hank Williams."

Muddy had a look that could be menacing or friendly. He was cautious and wary when I was first shown in, but now he grinned and extended a hand to me around the woman on his lap.

"Well hey there, partner. I know your music, man."

We shook hands. His grip was firm and strong, the kind of handshake a man likes.

Delilah regarded Muddy with an arched eyebrow. "Well, I'll be. Do you mean to tell me that the great blues singer Muddy Waters listens to hillbilly music?"

He spanked her ass good-naturedly. "Not hardly. But you can't travel south of the Mason-Dixon without hearing that cracker noise everywhere you go."

Straight Johnson said, "Told me he recognized your voice, Muddy."

I said, "Muddy, I'd know your voice anywhere. I'm a fan. Y'all cut to it, and no mistake. These days my favorite is 'She's Into Something.'"

He laughed and sang half a verse of that song, then me and the sax player joined in and we did a full verse, swinging it pretty good when we took it home. Me and Muddy laughed and the sax man was all smiles.

When things settled down some, Delilah said, "I understand you're going to be staying with us for a time, Hank. Welcome. There's a cot in the basement. No one in the world will know you're down there."

"That's mighty hospitable of you, ma'am," I said.

She arched a haughty brow. "Hillbilly, I run a whorehouse, so let's dispense with formality. Call me Delilah."

I said, "Well I do appreciate your hospitality." I glanced at the sax player. "I don't mean to interrupt."

Muddy said, "Naw, we're done here," and he said to the horn player, "You've got the gig, brother. Delilah had four horn players come by here and audition for me, and you're the best. You know The Boogie Woogie?"

The man was placing his saxophone in its case. "Sure enough. I appreciate this, Mr. Waters."

"Call me Muddy. We go on at nine-thirty."

"Yes, sir."

The sax player walked out with "so longs" all around.

During that lull in the conversation, I heard a car horn beep from out front, one extended bleat that was only slightly longer than normal so that it wouldn't draw attention to itself . . . unless you were listening for a signal.

Ava.

Trouble!

I said, "Miss Delilah, there's something I've got to—"

The crash of shattering glass came from the direction of the parlor. A window being busted in.

There was shouting. Men were yelling in surprise and indignation. Other men were barking commands that I couldn't make out, punctuated by women raising their voices, some in dismay, others in anger, all of it underscored by the pounding of many feet running through the house.

Straight Johnson unleathered his pistol.

"Stay here," he told us with a wave of his arm, and he stormed out of the bedroom in the direction of the melee.

Delilah rose from Muddy's lap and even in her cheap wrap with embroidered dragons, she looked towering and regal.

Muddy jumped to his feet, grabbing his jacket. "Son of a bitch!"

Delilah was reaching for her robe, which lay across the bed. She yelled, loud enough to be heard up front, "Who's out there messing my house?"

Straight Johnson could be heard shouting a command. Insults and racial epithets came in reply.

Gunfire. *Wham!-wham!-wham!* Different pistols, but the shots rolled together like a drumbeat.

There came a commotion from the alley entrance. The screen door slammed. Men were yelling there, too. The kitchen table crashed to the floor and a scuffle tumbled through the archway and into the hall outside the bedroom. It was all happening very fast.

Muddy started in that direction but before he could take a second step, the ruckus spilled into the bedroom.

The sax player was flung through the doorway, onto the floor, scattering some of the throw pillows. He scampered to cower in a corner.

I knew how he felt.

The ones who had flung him stormed into the bedroom. Huge, husky men but that's all I could make out because they were wearing Ku Klux Klan sheets over their clothes. The pointy white hoods covered their heads. One of them carried a heavy hemp rope tied in a noose. The other wielded an axe handle.

The one with the axe handle pointed at Muddy. "There's the nigger we want!"

The other shouted, to the front of the house, "In here, boys! We've got him!"

And they went for Muddy.

Chapter 12

Muddy

I'll tell you one damn thing. There ain't nothing makes a brother move faster than a pair of kluckers coming at you with a noose and an axe handle.

I stepped in to meet the one to my right, the one with the club, just as he was raising it and yelling something from under his white hood. I gave him the toe of my right shoe square in his nuts. He doubled up like an accordion and fell to his knees. He started moaning. I took the axe handle and popped him in the head with it. He stopped moaning and fell onto his face.

I saw Delilah reach down and scoop up one of those throw pillows laying about. She didn't pitch it at the other hooded head, but aimed it between his ankles and tripped him.

And damned if Hank didn't come to life. That cat was whiter than white, all shook up. His eyes were saucers in his head. But he thought to grab the bottle of Chivas Regal from the dresser and he swacked it down across the falling klucker's head. There was a *clunk!* sound. The force of the blow knocked the man's pointy hood loose and it slipped off as he pitched onto the floor.

I threw away the axe handle and dug the .32 automatic out of my jacket pocket. I got a look at the guy that Hank and Delilah had taken down.

I said, "Shit. That there's John Law."

The klucker who'd lost his hood was Jerry, the cop from Crowley, and he hadn't been KO-ed by that bottle to the head. He was trying to sit up, propping himself on the floor with one arm while he felt the back of his head. He was dazed and groaning.

I snapped the .32's butt upside his head.

His eyes rolled back and he stretched out next to his partner, curled up in a ball like he was inside his mama.

Not but a few seconds had flown by. There was still commotion coming from the front part of the house. Another window shattered. Another gunshot.

A woman yelled, "Fire! Oh my God. *Fire!*"

I started in that direction.

Delilah stepped between me and the door. She put the palms of both her hands to my chest.

"No, Muddy. Don't get into this!"

I started past her. "Out of my way, woman."

She shifted like a dancer, smooth and muscular, and got in my way again. A trace of that musky lovemaking scent lingered about her from when we had got us some, in between auditioning saxophone players.

She said, "No, you stop right there, big man. Muddy Waters ain't about to get himself killed in *my* whorehouse!"

"This here's my fight," I told her. "I brought it here with me. I ain't running."

"Yes, you are. I can handle this. I own this town." She spat at Jerry's unconscious face. "This cracker brought his klucker buddies in after you but this here's *my* turf."

She crossed to a closet and yanked it open.

Hank flinched and drew back, spooked like he half expected a body to fall out of the closet.

Delilah reached in and came out with a sawed-off shotgun. She brushed aside lacy woman things on hangers and nudged open the back wall of the closet, which gave way to reveal a steep, narrow stairway leading down.

She said, "Lover, we got us white man's justice in Louisiana. You're Muddy Waters. Big recording star from up north. They'll make an example of you. I can fix this. You and Hank get yourselves out of here."

Hank approached the closet and peered in and down. "Where does this lead?" He made me think of a rabbit, fixing to bolt.

"To the park across the street. A bootlegger built this house during Prohibition. He dug an escape tunnel and I still use it."

Hank said, "I've got a girl in a car, waiting across the street."

Delilah said, "Go to her then. Git, both of you." Then her free hand reached up and stroked my face with warm fingertips. "You be careful, Muddy."

I said, "I'll see you again, babe," and I slipped my arm around her and jerked her to me so hard, she almost lost her balance, and that big, bold, bronze beauty was plastered against me with my hand on her ass, pressing her close. Our lips locked. Hers were writhing and wet and our tongues made love. She'd have wrapped her arms around me except she was holding that damn shotgun. I broke the clinch and released her. I said, "All right, sugar. I don't like it, but me and the hillbilly are gone."

But I was talking to her backside. Soon as our embrace ended, she whirled and stormed out of the bedroom, striding regal as ever, holding that shotgun in both hands.

I said, "Come on, Hank. Let's hit it."

He disappeared down the hole. He was a peculiar combination of grit and looking like someone frightened of his own shadow.

I followed, closing the fake closet wall behind me. At the bottom of the steps, low-watt bulbs were strung up at even intervals along a low tunnel. There was the smell of earth and a musty, decayed smell too. When I left the bottom step, Hank was already well on. His thin shadow danced off the close walls and ceiling of the tunnel.

He called back, "There's something up ahead."

The tunnel ended where a big sewer line bisected it. Wooden planks were permanently affixed to the pipe for footholds, and once you made it to the top of the pipe, a metal ladder reached up to a manhole.

Hank scrambled atop the pipe and up the metal ladder. He started loosening the manhole cover.

He said, "Home free."

A *boom!* sounded from up there beyond the manhole cover. I recognized the sound. A shotgun. It boomed again. I could hear shouting.

I grabbed one of Hank's arms as he finished sliding the metal cover aside. "Play it cool, man. Sounds like a war going on."

He lifted his head and peered around, and eased himself out into the daylight.

I was right behind him. The day had cooled. There was no one in the park. The manhole had let us out near where Jimmy and I had stood earlier, across the street from Delilah's. The sun was dipping behind the trees, painting the cloudy sky a soft red. A breeze rustled the leaves of trees and dried my sweat except for the palm of my gun hand, slippery with nerve sweat around the grip of the .32. I crouched low to the ground next to Hank.

Flames were licking at the side of Delilah's cathouse. Shrubs and bushes were on fire around a cellar door. The flames were at window level. A couple of the whores, in their gaudy, flimsy work clothes, were manning a garden hose, watering down the fire.

Delilah and Straight Johnson were on the porch.

Delilah stood with her shoulders thrown back, shotgun in her hands, the wind nipping at the hem of her sheer robe.

A battered, paint-peeling pickup truck raced up the street. A Confederate flag flapped from its radio antenna. A half-dozen guys in Ku Klux Klan robes and hoods scurried from the house toward the pickup.

Delilah fired a blast that shattered the back window of the pickup's cab. The driver of the pickup panicked and slipped the heap into gear before everybody had a chance to climb aboard the bed of the truck. Kluckers started running after it, including a Klansman who stumbled from the alley, carrying a hoodless man— Jerry—over his shoulder.

Straight Johnson took careful aim and squeezed off a shot from his .38 that flattened the truck's front left tire.

The truck had been gaining speed but now it started to sway like a drunk. It jumped a curb. The truck veered back into the street, the driver struggling for control. Some of the Klansmen who'd made it into the truck bed toppled out.

When I was a kid, on Saturday nights down at the Stovall Store they'd rig up a bed sheet against an outside wall and show silent movies for a nickel. There were these clumsy clowns who made me laugh called the Keystone Kops. This bunch reminded me of them.

Another *boom!* from Delilah's shotgun and a load of buckshot ripped out a ragged hole through the Confederate flag flapping from the antenna, leaving the stars-and-bars in tatters.

The truck wobbled to a stop. Klansmen scurried for cover behind it, a few drawing pistols and returning fire but their shots went wild and you could tell those boys would rather be someplace else.

The Klansman who was carrying Jerry dropped him and ran for cover. Jerry looked only half-way conscious. He tried to get up but was dizzy and he fell to his knees. He shook his head a couple times and started crawling like a wounded animal toward the pickup truck.

Hank tapped me on the arm. "There's Ava."

A '49 Chevy was parked at the curb across from the alley, well removed from the line of fire.

Hank took off at a run. I paced him with no trouble. With a full-fledged gunfight in progress, no one paid attention to us. I reached the car first.

A chick sat at the wheel, a good-looking white girl with a cigarette stuck out straight from the corner of her red lips. Her eyes were glued to the street battle behind her, so I startled her when I came around the front of the car.

I noticed that the front end—the grill and hood—was banged up. I yanked open the driver's door.

I said, "Slide over, sugar." I was already into the car, bumping her across to the passenger side.

I don't like to drive. Muddy Waters is used to being chauffeured. But that don't mean I can't drive. Since it was my neck and my ass those Klan goons were after, I wasn't about to depend on anyone else for driving me the hell out of this, least of all some broad I didn't know.

She made a noise like she wasn't happy, but she wasn't sure what to make of me. She hugged the passenger door.

My side window grew a dimpled with a hole from a bullet that missed me by inches, buzzing like a hornet. I looked out over my left shoulder.

Behind us, the pickup truck was limping around a corner with Klansman huddling behind it for cover. Both sides ceased firing and hurled racial insults at each other instead. Straight Johnson stood next to Delilah on the porch. Smoke with no flames rising from behind them told me the fire had been extinguished.

The angle the bullet had gone through the window made an invisible line that ended right where Straight stood, staring dead at me. I was dead sure in my mind that he was the one who had pegged a bullet at me. I believe he purposefully missed, but he damn sure wanted me to know it was him done it. A warning. He could have been mad about this mess I'd brought with me, or maybe he was warning me off his woman. It was hard to figure him and Delilah. She ran things, but . . . it was hard to tell.

Hank was throwing himself into the Chevy's backseat, tapping me frantically on the shoulder.

"What the hell are you waiting on, man? Let's go!"

I popped the gears and floored the accelerator. The Chevy peeled a patch of rubber, hauling ass away from there.

There was a filling station on the next corner and we made it there in less time than it takes to tell. I yanked hard on the wheel and cut a sharp left across the street, right in front of oncoming traffic. We flew on through, under the station's overhang. An attendant went diving for safety. Our right front fender nearly clipped over a gas pump, and sent flying a nicely stacked display stand of motor oil cans.

We sped across the street, through a narrow gap I saw between the traffic. Drivers cussed me out. Then they were falling away behind us and we zoomed into an alley, which I'd only spotted seconds ago when we were tearing through that filling station. I cut my speed and tooled down the alley. I turned onto the next street and followed it away from there.

In my rearview, I saw Hank in the backseat, mopping at his brow.

He said, "Dang."

The girl's cigarette had fallen to the floor. She opened the largest black leather handbag I'd ever seen, reached into it and brought out a pack of Lucky Strikes. She shook the pack once, lifted it to her lips and drew out a cigarette. She shook the pack a second time under my eyes, and I snagged a butt the same way. She used the car lighter to give us fire.

She said, "You were good back there."

"Baby, if I got the Klan breathing down my neck, I'll sprout wings and fly if I have to."

Hank was staring out through the rear window. "I think you lost 'em."

The girl exhaled a stream of smoke that filled the car. "For now," she said.

Dusk was settling in. People were starting to drive with their lights on, though it wasn't strictly necessary. I switched on the Chevy's headlamps.

Hank turned from the rear window. "Muddy, you must have someone riled at you a whole bunch."

I said, "Damn husbands. Sorry I got you messed up in it, man. I'm driving us to the Jefferson. I'll get out there and you can be on your way like nothing happened. None of them kluckers got a look at you."

He leaned forward and rested both arms across the seat. "Hold on there, Muddy. Could be we could help each other out."

The girl was staring at me funny-like, her head cocked sideways, squinting at me through the cigarette smoke. She said, "Muddy. That's a funny name. Only Muddy I ever heard of is Muddy Waters."

Hank said, "Muddy, this here is Ava. We just met last night but we've been through some crazy shit since then. Ava, meet Muddy Waters."

"Well I'll be." The cigarette wagged from the corner of her red mouth. "I like all kinds of music. I listen to race records all the time. I'm a singer too, or I want to be. Hank says he's going to help me out in Nashville. Aren't you, Hank?"

"Well now, uh—" said Hank.

I drove with my eyes watching up ahead and in my rearview. Hank was right. I'd lost them. But the girl was right, too. *For now* . . .

She said, "Hank didn't tell you my last name. I'm Ava Proudfoot." She said it like I was supposed to recognize the name.

Hank nudged my shoulder with an elbow. "She's a bank robber's daughter, Muddy. Sure enough. Old Jud Proudfoot's little girl, all growed up. You know Jud Proudfoot."

I said, "I ain't from around these parts."

Ava stuck her chin out like she was daring someone to pop it. "My Daddy was the closest thing to a real life modern day Robin

Hood this country will ever see. We never got rich from robbing banks. Daddy gave away half of what he took to folks we met along the road. Me, Daddy and Mama. I drove getaway plenty of times with bullets flying and busting out the glass while Daddy returned fire. But always over their heads, which was better than the bastards deserved." She took a drag on her half-finished cigarette and pitched it out the window with a curse.

I laughed. I've always been crazy about crazy broads. "Honey, that ain't no way for a music star to talk."

She reached into her handbag and went through the cigarette routine again. "Well anyway," she said, "I know something about driving getaway cars. You did all right, is all I'm saying."

Hank chimed in with, "Y'know, Muddy, you going back to that hotel ain't going to do you no good if the Klan knows where to find you."

I thought about the Shreveport cop who showed up at the gig last night. I wouldn't be surprised if he was the Klansman with Jerry.

Ava said, "If they want to, Muddy, they'll hunt you down no matter what you do or where you go."

Hank nodded. "Best thing for you to do," he said, "is turn off the heat. Nip this in the bud."

I caught his eye in the mirror. "Why do you give a damn what happens to me? I figure you'd be glad to see this nigger bail out."

"Shoot, man, I'm *supposed* to help you out, same as Delilah was helping me. Folks like us got to help each other. Delilah knows that."

"I know it too," I said. "Delilah's a good woman. But she's a whore and she be working some angle, you can bet on that. Delilah's getting her a cut somewhere, most likely from whoever sent you to her."

"Don't matter," said Hank. "The woman loves music and, uh, I can tell she likes musicians." He spoke good-naturedly from the side of his mouth. "Way I see it, Muddy, you and me being musicians makes us kindred of a kind, though we're different in many ways."

Ava flicked ash from her cigarette. "You should trust us, Muddy. Daddy taught me to read people right the first time." She squeezed one of Hank's arms and said, "Hank is all right. He's one hundred per cent standup. And so am I."

We were idling at a red light, waiting on a left turn.

I said, "Y'all sound like you're ganging up to sell me on something. But you're right. If the Klan wants my ass, they'll get it. Ain't nowhere for a black man to hide in Louisiana. They'd burn down The Boogie Woogie if that's what it took, sure as they were fixing to burn out that whorehouse."

Ava laughed. "You boys make quite a pair. The FBI's after one, the Ku Klux Klan wants the other. I'd say in certain quarters, you're the two most unpopular fellas in Shreveport."

"Everyone seems to have us behind the eight ball," said Hank, "but I'm thinking that one fella could fix both our situations."

Ava frowned a pretty frown. "Fatty Hewitt?"

Hank nodded. "None other. Trouble's going to be trying to find him. It's too early for Fatty to be showing up at the club, and the G-men have the place under surveillance anyway, looking for me."

The stop light changed and I made the turn. Street lamps were going on.

I quashed my smoked cigarette in the ashtray. "Right about now I should be getting myself ready to go onstage at The Boogie Woogie Inn."

"It would be your last performance," said Ava. "The thing about kluckers, if you stomp their ass it just makes 'em more mean."

I said, "Who's Fatty Hewitt?"

"Big shot," said Hank. "The good old boy who runs this part of Louisiana."

Ava said, "Fatty wants to be Hank's agent."

Hank made a sour face. "He did. Now I wouldn't blame him for dropping me like a hot potato."

I said, "I reckon it's about time for someone to hip me to what your shit is all about."

"Someone stole my songbook," said Hank, "that's all I know. It's all I care about. All this other mess is messing up my mind. I need a drink." He slumped into the corner of the backseat and massaged his eyes with the fingers of one hand while the other hand waved like this was too much. "It's all balled up," he said. "I don't much understand any of it except someone stole my songs, the miserable bastards. I didn't kill nobody."

"So who did kill somebody?"

Ava said, "That's the mystery. Two tough guys named Wiley and Macklin are after Hank. They say they're G-men. They think Hank shot their partner."

"Why do they think that?"

Hank kept massaging his eyes. "The fella was killed with my gun, looks like."

I said, "Fuck."

Ava chain lit a fresh cigarette and offered me one. I lit it from the dash lighter.

Ava said, "Hank, there's something you need to know about back at Delilah's. Those two, Wiley and Macklin. I saw them."

Hank drew himself up straight. "What! Where did you see them?"

"They were in a car parked on the other side of the street from me. They were parked facing the wrong way, which I thought was peculiar, so they didn't see me or if they did, they didn't care."

"Are you sure?" Hank's voice was tight.

"Damn sure. I recognized one when he got out of the car and since there were two of them, I think we can safely assume it was both those rascals." She took a drag on her cigarette and exhaled nervously. "The reason the one got out of the car was that truck with those kluckers was turning onto the street in a hurry. There was three guys with hoods on riding in the front of the pickup and the rest were packed like sardines in the rear. I thought the guy was going to arrest them or something. I mean, he's supposed to be a Federal agent, right? And a truck load of Klansmen cruising through darktown in broad daylight has got to be breaking some laws."

I drew on my cigarette. "Don't count on it," I said.

Hank said, "So what happened? I don't like the sound of this."

"He spoke to the men in the truck. Then he waved them on past and they did what they did. Our two buddy boys drove off real fast after that. That's why they were parked facing the wrong direction, so they could intercept those kluckers because they knew they were coming, then they could get out fast before the trouble began."

Hank was slack-jawed. "But that means the G-men and the KKK are in cahoots."

"Wait a minute," I said. "You sure they were G-men?"

Hank lifted both hands and massaged his temples. He groaned. "See what I mean? This gets more confusing by the minute." He sank back against the seat. "I don't feel so hot."

Ava extended a hand over the seat and gave one of his bony knees an affectionate pat. "Now Hank, everything's going to be just fine. We'll get to the bottom of this."

"I just want my songs back. That's all I want. That and a goddamn drink."

She told him, "We'll get your songbook," those bright eyes of hers swung to me, "now that we've got three heads working on this, now that Muddy's with us."

I said, "Uh, now wait a minute, sister—"

"What?" she said innocently. "Didn't we just decide that you've got a big problem too? We can help each other."

I said, "I'm just a dumb country boy raised on the plantation, sweetheart. I ain't up to following this fancy thinking of yours. First thing, are we talking about real G-men or ain't we?"

Ava raised an eyebrow. "Honestly? At this point we can't be sure, but here's why I don't think so. Hank, you've been telling me that you got involved with a murdered FBI man and a Russian spy."

I eased the Chevy onto the street that would take us past the Jefferson. I said, "Russian spy? Now hold it—"

Ava pushed on. "But it doesn't make sense. Hank, we had the radio on all last night and most of today. If this is so all-fired important, why hasn't there been some sort of public announcement? Why aren't the police alerting everybody that the famous Hank Williams is a wanted man? You know what I think? I think it's because everything those men told you last night was a lie. They don't care if they apprehend Hank or not. They got the kluckers to do their dirty work."

I chuckled at Hank. "Man, this gal's got a lot of words in her but from what I hear, she's thinking clear. But it don't matter to me who those guys are. If the Klan is after me, and those boys are after you, how did they come to work together?"

Ava said, "Plenty of police in this town are Klansmen. Wiley and Macklin had that whorehouse under surveillance because they knew Hank was going to show up there. Then they saw Muddy show up. They knew the Klan was after him. So when Hank showed, they set it up for the Klan to stomp that place and Hank would stop a bullet in the crossfire. Only it didn't turn out that way."

Hank grimaced. "So they rang in those Klanners and told them that I wasn't supposed to walk out. But why do Wiley and Macklin want me dead?"

"Well, I don't know everything," Ava said with a turned up nose. "That's part of the mystery. But I've got a good guess how they knew you were going to be there."

We drove past the Jefferson Hotel. I took the next right and kept cruising.

I said, "Hank, sounds like your boy Fatty done double-crossed you."

Ava said, "My sentiments exactly."

Hank said, "Aw, don't be talking that. Fatty's giving me a break. Or, he was. Fatty's the best chance we've got."

Ava said, "Hank honey, you've got to slow down your brain and think this through." Her tone was like she was explaining something to a child. "One. Nothing on the radio about that G-man you're supposed to have shot. Nothing about a Russian spy. That should be big news. And two. Fatty's the one who sent you to that cathouse and lo and behold, Wiley and Macklin show up with a crew of kluckers who start shooting the place up and burning it down. I tell you, that big rat Fatty is in this up to his shit-eating phony smile."

I glanced sideways at the chick as I drove. "Sounds like you know the cat up close."

She blinked. "Well, I guess I do, sort of. We dated a couple times about six months ago, before I broke it off. Fatty Hewitt fancies himself a lady's man. He's always got himself a string. I doubt he even remembers my name."

Hank was staring at her. "You dated Fatty Hewitt?"

She chain lit another cigarette. "I thought it would help my career. I'm sorry. Maybe I should have said something."

"Heck, I don't care about that," said Hank. "There's a girl right here in Shreveport named Billie Jean that I'm fixing to marry and here I am running wild with you. I ain't got no right to judge. Y'know, this here's a good thing. You must know how we can get in touch with Fatty."

Her eyes flared. "Hank Williams, haven't you been listening to a word I've said? I'm telling you that I don't like the man. He makes my skin crawl. I don't trust him."

Hank said, "I heard you. And I'm telling *you* that I'm a-running scared because I don't know how to get out of this mess except to go to the big man who has all the answers, and that's Fatty. I understand you've got your reasons for thinking the way you think but so do I, dagnabbit."

"You're running scared," she told him. "What if Fatty's is in this up to his porky neck and it's him who's trying to pin a murder rap on you? You march us up to his front door and you're handing him your own empty head on a silver platter."

We left the Shreveport city limits sign behind. The traffic, the businesses and the dwellings began to thin out.

I said to Ava, "Uh, excuse me for butting in, doll, but you sound like you might know where Fatty's front door is."

"What if I do? Stay away from him, that's all you need to know. I'm telling you. Muddy, I see you're man of action and you're a competent lad. But trust me on this. Fatty Hewitt is out of our league. He's not a man to be meddled with. He's got an army of hoods to back him up."

I said, "You mean like Wiley and Macklin?"

"It's true," said Hank. "Going to see Fatty is a gamble. But it's a bet I'm willing to place. Hey, it's *my* life that's on the line here. That gives me the say-so on what we do next."

Ava was watching him coolly. "I don't think I like this truculent side of your personality, Hank. I haven't seen this side of you before."

Hank frowned. "Truculent? What the hell does truculent mean?" He looked to me. "Muddy, do you know what truculent means?"

I admitted that I did not.

Hank said, "Don't matter what it means. Now Ava honey, don't be difficult, darlin'. Ain't it right that I should have the say-so? I'm tired of being blown around like a leaf in the wind. What if those fellas weren't lying and they really are G-men? If Fatty Hewitt wants me dead, why did he have this fella Cantwell pick me up at the train station and get me loaded and take me over to play at Fatty's nightclub? I dare you to make sense out of that."

Her eyes grew narrow. Muddy Waters knows women and this one was fuming inside. I watched her from the corner of my eye as I drove.

"Baby, I know you want to be a singer. But why did you want a piece of this man's murder trouble?"

Without missing a beat she said, "Because I don't like to see genius trampled upon, that's why. But I don't want to commit suicide, either. I stopped seeing Fatty when I found out how deep he is into the rackets. I'm trying to live a right life. My father's dying wish was that I should go straight, and I'm trying hard to do that. I shouldn't want any part of this, if I had the sense God gave a goose. But I saw what they were doing to Hank back at that motel and I just flipped out. But that does not mean I'm going to follow you boys over a cliff."

"Now, sweetie," said Hank. "Think ahead. This will work itself out and when it does, I aim to do everything I can to get you a recording contract. Why, you'll be the next Kitty Wells."

She thought this over longer than I thought she would, then she sat with her back stiff as a metal rod and stared straight ahead through the windshield with her arms folded under those fine melons.

"Oh, all right, damn you. You know what I want more than anything, don't you, you bastard?"

Hank leaned forward to touch her on the shoulder. "Don't pout, hon. You know going to see Fatty is our best bet."

She jerked away from his touch. "I know no such thing. And truculent means cruel and belligerent."

Hank said, "Well shucks, that ain't nice."

I brought in some cool jazz on the dash radio. We cruised through the gathering darkness.

Chapter 13

Hank

Have you ever known a man who could whup his weight in wildcats, steal your woman if he wanted to, and he got your attention right off because there was something dangerous simmering just below the surface? And with all that, you *like* the guy.

Then you've known a man like Muddy Waters, though I doubt it. He was a strongly drawn personality, is the best way I can put it. As Ma would say, he draws from a deep well.

Muddy was a striking, handsome fellow, a chocolate-skinned man with Cherokee ancestry clear in his features. His straightened hair was artistically conked. I knew from his records, and from the way he spoke, that he was a ladies man. Now there are some ladies men—most of them, I think—who other fellas don't cotton to. But there are some who have the touch with women, but they've got the gift of getting along with other men too. Muddy was like that.

We had stopped at a rest area on the highway seven miles out of Shreveport. Ava had informed us that we were on our way to where Fatty had a home in the country, a thirty-minute drive from his club. The rest stop had a graveled parking area with mowed grass and picnic tables under a stand of cypress trees, with outhouses set back. The scene was gilded with moonlight. Cicadas cricketed around us. I could smell the bayou somewhere out there, not far away; a ripe mixture to the senses of murky dampness and peculiar noises from bullfrogs and other unidentifiable creatures.

We had the place to ourselves. It was on a secondary highway, and only the occasional vehicle whooshed by.

Driving out of Shreveport, Muddy had said, "Me and my boys slid into town yesterday and did a slick job of laying low. That's the route we're taking."

We'd stopped at an all-night diner where Muddy and I waited in the car while Ava went in and had them fry up a chicken and bag us up all the fixings to go.

As we'd left their parking lot, a spindly, gray haired woman was leaning out from the front screen door of the diner, watching us drive off.

Ava said, "The old crone waiting on tables back there gave me the third degree. I told her we were picking up dinner on our way to see a friend."

Several miles on, Muddy pulled over to the rest stop and the three of us had a picnic in the starlight. We ate without much conversation.

There'd been enough of that during the drive here. Naturally, Muddy wanted a detailed account of what had transpired thus far and so that's what I gave him. Ava supplied running commentary, filling in some details.

I took it from when I woke up in the motel. I told him about Cantwell and Fatty Hewitt and about finding a body stuffed in a closet. Muddy knew about my missing songbook but I told him that part again anyway because it sure was troubling my mind, like a part of me was missing. I told him about Wiley and Macklin roughing me up and about Ava crashing in to my rescue like gangbusters and about Fatty sending me to Delilah's.

When we were finished eating, Ava picked up after us and stowed the trash in a barrel provided for that purpose. Then she walked off toward the outhouses.

Muddy and me watched the action of her hips and behind rolling against the fabric of her tight summer dress as she walked away.

When she was out of earshot, Muddy said, "Make a poor man shuffle, make a rich man want to build."

I said, "Rootie tootie."

"Hillbilly, I might have to cut myself a piece of that."

I shook a cig out of my pack, offered him one and fired us both up. "Uh, I was sort of thinking the same thing."

"Don't matter. Get what you can, man. But I ain't never lost a toss yet," and he blew smoke not into my face but so that it drifted into my face.

I chuckled. I liked this fucker.

"Shoot, man, you're welcome to try. She's a sharp kid, right enough, but I've got enough woman trouble in my life. I don't need no more."

Muddy patted his conk to make sure every hair was in place. "Sounds to me, man, like you walk a hard road. Why you do it like that?"

"Like what?"

"Getting all tangled up in it, man. That ain't no way to enjoy life. The women, you've got to love them when they come along." He pronounced it "womens."

I said, "I just ain't put together like you, Muddy. I get to going with some gal, man, I fall in love with her. Happens every time. When I first started on the road, I used to have me honky tonk angels on the sly but they just made me miss my wife that much more. Audrey's my wife. My ex-wife. Aw hell."

A lengthy silence ensued. A car passed on the highway.

I had gotten myself blue, the way I always do when I think about Audrey. I recall what me and that woman felt for each other, what we had and how it slipped away and ain't never coming back and, yeah, I get the blues. I get that lump in my throat and my heart aches.

Muddy broke in on my thoughts. "So what do you think about this broad, Ava, besides she has a nice ass?"

That brought me back, maybe the way he intended it to. Audrey vanished from my mind.

I said, "Guess I'm worried that maybe you and her are right about Fatty pulling a double-cross on me."

Muddy drew cigarette smoke deep into his lungs and exhaled slowly at the faraway stars. "We've got to be careful." He reached into his back pocket and brought out the .32 he'd flashed at the cathouse. He checked the pistol's action. "Trouble can come at you from some crazy places."

"You're talking about Fatty and his boys?"

"Them, and the broad."

"Ava? But she's putting everything on the line to help us."

"A bank robber's daughter. Girl like that will turn on a dime."

"What do you mean, a girl like that?"

"That chick, Ava, she's got the heart of a thief."

"Naw, she's just rambunctious. Y'all are too cold on people, Muddy. Like with Delilah, you calling her a whore after all she's done for us."

His eyes narrowed and locked with mine. Then he grinned and tossed away his cigarette. "I see what you mean about your feelings getting you all tangled up. Son, Delilah is a whore. She'll tell you so herself. I call 'em as I see 'em. But that don't mean I ain't crazy about that stuff, no matter if she's a whore or a thief."

I said, "Speak of the devil," in a low voice.

Ava was sashaying up to us and the view from the front was every bit as delectable as watching her walk away. She sat with us at the picnic table and I lit her a cigarette.

She said, "You know fellas, I've been thinking. Did you notice something funny on the way out of town?"

Muddy pasted on a sideways smile that stretched across the width of his face. "Sweet girl, when you walk by, Muddy notices everything."

She made a coy gesture. "Oh, Muddy. You're bad."

"No, I ain't." He chuckled. "I'm *good*, sugar. Want to find out how good?"

I said, "Uh, excuse me, Muddy. I don't mean to be stepping on your action—"

"Then don't."

"But I want to hear what Ava was about to say."

Ava said, "Why thank you, Hank. I was only going to point out how easy it was for us to drive out of town without being stopped, without us seeing a single cop. That's normal, I guess, but that's my point. You'd think if there was both a commie spy *and* the killer of an FBI agent on the loose, they'd damn well have the city sewed up like Fatty told you they did."

Muddy said, "I believe she's got a point."

I rolled my eyes. "Now don't you start on me again, Muddy. You've got as much to lose as I have. Them Klansmen and cops weren't looking to invite you to an ice cream social."

He turned to Ava. "Hank thinks maybe we're right about this Fat cat."

She studied me with a sassy look. "Is that so?"

I got busy animating a cigarette. "Dang, Muddy. That was a private conversation between me and you. What are you going to do next, tell her we was talking about you getting a piece of her tail?" That ought to fix his wagon.

But Ava smiled demurely before Muddy could reply. "I certainly hope you boys were talking about me. A woman likes to think she has that power."

Muddy still wore his face-wide grin. "Oh, you've got the power, sugar, and that's a natural fact."

She tickled him under his chin. "Well just so you know, big man. I flirt like the devil's daughter, but I'm no pushover."

Watching Ava handle Muddy was like watching a child tame a mountain lion.

Muddy beamed. "Reckon I'm the pushover. Girl, you've got a way."

Ava said, "Fine then," and, like flicking a wall switch, she continued speaking in a different, brisk manner. "I do wish I could use some of my alleged charm to convince you two that, since getting out of Shreveport was so easy, well damn Sam, why don't we just hit the highway and keep going?"

Muddy's beam faded. "Can't do that, hon. You'd best learn something about this here music business. I'm on the road with my band, dig? Those cats are my boys. They be depending on me to keep them working. And there's the people who buy my records and go to the clubs when I come passing through, wanting to hear me. No, I've got to straighten this here mess out tonight, so I can get back to making a living."

I said, "That goes for me too. I can't very well just pack it up and disappear. Who knows, maybe the G-men and the cops are keeping that stuff undercover because of what you call classified information. Have you thought of that?"

Ava's gaze dropped. "No, I hadn't."

I pressed on. "And what about my songbook? I won't sleep until I get my hands on that. I ain't letting nobody take the only thing I got left, and maybe Fatty could help me with that too. If someone's trying to frame ol' Hank for a murder, by blazes I ain't going to just sit by and let them get away with it."

"No, Hank," said Ava, "of course not. That's not what I want. I just don't like the idea of go see Fatty."

"Ava, I know what you think. The point is, are you in this with me and Muddy or not?"

"I'm not going to back out on you this far into it," she said. "Just as long as we do like Muddy says. We've got to be real careful with these people. That dead guy at the motel was shot once in the head, once in the heart. My daddy would call that a professional hit. These are not people to be fooling with. Matter of fact, I aim to hang back and watch you two walk into that lion's den without me, if you're crazy enough to do it."

Muddy said, "You're right about not heading straight up to the cat. But Hank, you're right too. Sounds like this guy Fatty is a chance worth taking. Hell, sounds like he's the only chance we've got. Okay. I'll tell you how we're going to play this—"

A car cruised down the highway, decreasing its speed as it approached the rest area. A spotlight beam lanced out, directed not at us but panning steadily in our direction as the vehicle quit the highway.

Ava said, "Cops," under her breath.

Muddy said, "Shit."

And Muddy was *gone*.

He just flat wasn't there any more, gone with nary a sound. He had vanished into the night.

Ava and I exchanged a look and I'll bet she saw the same concern in my eyes that I saw in hers. There wasn't time for us to say or do anything because the car braked to a stop, tires crunching on the gravel before of us, just behind Ava's car. Up close I could see that it was a police car. It said *Crowley PD* on the door. Then I couldn't see anything because the driver turned the spotlight dead on Ava and me, blinding us.

"Evening, folks."

I raised my arm to shield my eyes. "Evening, officer."

Ava said nothing. She reached over and slipped her hand into mine, entwining our fingers.

The cop said, "I said good evening, miss."

Ava lifted that pugnacious jaw of hers. "I ain't no miss. I'm married to this here lazybones."

The beam left us and glided along the tree line that bordered the rest stop. Not having the spotlight burning into my eyes was almost as blinding for several seconds until my night vision returned.

The cop snapped off the light. I got a brief look at him. He was salt-and-pepper haired, with a trimmed mustache, pressed khaki and a wide-brimmed western style hat. His right hand was on the pistol holstered at his hip.

"How long you folks been here?"

Ava said, "We're coming back from seeing my ma in Bogalusa. She's in a nursing home." Her voice got a tight, choking sound to it. "It breaks my heart to see mama like that, all shriveled up and dying by inches." Her answer came so spontaneously, with just the right amount of ache in her voice, that she almost had me believing her until I remembered that her mother was deceased.

The cop spat. "I'm looking for an uppity nigger. Had a riot in darktown today and this crazy coon started it."

I dropped my eyes from looking at him dead-on. "Uh, officer, may I ask why you're questioning us about that?"

And that's when I got a good look at his face, and my knees knocked and my jaw dropped. He had to notice me gasp in surprise but he must have figured it was just a nervous hillbilly reacting to being interrogated by a cop. And come to think of it, that's exactly what I was. But I recognized him, sure enough.

It was the Klansman, from Delilah's whorehouse, whose hood had been knocked off when I beaned him with a bottle of Chivas Regal. There was a big white bandage taped to the side of his head.

And he didn't seem to recognize me!

He said, "Ma Grissom back at the diner called in a report and Shreveport HQ radioed me because they knew I'd be traveling by on this road on my way back home to Crowley."

Ava said to me, "I told you that old biddy couldn't keep her witch's nose out of my business."

I said, "Ava."

The cop's eyes narrowed. "What's that, ma'am?"

I said, "Don't pay her no mind, officer. She's under a world of worry."

His eyes grew skeptical. "Uh huh. Ma said they don't get much traffic out here this time of night. Too late for the dinner crowd, too early for the sober-up-on-the-road-home bunch. Folks who do stop in this time of night, why, they always come in and at least buy them a cup of coffee. But Ma Grissom says a lady stopped in a while ago and the two gents with her waited in the car the whole time that three chicken dinners was being fixed. Ma says one of those gents was a colored boy; like maybe a sympathetic white couple was helping some uppity nigger get out of town."

My hillbilly brain was crackling. Back at the whorehouse, he'd only caught half of a sideways glimpse at my face when he and that other klucker first stormed in, and that glimpse wasn't enough for him to remember me now.

Ava leaned against me, placing her head on my shoulder, and my arm naturally slid around her curvy waist. She was a nice bundle, and the scent of her tantalized me.

She placed both of her hands to her stomach and said, "Honey, I don't feel so good." Then she looked at the cop with a pathetic expression on her face. "Officer, we ain't with no colored man and that's the truth."

The cop said, "I've had me a bad day, folks. Drove all the way over here from Crowley to help the local boys with a manhunt. This nigger's name is Muddy Waters. He's a singer, they tell me. He's known to have molested half a dozen white women and children. Why, he's committed obscene acts that would make God roll over in His grave. I best not find out that you're harboring jungle filth like that. I wouldn't take it kindly, and neither would a judge."

I looked at the gauze taped to his skull.

"What happened to your head, officer?"

He unholstered his pistol. "I'll ask the questions. You ain't hiding a nigger in them bushes back behind you?"

I said, "Heck no. We pulled off here because the missus was taking sick." I got into the act of contributing to Ava's story, trying to be as skillful as she was. I said, "We just found out that my wife's in the family way." I was thinking, *A sick mother and a pregnant wife. That ought to get it.*

The cop held his gun at his side, aimed at the ground. He looked in at the car's back seat.

"Woman at the diner was sure there was a nigger with you. Now where is he?"

Ava said, "Officer, that old busybody is either losing her eyesight or she's a drunk. That's right, there ain't any nig . . . any colored man traveling with us. Honest."

The cop sneered. "Sensitive about niggers, huh?" He stepped past us, his eyes scanning the rest area in the moonlight. "Think I'll look around. Either of you folks try anything, something bad is going to happen. Stay right where you are, understand?"

Ava said, "But we didn't do anything!"

He said, "Stay here," and he stalked off toward the cypress trees where deep, inky shadows waited.

I whispered to Ava, "Now what the hell are we supposed to do?"

A car passed by on the highway without slowing.

The cop disappeared from our sight where trees blocked the moonlight.

Ava said, "If that cretin gets a hold of Muddy, we're stepping in."

I remembered the gun in her handbag resting on the picnic table. I heard myself gulp and it sounded loud to my ears.

"I dearly hope it doesn't come to that."

There was a shout in the night. The sound of a violent struggle rustled in the shrubbery and tall grass within the shadows.

Ava started toward the commotion. "Come on, Hank. Muddy needs us."

She pulled up short when a figure materialized from the shadows.

Muddy emerged into the moonlight, dragging the unconscious cop behind him, using one hand to grip the man's collar, hauling him like a sack of laundry. In his other hand, he held the man's pistol. He came to a stop before us and released the cop's collar.

The officer was out like a light. His head bumped onto the grass with a *ka-thump* that sounded like a dropped watermelon.

I had to laugh. "Damn if this peckerwood cop ain't making a habit out of getting KO-ed."

Muddy reversed the pistol he held and extended it to me, grip-first. "Here, take this. You need to be packing."

I waved the gun away with both hands. "Uh, I don't think so! That's a cop's gun. They find that on me, I'll be in more trouble."

"You'll be dead if you need a piece and you get caught without." He leaned down and patted the cop's pockets. He withdrew a wallet with his thumb and forefinger from a back trouser pocket and removed a handful of bills. He tossed the wallet aside with a chuckle that sounded like marbles rolling around in a pail. "First time I ever fined a cop. I don't like punks coming after me." He folded the money and it disappeared into his pocket. He hefted the pistol. "You sure you don't want this?"

I found myself waving both hands again. "Naw, I don't want no guns around me tonight. There's been enough shooting. And dammit, that is a cop's gun."

Ava lifted the pistol from Muddy's finger like it was a toy. "I don't care if it belongs to John the Revelator. You're a damn fool, Hank Williams." She balanced the pistol in her hand, gauging its weight. "Now me, I was born with brains enough to know when to pack."

She stared down at the unconscious policeman. Her expression was like she'd just tasted something rotten. "I ought to cork the son of a bitch right here and now."

Muddy grinned. "Now don't be doin' that, girl. We ain't going to be killing cops."

Ava sighed regret that sounded genuine. She drew a deep breath and threw her shoulders back, which did wonderful things for her bosom.

"Well then boys, let's get to it before I do something sane like walk out of this. Come on. I want to see Hank Williams and Muddy Waters in action."

Chapter 14

Muddy

There was a light over a ten-foot-high chain link fence that shined on a wooden sign that read *The Hewitt Spread*. Winged bugs swarmed like a black cloud around the light.

The moon hung heavy in a hazy night sky. The mosquitoes were bad. The air was thick with the sounds and smells of the bayou, like breathing through a wet cloth. The nearest inhabited property was more than a quarter mile away in either direction and not visible because the road angled and curved as it followed the uneven rim of the bayou.

We stood across the lane—me, Hank and the broad—looking across at the property that was spread before us. I'd parked the Chevy twenty feet off the blacktop, in among drooping willow trees set back far enough so passing headlights wouldn't reflect off the chrome. Not that there was any traffic at this hour.

The main house was a big deal in the center of the property, surrounded by a lawn and trees. There were lights on at one side of the house and you could make out a patio and a swimming pool. A curving driveway lined with oak trees looped past the front of the house. There was no sign of anyone or of anything going on in the house or anywhere on the property.

Behind the house was a pier and a boathouse and deeper shadows. The bayou. Bullfrogs and night birds and insects kept up a steady symphony.

Hank said, "Appears like no one's home."

Ava looked relieved. "Well ain't that too damn bad. It's about time things started going my way. Let's split."

I lifted a hand. "Now hold on. I didn't come all this way for nothing."

Her eyes swiveled to me with disappointment. "But, Muddy, we don't know what's waiting for you over there!"

"I ain't turning from it," I told her. "Y'all are white folks breathing free air. You ain't had a Ku Klux Klansman coming at you twice in one day and a whole damn town full of cops after your hide. If I've got a shot at making that go away by going over to that house and talking to that man, that's what I aim to do."

Hank said, "That gate's closed so I reckon it's locked."

I sneered. "A ten-foot chain-link fence ain't nothing to me. You can get good footing if you hit it right. Down in Mississippi I used to have me a woman in the boss man's yard and every morning when they was out working in the field, I'd pop over that fence, boom, slick as you please and get me something hot from the rich folks' kitchen."

Ava heard this and drew her head back to regard me. "So with you everything comes back to women, is that it, Muddy?"

I smiled modestly. "Well, I am the mojo man. And who says I'm talking about the same hot stuff you're talking about? Damn, I swear you got a dirty mind, child."

She laughed, "Oh, Muddy."

There was an edge to Hank's features. "Well I was the one pushing us to get here, so I reckon we'd best go through with it."

"I'll be standing right here by the car," said Ava. "First sign of trouble and I'm tearing down there to pull you out and you'd best be ready to git when I hit. You can count on me and Betsy." She patted the oversized black purse that held the gun. "Damn, I was crazy to try and walk the straight and narrow, booking deadbeats into a ratty motel." She looked at Hank with an apology in her eyes. "No offense, Hank. But what I'm saying is this here's the life I was born and raised to. I won't let you boys down."

She surveyed the house across the lane. "He's in his game room, by the pool. He calls it a library. Pool tables, big comfy chairs, wet bar. A game room."

I said, "Let's get on with this." I started across the black top lane. I heard Hank scuffling along to keep up behind me. He caught up with me and kept my pace. I eased us away from the light above the gate, over to near the front corner of the property. When we reached the foot of the fence, his step faltered.

"Uh, how are we going to do this, Muddy?"

I stoked up my pace and sprung onto that fence at a run, extending both arms up. I lodged the toe of one shoe between the links of chain for leverage, wedged the other toe hold, ready to hurl myself over and drop onto the other side. I held that position and twisted back toward Hank and extended an arm down to him.

"Come on, man. Hit it on the run."

He cussed under his breath, then did like I said and stuck his right arm up so I could grab his wrist and with his momentum and me already holding onto the fence, I helped him over with no trouble. Then I swung myself over and landed inside, right next to him.

He was laughing low. "Guess that wasn't as hard as I thought it would be!"

I said, "Lots of things in life are like that, man. Think on that sometime. Come on, now let's check this out."

I took off at a jog up the incline, heading for the lights around the pool. Hank kept pace next to me and the pair of us cut through the night like a couple of commandos closing in on an enemy target. Now why did that thought cross my mind? Enemy? We'd come to get help. Something deep inside of me was trying to warn me. I snagged the .32 automatic from my slacks pocket and thumbed off the safety.

We reached the corner of the house. I motioned for Hank to do like me and press himself flat against the house, no more than fifteen or twenty feet away from the swimming pool. French doors were open on the patio, with lawn chairs and some tables around the pool and a barbecue pit. There were sliding screen doors to keep out the bugs and mosquitoes.

I fought the urge to slap at a mosquito that was working on my neck. I moved my hand slowly and rubbed, mashing down where I'd felt the bite, but naturally by that time the little bastard had buzzed off.

Hank was looking itchy, standing there beside me. His face was pale in moonlight. His fidgety eyes watched me for a cue. He was swallowing large gulps of air, trying to keep quiet but wheezing, catching his breath after the short run from the fence.

Voices drifted out to us through the screen doors. Voices in conversation. I nudged Hank with an elbow and a wag of my head, and we inched along the side of the house, right up to the corner of the patio.

A voice was saying, "I don't mind telling you, T. J. I'm real surprised to see you popping up on my doorstep under these circumstances." It was a baritone voice, serious has hell.

Hank whispered in my ear, "Fatty Hewitt."

The other man inside the house said, "I snuck up on foot, Fatty, because I'm lying low. I didn't want to get caught in a bind with Wiley and Macklin."

Hank whispered to me, "Cantwell."

Inside, Hewitt said, "And why exactly have you been lying low, amigo? You're supposed to be my partner. Ain't partners supposed to trust each other?"

"You'd think so, wouldn't you," said Cantwell. "Uh, Fatty, mind if I freshen my drink?"

A chuckle. "You go ahead, you ballsy bastard. I've had crews out looking for you with orders to bring you in alive so I could go to work on you slow."

There was the *clink* of glass on glass. Cantwell fixing his drink. "Fatty, I want to clear up our misunderstanding. What other reason would I have for coming here?"

I thought, *Two mankillers staring each other down in that house.* Another mosquito went to work on my neck.

Fatty Hewitt was saying to Cantwell, "Let me spell out how this plays to me, T. J. Short and sweet. My ledger is missing. You know the ledger I'm talking about. If that ledger falls into the wrong hands, it's going to cause a world of trouble for a lot of people including me. That ledger disappears, then you disappear. How's that for making it simple? You stole my ledger, and I want it back."

Cantwell said, "Simple, hell. Two unrelated events."

"You've been incommunicado, T. J. and now you come here to what, clear the air? Okey dokey, son. Start clearing. I'm all ears."

Cantwell said, "After I got Hank to your club last night and he started his show, I went back to the motel. Thought I'd hustle a pretty gal they had working behind the desk."

Fatty made a grumbling sound. "What do you know about her?"

"Not a thing. I don't even know her name. The office was closed. No one answered when I knocked, so I figured the hell with it and went to the cabin to catch some shuteye. But there was a stiff on the cabin floor, so I got the fuck out of there."

"A stiff," said Fatty. "You said it was on the floor. Not stuffed into a closet?"

"He was on the floor, deader than Cincinnati on a Tuesday night. And that's it. That's my story."

"Sure, it is," said Fatty. "When you first came to me your story was that you were on the run because you double-crossed the wrong guys in Chicago. A punk on the run looking for a hole to crawl into, so I gave you a safe place to hole up. I took you on because you're a sharpie, T. J., and I can always use a sharpie in my line of work. Unless, that is, you get so sharp, you start thinking you can cut me."

"Fatty, I didn't take your ledger. I've got a sweet thing going, working for you. You've got nothing to worry about from me. I'm the one in the hot seat. Has anyone from Chicago been looking for me? I don't want to bring them in your way."

"No one's been around," said Fatty. "And no one gets in my way. Best you not forget that. You're talking to Fatty Hewitt."

"I know. That's why I want you to see me side of it. There are things I don't know, like who was that dead guy? What happened to him? How's Hank doing?"

"Don't you worry none about what happened at that motel," said Hewitt. "That dumb bastard that got himself killed was one of mine and I've cleaned up that mess. Made the payoffs, disposed of the body. You know how it's done. As for Hank, well, that's a real good question. Hank and some coloreds have joined forces is the last I heard. At a whorehouse in darktown, no less. Damnedest thing you ever heard. But Hank ain't what's got me worried, T. J.

It's you that worries me, son. Ol' Fatty don't know what to make of you and that's a natural fact."

"You checked on me in Chicago before you took me on."

"Yeah well, my contacts up north ain't that good. I could've been snowed."

"I haven't snowed anybody," said Cantwell. "I took to ground for a day to cover my ass and in doing so, I protected you too. You've been good to me, Fatty. I don't want to bring heat on you."

"So it wasn't a run-out powder?"

"Run out? Do you call showing up on your doorstep, running out? Shit, I didn't steal your ledger and I don't know who did. If anything, I want you to give me a promotion"

"A what?"

"Hell, I appreciate the small jobs and the odds and ends you've been throwing at me but you ought to utilize my talents more than you do. How about some action in darktown? I can handle a gun. Send me down there with some boys and I'll put all those concessions in your pocket; numbers, protection, girls."

"I've already got that sewn up," said Fatty. "You damn Yankee. Wish I knew what to make of you, T. J."

"You can trust me, Fatty. Go on, take a chance. Give me a concession. You won't regret it."

There was a knock at the door.

Fatty called, "Yeah?"

The door clicked open and a new voice said, "Uh, chief, there's something you ought to know."

Something else was said but I lost track because Hank bumped me with his elbow and whispered in my ear.

"Shit. That's Wiley, one the G-men."

I whispered, "Shut up."

Fatty was saying, "You make yourself at home, T. J. Have another drink. I'm enjoying our little chat and I will return directly so that we may continue."

The door clicked shut.

Hewitt was gone with Wiley. Maybe half a minute passed. Sweat greased my forehead and rolled down my neck. I wiped at the sweat and wondered what the hell to do next.

Inside, Cantwell started to speak in that voice folks use when they're on the telephone. He said, "Yeah, it's me. Can you talk?"

I eased an eye around the edge of the nearest glass door and caught a gander of a room like what Ava had described, a game room done up in oak with throw rugs and a seven-point buck mounted on one wall and the biggest swordfish I ever saw over a fireplace. There was a gun case across from the fireplace.

A squirrelly little dude in shirtsleeves and brown slacks stood with his back to me, saying into the telephone receiver, "Never mind where I am. I've only got a second. Have you got it?" A pause while he listened. "Okay, we're set to head out and make a break for it." Pause. "I said, never mind where I am. You have your black ass and that whore's papers at the station. The six-oh-five to New Orleans. Contact me on the train after you're sure you're not being followed." Pause. "Be there, Straight," and Cantwell slammed down the receiver.

I thought, *Straight?* That would be Straight Johnson he was talking to. . . .

Without warning, Hank plowed into me with enough force to send us both stumbling into the light pouring onto the patio from the screen doors. Hank tripped over his own boots and went down.

I almost lost my footing but came about in a fast crouch, ready to bolt in any direction. I brought around the .32, then froze.

Wiley stood there holding a Thompson submachine gun in both hands. I'd fired one of those babies once when we played a moonshiner's barbecue outside Helena, and I could see that he had the bolt back on full cock and his finger curled around the trigger.

He said, "Drop the piece, nigger, or I'll stitch you open right down the middle."

Chapter 15

Hank

Muddy dropped his pistol and it seemed to make an extra-loud clatter when it fell to the patio.

I'd drawn around and straightened slowly so as not to agitate Wiley into squeezing off a burst from the Tommy. Pain was pulsing from the base of my spine out through every artery and muscle in my body and I ground my teeth against it.

Macklin stood next to Wiley, holding his big .45 automatic aimed right at me.

It was like last night at the motel when they'd stormed in on me after I'd found the body; a pair of bookends, hulking and broad-shouldered with matching mean-ass features. The trench coats of last night had been replaced by matching blue serge double-breasted suits with wide lapels and loud ties.

Macklin sneered. "Well if it ain't the hillbilly Shakespeare."

Muddy had raised his hands too. "Hey, put down the Tommy gun, man. We ain't going nowhere."

Wiley said, "You got that right," and kept right on aiming the Thompson at us.

There was movement inside the game room.

Cantwell had quite naturally turned from the telephone to face the commotion so he was clearly visible to me where he stood just inside the screen door. His expression showed surprise when he saw me. Then his eyes swung to Fatty Hewitt, who stepped into the game room through a doorway behind Cantwell.

Fatty came in with a gun drawn, aimed between Cantwell's eyes.

Wiley called into the house, "The situation out here is under control, boss."

"Boss," I said, "I knew it. Dang me, I should have known it from the start. You guys ain't no more G-men then I am and there sure as hell ain't no Russian spy on the lam. Y'all made that whole mess up to intimidate me and appeal to my patriotism and con me into cooperating."

Macklin drew back his arm like he wanted to pistol whip me. "Shut up, bed wetter."

Wiley snickered.

From the game room I heard Fatty say to Cantwell, "I know you're packing, T. J. Reach for the gun real slow with your thumb and index finger and hand it to me with the butt first."

Cantwell slid open the screen door and joined us in the rectangles of light next to the swimming pool.

Fatty was right behind him, covering Cantwell with two guns, his and Cantwell's. Fatty looked like some big ass villain in a cowboy movie. He wore a brown western suit. His mismatched necktie was dark polka dot. He tossed his head back and cut loose with a guffaw like he was having the time of his life. But the guns in his hands stayed steady.

He said, "Well goddamn boys, we've got ourselves a quorum. The stooges who've been on the run—that would be you, Muddy, and you, Hank—and them who've been hunting you. That would be me and my boys here."

Muddy said, "I don't know you, mister. You ain't got no reason to aim a gun at me."

Fatty said, "You're trespassing. You think I couldn't have a colored killed for trespassing and get away with it? I've got that kind of pull in this parish."

I was keeping an eye on Muddy. I'd seen the man in action, so I knew what he was capable of. But he took a step back and lowered his eyes and I saw at that moment how he'd trained himself to do that as part of being Negro and knowing how to stay alive in the South . . . or anywhere else.

Muddy said, "We don't want no trouble."

"Well then," said Fatty, "you came to the wrong place. I'm the one sicced that Klan cop from Crowley and his Shreveport buddies down on your ass at Miss Delilah's. You've got plenty of reason to hate me, Muddy Waters."

Muddy said, "I don't want to see nobody dead."

"Fatty," I said. "I thought me and you was friends." I tried not to sound like I was pleading for something.

He sighed and shook his head. "Shit, Hank. I love your records, hoss. I've gotten me a heap of pussy with your voice moaning in the background, putting them fillies in the mood, so I'm sort of partial to you, son. But ol' Fatty's got himself too much riding on this one to cut you any slack."

I said, "So after Delilah's whorehouse was burned to the ground, the cops were going to say some kluckers did it to get Muddy. But they'd find me dead too. Damn, Fatty. That's cold."

"Business," he said. "But you two busted out. You're a real team, that's what you boys are, like salt and pepper. But you're not going to get out of *this* one."

Wiley said from behind his machine gun, "Shit. Three stiffs to bury. I say we make them dig their own damn graves."

Macklin spat near Muddy's feet. "Good idea."

I said, "Fatty, I don't understand. What did I ever do for you to want me dead?"

"You're a loose end, Hank. That dead guy in the motor court cabin, remember? You know that there's been a murder and if you were leaned on hard enough, you'd testify to that in court. With people out to take me down," his eyes moved to Cantwell, "government people who could use that sort of thing against me in a court of law, well, I can't have anyone testifying about a murder whether I'm guilty or not. The Feds don't care how they get me behind bars and if it's the death house on a murder rap, that would suit them just fine. I've got to make sure that doesn't happen. And that means take care of the loose ends. That weasel Cantwell thinks he's got everything he needs to put away me and Delilah Buie. Too bad he didn't stop to think about telephone extension lines. He thinks he's meeting Straight Johnson and catching the 6:05 to New Orleans tomorrow morning. Truth is, he's not leaving Shreveport alive. And neither are you."

Cantwell took a step forward, taking care to keep his hands visible. "Fatty, you've got me all wrong if you think I'm a Federal agent."

Fatty sneered. "I *know* you're an FBI man. I was just leading you on to see what I could get out of you before I turn you over to my boys. Yeah, you're a ballsy son of a gun and no mistake, T. J. You saw one of my boys, the one who got killed, watching the cabin before you took Hank to the club. You went right out and confronted him in the rain, told him some bullshit that bought you time. Ballsy, yeah."

Cantwell said, "Not that ballsy. You've got me so wrong, Fatty."

Fatty said, "I don't think so." He looked at me and Muddy. "And now these two mugs lurking outside, eavesdropping."

I said, in as reasonable tone as a man could summon with a shitload of guns pointing at him, "Now wait a cotton picking minute here, Fatty. Only reason in the world that I'm in this mess is because T. J. came up to me at the train station. All I want is my gol-dang songbook and I promise not to say nothing to nobody about nothing."

Fatty pursed his lips but shook his head. "Sorry, hoss. With what I've got staring me down, the word of a broken-down hick singer just ain't good enough."

Cantwell said, "Fatty, I swear I'm no G-man!" Desperation was creeping into his voice.

Fatty sneered. "You got into my organization with that bullshit story about being on the run and all the time you were running jobs for me, like lining Hank up to play the club, the real thing you were after was that ledger. Well you finally got your hands on it and you've been lying low because you know what you've got is dynamite and you don't want it to blow up in your face."

Cantwell said, "Think, Fatty. If that's true, why did I come out here and show up on your doorstep?"

"Because you're a ballsy bastard for a little fuck. You came here to stick your head into the lion's cage one last time before you split to Washington with my ledger for your Federal prosecutors. That's why you were asking all those questions, like you were looking for a new position with me. You were fishing for one last thing that would nail my coffin shut. Ballsy, yeah. But you're stupid, T. J., and you're just about dead. You're going to die by inches, pally, screaming every inch until I get my ledger back."

While Fatty prattled on, enjoying the sound of his own voice, I copped a sideways gander at Muddy to see how he was taking this in, and Muddy picked that exact instant to glance my way. Trouble was, I couldn't read the message his eyes were sending me. The lines of his Cherokee features were tight and his eyes made me think of smoldering coals.

The roar of an accelerating car engine from not far away ripped through the night, and a metallic smashing sound drew everyone's attention. I looked down where the driveway curved in moonlight. Pieces of the main front gate were airborne, glittering like falling comets in the headlight beams of the Chevy as it busted on through at full-throttle, speeding up the driveway. A firearm discharged from the driver's window once, twice, three times as the heap came barreling up the drive.

Macklin said, "What the—"

Wiley said, "Holy shit."

And Fatty was yelling at Wiley, "Shoot, damn you. What the hell are you waiting for? *Shoot!*"

Wiley showed his back to us and planted his feet squarely and took aim with the Tommy gun.

I yelled, "No, *don't!*"

Ava, for it could have been no one else, fired another round out the car's side window. The Chevy was eating up the distance, zooming in not more than a couple hundred yards out now, the headlight beams sweeping across us as the driveway curved on its final approach to the house.

Then the night was torn apart by the hammering of the Thompson. The recoil made Wiley's whole frame shudder. Saffron flashes spewed from the tommy's muzzle like spitting fire.

Shattering glass. The Chevy decreased its speed and swerved, traveling too fast when it left the driveway and plowed into one of the mighty ancient oaks that lined the drive, slamming into the massive tree trunk with such force that the vehicle's rear tires lifted while the front end crumpled in on itself like an accordion.

Gasoline from the ruptured gas tank spilled onto the hot engine and there was an enormous *ka-whumph!* that sounded like an oversized bass drum being struck. The Chevy disappeared into a blossoming ball of orange-red fire. The fireball rose into the darkness like a giant firefly.

For a single heartbeat, Macklin's eyes flitted in the direction of the explosion, and at that instant Muddy went into action with the eye-blurring speed of a professional boxer in the ring. Muddy's right fist shot up and popped Macklin on the jaw. Macklin jarred back. Muddy grabbed the wrist of his gun hand with both hands and tried to twist, to force the gun from Macklin's hand. But Macklin must have been used to getting punched in the jaw. He twisted to break free, but Muddy kept hold of that wrist.

The .45 went off.

Fatty ducked to the side with a funny little squeal. The bullet shattered glass in one of the French doors.

Muddy swung Macklin about like an over-zealous dance partner, and the pistol fired again, this time sending a bullet into the night.

Wiley was whirling around to bring his machine gun to bear on us but before he could do that, Muddy sent Macklin sailing into him and the two gunmen and their guns tumbled into the swimming pool amid a tangle of arms and legs, angry shouts and much splashing.

Fatty recovered his balance and brought his pistol around in Muddy's direction. Muddy was his only concern.

I had to do something. Fatty didn't expect anything from me. I'm just an alky hillbilly. He should have been watching me too, because I only had to take three steps on his blind side.

I said, "You fat double-crosser," and gave Fatty my shoulder with everything I had. I'm on the bony side, I'll admit, but angling at him like I did, I sent him off his balance and he followed his boys into the swimming pool with a cry of outrage like a wounded buffalo. There was more agitated splashing.

I pivoted to find Muddy running for the wreckage of the Chevy. I went after him, away from the patio and the lights. I looked around for Cantwell. G-man or not, he was nowhere in sight. From the pool behind us there was still plenty of splashing and I heard Fatty shouting.

"Get them. *Stop them, goddamn it!* Jesus fucking Christ—"

I caught up with Muddy and we reached the wreckage together.

The tree had caught fire. Not a blazing conflagration but the moist bark of the upper limbs smoldered, loading the air with a pungent nip. Fire crackled at the base of the tree where the frame of the Chevy was engulfed in flames that illuminated everything in a shimmering amber glow.

I had to raise a forearm to shield my face from the heat of the flames.

I cried, *"Ava!"* but I knew it was no use. No one could survive those flames licking the interior of what had been a car.

Muddy tugged at my arm. "She could've been tossed out and rolled."

That made sense, for I could not see any sign of a human form inside the flaming car. Of course she could have fallen onto her side, onto the car seat, but I'd follow Muddy's lead.

I swept my line of vision across the sloping grounds. There was a hedge on this side of the driveway some thirty feet down, away from the house. It was difficult to see in the flickering amber shadows. I started in that direction.

"Ava! Ava, can you hear me? *Ava!"*

Muddy was looking in another direction, though he wasn't calling her name.

A gun blasted from the direction of the house, a noisy *boom!* that could only have been a shotgun. Buckshot whistled over my head, which made me draw my head down level with my shoulders like I didn't have a neck. Handguns opened fire from the patio. The reports sounded like someone popping air-filled paper bags in the outdoors. But the bullets whistling close by me sounded serious enough. There was a keening whistle as a ricochet careened off a rock and something stung my cheek. I knew I'd received a laceration from a flying chip of rock.

The shotgun boomed again. Fatty and his boys had made good time climbing out of the pool and acquiring guns that weren't waterlogged, most likely from the gun case in the game room. And I was giving them a dandy target, shouting my fool head off and darting about in the firelight. The best thing I had going for me was to keep the fire between them and me. I glanced around but I couldn't see Muddy. He was either keeping his head down too or one of those bullets had got him.

The shooting tapered off. I could make out Fatty and his men advancing.

Muddy ran up to me and whispered, not panicky but with the words coming rushed together. "We've got to make tracks. Come on, this way," and he took off, not toward the road but toward the bayou.

I dug in my heels.

"But Muddy, what about—"

"She's burnt to a crisp or she's laying where we can't find her. Ain't nothing we can do to help her if we're dead.

My heart was pounding like it wanted to bust out. I said, "Poor Ava."

Another handgun *pop!* I heard a bullet whistle past.

Muddy said, "Suit yourself, man," and he bolted off in the direction of the bayou with its croaking, its symphony of night birds and owl hooting and its dozens of other unidentifiable sounds. I thought of a gigantic salivating monster lurking out there in the humid night. That's what the bayou sounded like.

I said, "Damn. Here I come," and I ran after him.

Chapter 16

Muddy

The hillbilly and me hit that cold, clammy, knee-deep water at a run, sending night birds from their perches with their wings flapping and angry cawing at us.

Then the bayou closed in. The moon got covered up behind cypress trees and vines that made a canopy over us. The air got thick and hard to breathe. Vegetation and vines and stands of reeds grew and there was a swampy, stagnant feel to the water that made me think on the marshlands back in the Delta where me and my boyhood running buddies would hunt and fish and drink 'shine and smoke reefer, or row out into the weeds with a gal in a pirogue, to grab some loving if you was lucky.

I've always hated the water except for bathing, of

course. Never cared much for swimming. And right now I was ruining a damn fine set of trousers and my beautiful alligator shoes trying to get the hell away from those boys who were hot on our heels.

Fatty was yelling at Wiley and Macklin, "Don't let them get away! Stop 'em, goddammit! *Kill 'em!*"

The shotgun went *boom!* Buckshot tore through rotting vegetation close to us.

I picked up my pace and the water got waist-deep, icy cold. Thick and clammy. I felt my dick shrivel up to a nub from that frigid water. The moon eased into view, glittering off the dark water. The water was black like oil, and felt just as thick. The bottom was muddy and mucky and damned if I didn't lose both of my shoes within a couple yards. Each step was an effort, like the mud was trying to suck me on down into it. But Hank and me were pushing on deeper and deeper into that dark world.

Handguns started popping off behind us. The vegetation and the cypress trees and the marshy weeds we were pushing through muted the gunfire. Fatty was shouting some more but I couldn't make out the words. Then they ceased firing.

It looked like we'd made our getaway.

In the moonlight, dead trees poked up from the murky, stagnant water like giant fingers reaching up from underwater to claw at the moon.

I'd lost my sense of direction.

A small outboard motor chugged to life.

Hank threw a look over his shoulder in the direction of the sound. Instinct will make a man do that even at night when he knows there's nothing to see. Then he let out a yelp and he tripped forward. Maybe over his own boots, maybe tripped up by the mucky bed of the bayou. He went pitching face-down and the splash he made was loud enough to be heard in New Orleans, much less in that boat, which started to *put-put* in our direction. I reached down and slid my arms under his shoulders and helped him stand. He was shivering like a wet kitten.

He said, "Gol-dang, Muddy, what are we going to do now?"

The silver beam of a searchlight pierced the dark, directed at first in the opposite direction from us. But the boat was coming in our direction. One man held the light while another sat at the motor, steering the boat, and you could bet the cat with the shotgun was sitting there, waiting, watching, ready to open fire at the first sight of us.

I whispered to Hank, "Over here," and grabbed his arm and drew him with me to behind the trunk of a dead tree that was thick and tall, a tree long dead but with its roots sunk deep below the waters. The heavy limbs that reached out at angles were like a statue with its arms uplifted to the sky.

The searchlight beam swept past the tree. We hunched down behind it and the light flitted right on past. From the puttering of the outboard motor, they couldn't have been more than a few yards away. After the light swept on, I eased an eye around one side of the trunk as Hank did around the other.

I could make them out in the reflection of the spotlight off the black water. Three of them were in the boat, just like I figured. The light made their white faces look like they were hanging there suspended. The three of them were in shirtsleeves. Fatty wore suspenders. He worked the outboard, and right now the boat was sitting still. Macklin crouched in the bow, directing the searchlight. Wiley sat between them and reflected light glinted off the barrel of his shotgun.

"What's that?" said Fatty.

Macklin brought the searchlight about and I saw what Fatty had heard.

The spotlight showed, clear as day, the long bodies and tails, the hungry eyes and the jaws and sharp teeth of alligators. They were slapping their tails upon the water and snapping their jaws. The gators were slithering about, irritated by the light.

I heard Hank inhale a ragged breath and I figured he was about to let out a cry of surprise or fear, and they would hear us. I twisted in the water there behind the tree and I pasted my right hand to the back of his head so that it held steady when I placed my left palm flat against his open mouth, and not a sound came from him.

I whispered in his ear, "Cool it, hillbilly. You'll get us killed."

His body relaxed then and he didn't try to resist. His right hand gave me an index-finger-to-the-thumb "okay" gesture.

I took the chance and released him.

He whispered, "Thanks, man. I almost lost it. Goddamn, them are gators! What are we going to do?"

"Wait," I said.

I went back to peering around the tree trunk.

Wiley was standing in the boat, and I heard the *ka-klick* as he worked the shotgun's pump.

"You want me to pop one of them gators, Fatty?"

Fatty said, "Naw, let 'em go. We're heading back. We've got more important business to attend to. That son of a bitch, Cantwell, he's my main concern. We've got to nab that boy. We're getting my ledger back."

Macklin snickered. "Hell, yeah. Let the gators do the dirty work."

Fatty nosed the boat around and they *put-putted* into the darkness back in the direction from which they'd come.

Fatty was saying, "Damn right. Those boys are alligator bait and I ain't proud to be the man who ended the career of Hank goddamn Williams. That's something else I need to settle with Cantwell for, putting me in this here situation."

Wiley said, "What about the nigger?"

The last thing I heard before they motored out of earshot was Fatty laughing. "Muddy Waters should've never let them gators see him wearing alligator shoes!"

I felt a sting on my left forearm, like someone branding me underwater with a red-hot poker. *Leeches*, I told myself. I was soaked and cold to the bone and I *had* to get out of that damn water. I brought an arm from underwater and looped it around the lowest part of the bare tree limb that jutted out above me. I used my knees and my feet and got leverage below the water and hoisted myself up. I've got strong muscles in my arms from playing the guitar every night, but that tree limb was damp and slippery and I slipped back twice before I got a good footing above the water line. I braced myself with my right hand to the tree trunk and brought myself all the way up and I got situated in the nook where the tree limb and the trunk met, using my right hand to swat off the leeches that had attached themselves to my arm.

I looked down at Hank and extended my right hand to him. "Come on, man. Get up out of there. Them gators—"

He said, "Oh my God. Oh my God." There was weeping in his voice. "I've come to this. We're gonna die, Muddy. There ain't no hope for us. We're done for."

The black waters shifted and rippled behind him under the moonlight. Leathery, ridged backs slithered toward him.

I said, "Screw that, whitebread. Get your skinny ass up here."

I clamped my fingers around his wrist, like I had when I'd helped him over the fence. I braced myself extra secure with both feet and yanked him up a split second before there came an angry upset in the water where he'd just been.

Then there were two of us in that tree, him in the crook of the bare branch opposite me. We must have looked a sorry-ass mess. I sure as hell felt sorry-ass, dripping smelly, oily water, perched in a tree like a fat-assed bird, listening to gators slither and snap in the water just beneath us. They sounded evil at having missed a meal and knowing that we were inches from reach of their snapping jaws.

Hank held onto the rotted tree trunk, hugging it with both arms, shivering so hard I'm surprised the vibrations on that tree didn't knock us into the water. His stringy hair was plastered to his skull like seaweed clinging to a wet rock and I saw for the first time how near-bald he was. He'd been doing a good job of combing what hair he had in over his bald spot. Funny what a guy notices at a time like that.

Then I started to get pissed off and surly and I said, before I could rein it in, "So that was the fat fuck who was going to help us out, huh?"

Hank made a pathetic moaning noise that I hoped Fatty and his boys couldn't hear. "And we lost Ava. Oh Lord, the poor child. Muddy, she's dead—"

"I wouldn't count that girl out until you see her body or read about it in the newspaper."

He lifted his head and the moonlight fell on his face. "You think she could have survived that crash?"

"How the hell should I know? Shit, right now me and Jimmy and Elgin should be onstage playing at The Boogie Woogie Inn. But no, I had to be talked into helping you out because you're too fucked up to help yourself. Shit, I must have been out of my mind throwing in with a tanked-out hillbilly singer on a losing streak. You ain't nothing but a bad luck child. You're what they call an albatross around my neck."

Below us, the alligators slithered away with a sneaky sound of rippling water.

Hank said, "What're we going to do, Muddy?"

"We're going to sit it out up here for a spell. Let them gators move off. Let Fatty and his boys make it on out of here."

"But what if them gators don't swim off? What if they're just laying out there waiting, to snooker us and move in for the kill and chaw us up soon as we set foot down off this tree?"

I said, "Hank, we ain't spending the rest of our lives in this bayou."

There came a spell of nothing said between us. Then he said, "Muddy, I believe in God. Do you believe in God?"

I felt my temperature starting to rise again.

"Don't be calling on Him just yet, fool. We'll get ourselves out of this."

The bayou was back to normal. The boat engine had stopped. The sound of voices had gone away. Just the bullfrogs, night birds, insects and too damn many mosquitoes.

He said, "Sweet Lord, I wish I was lying safe and warm in Miss Audrey's arms up in Tennessee."

"Miss Audrey? I thought your fiancée's name was Billie Jean."

"That is my fiancée's name. My wife's name is Audrey. She's the mother of my children. And Lord help me, I still love her cheating heart."

"Now that," I said, "would make a good title for a song."

"Aw heck. You know, Muddy, the people I love the most, reckon I'd be worth more to them if I was dead. The world's already got my music, I gave it to them from my heart and my soul. My music's going to *last*. But without ol' Hank around, mucking up the works, whoever owns the rights to them songs will be making money forever. Reckon that's what they'd rather."

I said, "Knock it off, man. Talk like that don't get you nowhere."

He didn't reply. I leaned in to check him out. His head was against the tree trunk and damned if he wasn't asleep. I let him sleep for close to a half-hour. He needed a break, and so did I.

I almost drifted off to sleep, or maybe I catnapped without knowing it.

His cry tore me awake. *"Daddy!"*

The moon had drifted out from behind the trees, tossing light down on us and the oily water around the tree. Something long and dark slithered past, making the water ripple.

"Hank, wake up. You're dreaming."

He made a gurgling sound like water going down a drain, then he shifted in his perch and said again, in a lower voice, "Daddy . . ."

He started to slip sideways. I kept my left arm looped around my branch and with the other I caught him and heaved him back so hard, his head banged against the tree trunk. He came awake with a start.

"Huh? What?" He looked around and his vacant eyes rested on me and started to focus.

I said, "You were dreaming. You almost fell in. Them gators are still down there.

He gave a pitiful moan. "Nightmares when I'm asleep, and a living nightmare when I'm awake."

"Stow that. You've got to toughen up, man. I'm tired of listening to you piss and moan."

"You're right. I'm sorry. I'm supposed to be your partner, and I get you into a pickle like this." He kept scanning the water around us.

"That's right, and I ain't happy about it. But we got to pitch in together, Hank, if we're going to make a way out. I don't need you falling to pieces on me."

"I said I was sorry. Shoot, Muddy. A strapping, hearty fella like you, who knows how to take care of business . . . how would you know what it's like to be a skinny, sickly little fella like me? My daddy got his brains messed up in France in the First War and they took him away from me and Mama when I was but seven years old. Locked him up in the insane asylum. I was a grown man before they let him out. Maybe that's why I went wrong. I didn't have no one but a no account Negro street singer to look up to when I was coming up. That's why I'm this way. I can't help it."

I said, "They had me working in the cotton fields, on Stovall's Plantation, when I was seven years old. You're the way you is, Hank, because you ain't thinking right. What is it? They got you on drugs, messing with your mind?"

"It's my back. My spine's all messed up since when I was born. Yeah, the doctors, they give me medicine for my pain, but—"

I said, "What kind of medicine?"

His shoulders twitched. "Well, I don't rightly . . . well, hell, Muddy, they been giving me morphine and Demerol, and of course I need my bennies and my Seconal just to keep my life together."

"Your life ain't together," I told him. "Your thinking's messed up. You've got to dry yourself out from that junk they been giving you. Good pussy on a regular basis, that's what a man needs to keep him fired up and moving right. Them drugs, man, they steal your soul. I've seen it happen."

"I got troubles, man. The pills help."

I said, "I don't want to hear *why* you're doing that shit. You know you need to be thinking on your troubles clear-headed, without using that junk. Letting your head get messed up, man, I hate to see it. I'll tell you something, man. I like your songs. And that's you doing those Luke the Drifter records too, or somebody trying to sound just like you."

"Yeah, that's me. I'm Luke the Drifter. Well, I'll be damned. Muddy Waters digs Hank Williams. Heck, man. I been digging your low down blues since I first heard 'em."

"Well, that's hip enough," I said. "But don't be telling nobody that Muddy Waters digs hillbilly music. I've got me a reputation to maintain."

"Muddy, if you was me, what would you do?"

"About what?"

"I don't know. About my troubles in life. About Miss Audrey and Billie Jean. About thinking too much on never knowing my daddy, and—"

"Hank, life's a twisty road."

"Yeah, ain't that the truth."

"You spend all your time looking into your rearview mirror at where you've been, and you're liable to drive your car off a cliff."

Silence from him. I thought, *My big speech and the hillbilly falls asleep.* . . .

But then he said, "Well, goddamn, you sure know how to nail it to the barn door, don't you, bluesman? Those are wise words. I'll remember that, and I'll think on it. Uh, er . . . and I reckon there's something else we need to talk on."

I said, "If you want to talk about anything except me and you getting out of Louisiana, I don't want to hear about it."

The moonlight was a silver slash across the bayou. The water was flat like black marble. The black marble wavered. A pair of gator snouts and glittering eyes and long menacing bodies rippled past.

Hank moaned. "Oh Lord, Muddy!"

Gator jaws flapped open and lifted. A flat ugly head dripping oily water. Rows of sharp crooked teeth snapped at me, just missing my backside. I shimmied higher up into the crook of the tree with my legs hugging the limb, and pressing myself to it like a monkey humping his mate. Then the gator was gone. The water was back to looking like black marble in the moonlight.

Hank said, "I was just going to say that, well, you're so all-fired hard-ass and sure of yourself, you've got *me* putting faith in you. I know we'll get out of this. God *will* provide a way. But then what?"

"Say it clear, man," I said. "Talk in words a bluesman can understand."

"Well, what about Fatty Hewitt and Cantwell, and that dead guy back at the motel?"

"What the fuck about them? Get hip to yourself, Hank. You heard what I heard back at the house. Fatty cleared things with the cops and got rid of the stiff, so it's like there never was a murder. And your buddy Cantwell—"

"He ain't no buddy of mine. That son of a bitch got me into this when he accosted me at the train station. And me, just minding my own business, fresh in from California and wanting nothing more than to spend some time with Billie Jean. But look at the fix we're in! Would've never happened if that bastard Cantwell—"

"Fatty's right about one thing," I said. "Cantwell's a G-man. He was working undercover to bust Fatty."

"He sure disappeared fast. What do you think happened to him?"

"Maybe the gators are working on him. I don't give a shit. Just don't you try talking me into nothing else. We get out of this alive, I just might kill you, I don't get over this mood I'm in."

"But what about Straight Johnson?"

"What about him? Damn, I'm freezing in these wet clothes! And my conk . . . Jesus, my beautiful process has done been destroyed. But Straight, that bastard, took a shot at me. You heard that phone call the G-man made. Straight's working with him. Cantwell wants to go back to Washington, making a clean sweep down here. He's got Fatty dead to rights with that ledger and Straight's turning over Delilah's paperwork. Sounds like she's going down with Fatty."

"Don't that bother you, Muddy?"

"Why should it? I've got me a living to make, man. I want to get back to playing my music, that's all."

"Well shoot," he said, "so do I. Muddy, they've got my songbook."

I said, "Oh . . . yeah."

"I do want to get on with my life without looking back, like you said. But I can't do that without my songbook. It's who I am. It's *what* I am. You've got to understand that, because I need your help."

"You think Fatty's got your songbook?"

"Could be. Maybe that's why he had Cantwell track me down in the first place. Think about that. Fatty wanted to get his hands on great songs by a washed-up hillbilly, and then make a fortune getting someone else, someone new to sing them. Someone he could make into a star, like that Elvis kid he's got pushing a broom at his club. The right kid with good material could go a long way."

I slapped at a mosquito, or maybe it was a dozen of them buzz-bombing me. Damn but they were thick.

I said, "Reckon it could have happened that way."

"My songbook went missing the same time I found that dead guy in my cabin. You think that there's a coincidence? Way I see it, they're all fixing to come together at the train station in the morning. Fatty and his boys are going to be there and so is Cantwell and Straight Johnson. Delilah, she'll be around too. Bet on that. I don't get it either, Muddy, but my songbook is going to be there with one of those people. I feel that in my bones. This will be my last chance to lay my hands on it."

"Okay, okay."

"I aim to get that songbook back or die trying."

"That's mighty big talk."

"Well, it's what I aim to do. And if I had you in my corner, I know I could pull it off."

I couldn't help but laugh. "Yeah, I reckon you could. But Hank, it ain't gonna happen. I done carried my weight and then some since I hooked up with you, but I'm tapped out. Being in your vicinity has brought me nothing but shit. Damn, my pecker's done froze away to nothing, sitting up here in this tree."

He said, "Mine too. But uh, look, man. I hate to remind you, but I saved your life when I took a bottle to that cop's head back at Miss Delilah's, when them kluckers came for you."

"Yeah, and I just saved your skinny white ass from an alligator. That makes us even."

"Aw now, Muddy, don't be cross with me. Won't you kindly reconsider—"

"Cool it," I said. "I hear something."

He quieted down without finishing, and listened along with me.

The *putt-putt* of the boat's outboard was back and coming closer. The searchlight beam stabbed again into the dark and skipped across the water, cutting through the cypress and the dead trees.

Hank whispered, "Oh, criminy. Fatty's decided to track back and finish the job. We're done for!"

I whispered, "I don't think so. He wants to make that train and get his ledger back more than anything else. That's *his* life at stake, and ain't nothing going to stop him from that."

But in case I was wrong, I got ready to dive into the water if the searchlight beam came in our direction, which it would.

I thought, *Hell of a choice, gunsels or alligators.*

A woman's voice called, "Hank! Muddy! Are you out here?"

Hank whispered to me, "Ava." Then he stood up and started shouting and waving. "Ava! *Ava!* Over here! We're over here!"

You'd have thought he was Pentecostal, witnessing the Second Coming. He almost fell out of the tree, waving and holding on.

The beam of light swept past, stopped and returned to stay on us. I stayed where I was. I didn't look into the light. The boat *putted* over and bumped its bow against our tree.

Ava held the light to guide whoever was manning the outboard engine. She'd changed into a freshly pressed blue summer dress that showed off her tanned arms and just a hint of the tops of smooth white breasts.

She reached out an arm to steady the boat against the tree, and said, "Well howdy there, you two. Reckon you didn't expect to see me again, didja?"

Hank said, "Glory be to God, Ava. I didn't expect to *ever* see you again. Dang!"

I said, "Good to see you, girl. Glad you brought the boat with you. Had me a hunch you wasn't burned up in that wreck."

She set down the flashlight, braced her footing and reached both arms up to Hank. He started to ease down from the tree, but that skinny hillbilly was so wet and miserable and uncoordinated, he'd have fallen in if I hadn't thrust out an arm and steadied him while Ava got him into the boat, which commenced to rock violently with his added weight. She returned one arm to the tree to steady them while with the other she guided Hank into a sitting position. The curves inside her dress moved with a sly way that made me think of a healthy cat. Hank was holding out his arms like he wanted a hug from her, but she wasn't having any of that.

I stepped into the boat, and let go of the tree only when I was sure of my footing. I stood there steady and the boat stopped rocking.

I said, "Woman, you've got too much spunk to roll over and die for anyone. Sure, I knew that. So where you been? Damn alligators almost had us for dinner." I picked up her flashlight and turned its beam on the figure who sat with one hand on the idling outboard, ready to steer us off. "Who's that you got with you?"

He was a button-eyed guy with a freckled face, chewing gum. A toothpick stuck from the corner of his mouth. He jerked an arm up to block the light that caught him square in the eyes.

"Hey! Nix the light!"

I said, "Who the fuck are you?"

His back straightened and for the first time I could see the grip of a revolver tucked in his belt.

He said, in a cool voice, "I'm nobody to get surly with, pal. Ava brought me out here to rescue you two so I'd appreciate not having to take any lip. Now get that light out of my eyes. I've got to keep sharp. I'm driving."

I said, "Damned if you are."

Ava said, "Muddy—" in a troubled, warning voice.

But I wasn't paying her no mind. I was dripping wet and I was mad. Part of me had thought I was going to die in a Louisiana bayou, eaten by gators. I had me a mad fever beyond common sense.

Then Hank lit up, like he did at unexpected times. "Wait a minute!" he hollered, and he was pointing a finger at the freckle-faced man. "I *know* you—"

Chapter 17

Hank

The freckled face got friendly. He wore his cabby's cap at the same jaunty angle as before, over his unruly red hair.

"Howdy, Mr. Williams."

"Well dog, hoss. I'll be danged." I was trying to get over my surprise but that was the best I could do.

Muddy lowered the flashlight and its beam reflected from the bottom of the boat, illuminating our faces.

The boat nosed around, the fella in the stern guiding us back in the direction they'd come from. There was no sign of gators. We hadn't gotten that far, me and Muddy. House lights from the Hewitt place slid into view through the cypress trees.

Muddy swung to face me and his eyes glittered in the reflected light. "Who is he?"

As the man steered the boat, he said, "I can speak for myself."

By this time, I knew Muddy's hair trigger anger. And I figured it was best to keep it from going off.

I said, "This here's the cab driver who picked me up at Fatty's club after I got done playing." I felt my face screw up, and I looked at the guy. "What was your name again, old son? I've been through so much since I seen you last, feels like my head's inside a cement mixer."

He looked real happy. "Mr. Williams, it's a pleasure to find you." He tossed me a dark shape. "Here's a blanket. Y'all look about as happy as a wet kitten. I'm Driveabout, Mr. Williams."

I wrapped myself in the blanket and it helped take off the chill. It was a warm night, but I was cold through.

I said, "I told you to call me Hank. You still carrying that flask?"

He chuckled and produced the flask, in a stitched leather pouch, which he handed to me. He said, "You want a blanket, Mr. Waters?"

Muddy said, "I don't want no blanket. Tell me about yourself."

Driveabout did not take offense at Muddy's tone.

"I drive around in my taxi," he said. "Got me seniority down at Yellow, so they let me cruise my own hours. I don't follow no rules or regulations. Never could stomach that way of life. I just about live in my ol' Yellow. I told Hank that he could call on me, he ever needed me."

Muddy said, "Yeah. So when did you call him, Hank?"

I said, "Uh—"

Muddy said to Driveabout, "How'd you show up here?"

The cabby brought the boat in gently against a pier, then went about securing the line. We were down a pebbled path from the main house.

Driveabout said to Ava, "Maybe you'd better tell them, hon."

That brought my eyes to Ava, fast. "Hon?" I echoed.

Muddy gave me that low, gravelly chuckle of his, like he knew everything. "Don't act so surprised, hillbilly. What did you expect, a girl pretty as this," and he his eyes roamed over Ava's figure in a way that made brassy little Ava turn away. I'll bet she was blushing.

"I'm sorry, Hank. I guess you could say that . . . well, Driveabout here is sort of my boyfriend."

Driveabout frowned. "What do you mean, hon, you sort of could say?"

She stepped from the boat and rested a slim hand on one of his broad shoulders. She lifted her chin.

"All right, you are my boyfriend." She looked at me straight. "He is my boyfriend, Hank. Don't be sore. I was just waiting for the right time to tell you."

She offered a hand to help me out of the boat, onto the pier. She was a fine figure of a woman, tight and sassy and in her prime. I shucked the blanket and brushed her hand aside.

I got out of the boat my own damn self. "When were you going to tell me? After I got you that recording contract in Nashville?"

She pouted. She was very pretty. "Now Hank, that's not fair."

Driveabout said, "Yeah, that ain't fair. I spend time dropping by at the motel in between driving about, to romance Miss Ava who, by the way, is as fine an upstanding a young lady as you are likely to find anywhere despite her, uh, notorious past. Point is, Hank, I've been sparking this gal since before you showed up."

Muddy joined us on the pier. His eyes kept darting about, probing the dark. "I need me some dry clothes. Let's get out of here."

"This way," said Driveabout, and he started off up the path.

Muddy stayed right beside him. Ava followed briskly, and I struggled to keep up with her. I was gulping air to catch my breath because Driveabout and Muddy set a brisk pace.

I said, "Things are happening too fast for me to keep square, dagnabbit."

Driveabout said, "Hank, after I dropped you off at the motel the other night, I stopped in to smooch it up some with Ava. We were together when those goons, Wiley and Macklin, showed up and started roughing you around. I know those boys from hanging out around Fatty's club, waiting on fares. They're poison. I thought me and Ava should make tracks and disappear and let you take care of yourself."

I said, "Then I reckon you can go back to calling me Mr. Williams."

"Point is, Ava insisted that we stay and help you. And we're still helping you, so go easy." Driveabout motioned for us to slow down when we reached the side of the house. He added, "I was just doing what Ava told me."

Muddy made that gravelly sound in his throat. "How long you been bird-dogging us?"

Ava spoke up. "Drive stayed behind at the motel when I took off with Hank, but I called him from that diner where we got the chicken dinners. There was a pay telephone in the ladies room. My daddy taught me to always have backup."

We grouped into a small cluster at the corner of the house, and I reckon I was gawking at Ava in the light of the moon.

"I'll be horn-swoggled. You could've had Driveabout back you up when you first busted into that cabin with your car, but you wanted me to think that you was doing it alone so I'd be more impressed and help you in Nashville."

She said, "Well what's wrong with that?" in a tone like I was stupid and the matter was closed. "Hank, I did help you at that motel and now too, when it looked like alligators were going to feed on you." Then her fingers were touching my cheek. Her caress was warm. So was her voice. She cocked her head slightly and said, "I think you're a musical genius and a swell fella. Please don't be sore."

I said, "Oh, all right." I would have melted like butter in the July sun if she hadn't taken her hand away.

The four of us peered around the corner of the house, at the front.

The wreckage of Ava's Chevy was nothing but an inky clump on the far side of the driveway. The yellow taxi was parked about a hundred feet away, near the front entrance of the house. There was no trace of anyone around. Cicadas chirped. Night birds sang. Tranquility reigned.

My gut felt tight. My bowels felt loose. I said in a whisper, "What now? Why ain't there anyone around after the explosion when Ava's car crashed?"

Driveabout said, "Even if it was reported, Fatty owns the law out here. The cops wouldn't check it out unless Fatty called and ordered them to."

Muddy eyed Ava. "Busting through that front gate and driving like the devil, raising hell, you gave me and the hillbilly something to work with, so we could get out of that jam."

She said, "That was my intention.'

Muddy smiled a quick smile. "You're a lucky gal."

"One time when I was driving getaway for my dad," she said, "the cops were hot after us, shooting up a storm. We blew a tire and the car went speeding out of control right near a cliff. Well, Daddy tossed me out the passenger side, onto the shoulder, and he jumped out after me into some high weeds. Our car went over the cliff and crashed onto some rocks hundreds of feet below and they thought Daddy was in it because no one had been seen jumping from the driver's side. They didn't see us before the car went over. By the time they got down there and figured out that he wasn't in the car, Daddy and me were long gone." She smiled to herself. "Mama was always waiting on us after a job with a special dinner. Anyway, when my tire blew tonight, that's what I did. I jumped out at the passenger side, so Fatty and his boys wouldn't see. Only I wasn't as lucky as I was that day with Daddy. I hit my head wrong and the next thing I knew, I was lying out cold in the weeds." She placed her arm through Driveabout's. "And it was my backup man who saved the day."

Driveabout was enjoying basking in the attention she was paying him, as any man would.

He said, "Ava told me that she was bringing y'all here to Fatty's and that I should drive ahead from Shreveport whilst you were having your moonlight picnic. Had myself hid in place when you showed up here."

Muddy said, "I didn't see no Yellow cab."

Driveabout flashed a grin. "A Yellow ain't that easy to hide, true enough. But you couldn't have spotted me, mister. I was down the road apiece beyond where you staked out Fatty's. I saw your headlights turn off. Ava told me to lay low, so that's what I did. Next thing I knew, Ava was blowing a gasket and crashing through that gate and before I could get over here, there's gunfire—a frigging machine gun! I came racing in with my headlights off and almost rolled because I took the turn too fast. I pulled up near the wreck just as Ava was coming to."

Muddy said, "Real convenient."

I said, "Muddy, why is it you're so distrustful of Driveabout? Here's how I figured it happened. Fatty and them mugs changed into dry clothes after they got out of the pool and came straight after us in the boat, not paying attention to nothing else. That must've been when this boy came on the scene."

Muddy said, "Maybe," and he turned to Ava. "It ain't just the cat I'm wondering about."

Ava's mouth tightened into a thin line. "Muddy, that's not nice."

Driveabout continued speaking as if these things had not been said.

"Only thing kept me in this from the start is making sure my gal stays safe." He patted Ava's hand, clasped in one of his, and he added, "No matter how harebrained her schemes get."

Ava pouted. "Now, you, that's not nice either."

Driveabout grinned and shrugged. "Truth hurts, don't it, toots?"

She withdrew her arm from his and her spine grew a steel rod. She crossed her arms and stared at him down the length of her pretty nose.

"I don't care to be spoken to in that fashion."

"Anyway," Driveabout told me and Muddy, "I loaded tootsie here in the backseat of my cab and made a U-turn and got the hell off the property. I parked and put some cold water on her face and she came around, and the only thing she wanted was for me to drive us back here and go up against Wiley and Macklin to pull you guys out. But, like I said, they're heavy opposition. Sorry, boys, but I took some convincing. I'm a lover and a cab driver, not a fighter. But then we saw a snazzy Buick go tearing off, I knew it was Fatty and his boys lighting out, so that changed things and here we are." He added for Ava's benefit, "Maybe I don't like it, doll, but I do deliver."

She sighed and uncrossed her arms. "Yes. But sometimes you're mean."

Muddy grumbled, "I'm glad as hell that we're up to date. I need me some dry clothes."

I said, "Me too."

Driveabout ran his eyes over my frame. "No trouble for you, Hank. You and me are about the same size. I got a spare set of clothes in the cab. They'll be a tight fit—"

Muddy started toward the cab. "I'll find some dry threads on the way. Let's go."

We toddled off after him.

Driveabout stayed abreast of Muddy as they approached the taxi. "Uh, pardon the hell out of me, mister, but you mind telling me where it is you want to go?"

Muddy said, "Going to be a party at the train station. Going to mess it up with the bad guys and with Miss Delilah and her boy, Straight Johnson, who thinks it's hip to peg a slug at Muddy Waters."

Driveabout said, "Say what?"

Ava said, "Now wait a minute. Wait one cotton picking minute."

Her eyes blazed from me to Muddy and back again. "Are you two out of your alleged minds?"

Muddy said, "Slow down, woman." There was a dangerous growl to his words. "That ain't no way to talk to a man."

Ava took a deep breath. "Okay." She exhaled. "Let me see if I have this straight. You, Hank. You get yourself in deep do-do with Fatty, involving a dead body in a closet and who comes to the rescue? Me. Then I provide you with wheels to get away from that whorehouse in tan town with your buddy here"—she wagged a thumb at Muddy—"during the course of which I dodge bullets from the Ku Klux Klan. I do my best to talk you out of coming here to see Fatty, but my advice is totally ignored. So I get shot at some more, my beautiful Chevy gets blown up and I'm knocked unconscious, trying to get you out of Fatty's clutches. Then I have to get in a gol-dang boat and dodge alligators to help you. Tell me, have I got that right so far?" Even in the dark, her angry eyes were boring holes into me.

I scratched the back of my neck and tugged an earlobe so hard it hurt. I scrapped the ground with the toe of my boot. "I reckon that is a pretty fair summation."

Muddy said to her, "Get out of my way."

"I will not. After everything I've been through, I deserve to be heard. You two are fixing to get yourselves killed!"

I said, "Now, Ava. Look, sugar, I've got to see this through. They've got my songs."

Driveabout muttered, "Hank, it ain't worth risking your life for."

I said, "Yes, it is. Damn well told it is. I done lived the life that went into them songs, and it ain't been easy on me. Believe that. Ain't nobody getting them songs but me unless I *am* dead."

Muddy placed a meaty hand under each of Ava's arms and lifted her as he would a child, turning to set her down before showing her his back, to again face the cabby. She started sputtering, calling him names. Muddy ignored this and said to Driveabout, "How about you, bo? How are you going to play this?"

Driveabout made a snorting sound. "Shit. What's a gee supposed to do?" he asked no one in particular. "All right, mister, you and Hank get yourselves killed if you have to. I'll take you where you want to go."

Ava wailed with despair. "No, Drive! You can't—"

Muddy said, "Give me the keys. I'm driving."

"Sorry, mister," said Driveabout. "Nobody steers these wheels but me."

"Don't tussle with me, son. I said give me the keys."

Driveabout stepped back. "And I said no one rides in my cab unless they're a guest or a fare. Tell you what. Me and Ava will take you to the train station, but after that we hold back with my cab so's you can make a fast getaway if you need to. But that's it. Don't involve either one of us in your business."

Ava said, "Driveabout honey, this is *not* a good idea."

He nodded agreeably. "That's why we're going to lay back after I get these guys to the station. But Ava, I've got to do this. You just listed everything that's happened so far. I can't run out on these fellows after all that."

She made a sound from deep in her throat that sounded like *grrrrrr*, and turned away.

Driveabout said, "But I'm driving."

Several heartbeats passed. I thought, *Be cool, Muddy.*

Then Muddy said, "Shotgun."

And I piped up with, "Uh, about those dry clothes. . . ."

Low, scattered clouds in the east were starting to turn from black to gray with the promise of dawn.

From a half block away, the lights from inside the train station shone weakly through what remained of the night. There were a few cars parked in the rectangular gravel lot adjacent to the tracks; folks waiting for the train that was due in eight minutes.

The Yellow cab was parked behind us, in the shadows of an alley that ran behind a Ben Franklin store, which was closed at this early hour, as were the other businesses along this street: a Walgreen's, a restaurant and some small shops and a movie theater with *An American in Paris* listed on the marquee. The humid air cast halos around the streetlights at each corner. The world was quiet. A pickup truck rattled by, but there was no other traffic.

Me and Muddy stood at the end of that alley and peered up and down that street one last time. Ava and Driveabout were there with us.

The roads were clear and Driveabout made good time after leaving the Hewitt Spread. The slacks and shirt he gave me were tight in places but felt like silk after those wet rags I'd been shivering in. It was funny how Muddy got his new clothes, a pair of gray slacks, a black T-shirt and a lightweight jacket. Muddy had wanted Driveabout to pull over on the way into town when he spotted dry clothes on a wash line, but Driveabout insisted that he had something better, and we went rapping on the back door of a secondhand clothing store. Driveabout's cousin ran the shop. Bleary-eyed, he answered our knock and Muddy got new threads and a pair of shiny-like-new shoes. He also grabbed a handful of new bandanas and disappeared into the bathroom for an extended period of time. When he emerged, he'd fashioned a do-rag, which made his appearance at least more acceptable than having to see the damage our ordeal in the bayou had done to his conk.

He wore the do-rag now, a snazzy red print number, stylish after its fashion.

After taking a gander up and down the street, he said to me, "Ready, hillbilly?"

I gulped hard, and wondered if the gulp sounded as loud to the others as it did inside my head. "I reckon. I just wish we had us a gun."

Ava seemed to tighten her hold on that big black handbag, which she wore by its shoulder strap. She was carrying her .38 in that oversized purse. There wasn't much light reaching us from the nearest streetlight, but I saw concern in her eyes.

She said, "I wish you weren't doing this. You two, this is your last chance to back off."

Muddy grinned his across-the-face, sideways grin. "May be the last time for you to be nagging on us."

She said, "I've got a right."

Driveabout didn't look happy, either. "You fellas go through with this, likely someone's going to get killed."

Muddy nodded. "That's why I want a piece."

Driveabout patted a pistol grip that was visible under his belt. "Sorry. This stays with papa. You boys listen to Ava. She's right. Stand down."

"Muddy," said Ava, "talk Hank out of this. He's not a fighting man."

Muddy took a moment, then he said, "I ain't a man for speechifying, so listen up. If there's a way to get the Klan off my back, I got to try for it. As for Hank, well, this hillbilly here went utsnay back in the bayou, when it looked like gators was going to eat us up, but he talked some sense in between getting on my nerves. He talked about having deep feeling for that special someone, y'know? I only ever had that kind of deep feeling for my wife. Chicks on the road, road wives, they're pleasant companions but my deep feeling is for the mother of my children, waiting on me in Chicago. But Delilah . . . well now, that woman's *got* something."

Driveabout removed his cap and ran fingers through his red hair. "But Muddy, she runs a whorehouse."

"Don't matter. I don't want to marry the bitch. But I got that deep feeling for her that Hank was talking on. Never knowed a woman like her. And I ain't quitting this mess until I know she's all right."

I could only scratch my hillbilly head and say, "Well, I'll be go to hell."

Ava was watching the train station. "I don't see any G-men," she said in a quarrelsome tone. "What makes you so sure everybody's coming *here* this morning?"

Driveabout replaced his cap to the back of his head. "If Fatty knows that Cantwell aims to catch this train, ain't that enough to make Cantwell change his plans? I sure would."

Muddy said, "Let's find out. Come on, Hank, if you aim to," and he took off, hoofing across the street without another word.

Ava touched the side of my face with her fingertips. Warm fingertips.

"Hank, please don't do this."

"Got to," I told her.

And once again I found myself hurrying to keep up with Muddy.

Chapter 18

Muddy

I've never been an early riser, even back on Stovall's, but I have seen many a sunrise because I've been up all night, like now; that time of day when the first light creeps over the world, little by little, growing lighter every minute. Birds start singing from the trees. The day would turn steamy hot in an hour or so, but right now the morning air was clean.

Me and Hank made it across the street to the mouth of the alley opposite from where Ava and Driveabout stood. I drew up to let Hank catch up with me. Across the street, the quail and the cabby stepped back into the shadows.

A city bus went past and then the air wasn't so clean because the smell of diesel fumes was thick. Down the street, cars were pulling into the depot parking lot and for the first time I could see people waiting for the train on the platform. Two soldiers with duffel bags from Fort Polk, shipping out for Korea. A man and a woman and their two little kids, waiting near a baggage wagon. And a group of nuns traveling together.

Hank was breathing hard from trotting across the street. "Now what?" he wanted to know.

"We're going to ease in on that station from the blind side. If they've got it staked out, they won't be expecting that. We're walking the tracks."

He started to reply, but I was done talking. I trucked on down this alley. There was no one around. There were still plenty of shadows. I angled across and walked down the railroad tracks. The gravel and cinder crunched beneath my new shoes. The creosote of the railroad ties didn't smell bad.

Hank crunched along after me, wheezing. But he kept up.

Short of the depot, I led him away from the tracks before the circle of the depot lights could reveal us to the people waiting on the station. At this end of the platform, the roof overhung a couple of sheds, side by side, and a narrow walkway between that led to the front. We started along the paved walkway.

Hank was crowding me from behind when he said, "Muddy, what the hell are we aiming to do?"

There was a shift in the shadows right ahead of me and a figure showed himself, stepping squarely into my path from where he'd been standing behind one of the sheds.

The shadow said, "I've been wondering the same thing. What the hell *are* you aiming to do?"

T. J. Cantwell didn't look so squirrelly, holding a .45. He held a briefcase in his left hand. He raised his right arm and the muzzle of that heavy piece touched my sweaty forehead with a cold metal kiss. He thumbed back the hammer and it sounded like the crack of a whip in that narrow space. The soles of my shoes glued themselves to the ground. I tried not to move a muscle.

I said, "We come looking for you, mister."

Cantwell grunted. "Well, I sure as hell wasn't expecting you two jerks to show up. I figured you'd both be on your separate ways out of state by now after what happened at Fatty's."

From behind me, Hank piped up. "We've come to set things right, T. J. This is one hell of a tawdry mess you dragged me into, you conniving bastard."

"Uh, hillbilly," I said quietly, "you might want to tone it down a notch, what with the man aiming a gun at my head."

Cantwell's eyes were cold as ice and so was his voice. "How did you boys know I was going to be here? No, wait. I get it. You were outside Fatty's when I called Straight Johnson."

I nodded. "You on the beam now, brother. Fatty will be skulking around here, I expect."

Cantwell sighed. "I know. Why the hell do you think I'm hiding behind a tool shed when I've got the power of the U.S. Government behind me? But that doesn't carry much weight in Louisiana." He made a disgusted sound deep in his throat. "This is a thieves paradise and I'll be glad to be gone."

I said, "Mr. Cantwell, Muddy Waters ain't no threat to you, so why don't you lower that gun?"

His narrowed eyes sized me up along the gun barrel. Then he blinked and lowered the .45.

"I guess I do owe you for starting that rumpus at Fatty's, dropping those boyos into that pool so I could get away. That was quick thinking.""

Hank said, "Thanks for sticking around to help."

Cantwell just shrugged that off. "You were doing okay. I had work to do."

I nodded at his briefcase. "You're getting Fatty's ledger to Washington, D.C. You got guts, G-man, I'll cut you that, showing up at Fatty's house like you done. I admire you, I'll tell you right. You a squirrelly little one but you got damn big balls, son."

Cantwell said, "There are people in Washington, at the Department of Justice, who need everything they can get to put these bosses away."

A train whistle carried through the dawn from not too far away. I judged it to be less than a mile. In the time since Hank and me had left the tracks, the dawning light had seeped into the space between the sheds and the depot, though we were out of sight from anyone else. When the train whistle hooted, Cantwell did the natural thing without thinking and for a second his eyes flickered in that direction. I thought on making a move to take him. I don't like for people to point guns at me. And I needed me a gun. But his eyes came back to me before I could try anything.

He said, "Look, both of you, my job for Fatty was doing whatever he told me to do. He sent me down to proposition you,

Hank. If I hadn't done that, I'd have lost my job and my cover and I'd have had to go back to Washington empty-handed."

"That still don't make it right," Hank said. "And what about my songbook?"

"What about it? I don't know anything about a songbook. And consider this, Mr. Williams. I wouldn't be in the danger I'm in if it weren't for you. I nicked Hewitt's ledger and was set to get the Buie woman's records from Straight Johnson and quietly slip out of town. But look at me now, slinking around like I'm the criminal. Everything turned to shit after you shot that man at the motel and stuffed his body into a closet. What in God's name possessed you to do that?"

Hank looked like he couldn't believe what he was hearing. "Me? I didn't kill that feller!"

"If you didn't, then someone sure as hell built a fine frame for you."

Gauging ways I could take Cantwell, I spoke up.

"Look here, sir. You're in deeper shit than you think you're in. You got that boy Straight Johnson to double-cross Delilah and bring you her books. Hell, if Fatty don't skin you alive, Delilah will."

He started to say something to that, but stopped when we heard a car turn into the empty lot at the end of the walkway. The car came to a stop, and Cantwell started to look in that direction.

I swung out my left hand fast enough to snatch the .45 out of his hand. At the same time I brought up my right hand, with the palm open, and caught the side of his head and smashed it hard into the side of the shed. There was a *thunk!* and his knees buckled.

I said, "Jive son of a bitch. Don't be pointing no guns at Muddy Waters."

But I was talking to a cat who'd been KO'ed. I stepped aside and he slid to the ground.

Hank said, "Whoa!"

I handed him the .45. "Here, hold this."

He took the gun. Moving fast, I unhitched Cantwell's belt and yanked it from around his waist. I used it to tie his ankles real tight, then I pulled the handkerchief from his breast pocket, rolled it into a ball and stuffed it into his mouth. He groaned, starting to come around.

Hank said, "Let me," and he rapped the .45's barrel across the side of Cantwell's head.

The G-man bumped his head against the pavement and stopped groaning. He started to snore.

I picked up the briefcase and snapped it open. Wasn't nothing inside except a ledger book. I snapped the briefcase shut and snagged the .45 from Hank's hand.

I said, "Let's go. Be careful."

I left the walkway and stepped into the corner lot with Hank right on my heels. I was doing an imitation of Cantwell, holding the .45 in my right hand and the briefcase in my left.

The car we'd heard was a cream-colored '51 Packard. The rear door opened and Straight Johnson stepped out.

He wore a Panama suit with a matching vest, slacks and white shoes, and a Panama hat. The white suit made his black skin blacker. He let on that he saw me and the hillbilly while he made a production out of lighting a cigarette with a gold pocket lighter. Sunrise was minutes away. Near the depot, folks were moving about and there was more traffic; people heading to work, delivery trucks, buses making stops. Kids pedaled by on their bicycles. No one was paying attention to this vacant lot. The train whistle piped up again. A longer hoot than before, drawing closer.

The Packard idled almost without sound. As me and Hank walked toward it, I got a look inside the car.

The little blond wench, who'd been hanging on Delilah Buie's arm that night at The Boogie Inn, sat erect in the front seat with both her hands on the steering wheel, looking pretty as heck, dolled up and proper in a chauffeur's uniform, complete with a visor cap.

Delilah sat in the rear. She wore a black summer dress with a low neckline. She wore a necklace with a ruby at her chocolate throat, and a white straw hat with a broad brim. She smoked from a long cigarette holder.

Straight exhaled cigarette smoke in two sharp streams from his nostrils, and our eyes locked through the smoke. I thought about those movies where pirates have sword fights. You know, like with Errol Flynn. I thought about the nasty *clink!* the steel makes when they cross swords in a duel. Locking eyes with Straight Johnson was like that.

He said, "Well well well. Wasn't expecting you."

I said, "You're the second person's told me that this morning. Reckon it's a day for surprises."

Hank strutted up to stand alongside me like he was cock of the walk, feeling ten-foot-tall and bulletproof after seeing what I'd done to Cantwell.

He said to Straight, with a smile that was a leer, "The fella you were expecting, old son, why he's been incapacitated."

Straight regarded Hank. "What are you doing here, chalk? I don't like hillbillies. Thought I made that clear."

"I'm looking for my songbook. I got all tangled up in this mess and someone stole it. I aim to get it back."

Delilah spoke through the open car window. "Mr. Williams, we don't have your songbook and I'm sure I don't know what happened to it. I hope you believe me." Again I caught the scent of hash.

Hank scratched the back of his neck. His face got scrunched up. "Well, you were willing to take me in and hide me out. I appreciate that. But you and Fatty are hooked up. That's why Fatty sent me to your uh, establishment. I'm all mixed up."

Straight leaned back against the rear fender of the Packard and crossed his ankles like he was relaxing but while he drew on his cigarette, his other hand lingered by the lapels of his jacket.

"Boys, you're in the wrong place at the wrong time. Going to be some blood spilled here this morning."

That's when I motioned with the .45, keeping it pointed at the ground.

"Anyone shooting at me today, I aim to shoot back." I said to Delilah, "I knew you'd be here."

She studied me from under the wide hat brim. "Good morning, mister blues." The sound of her voice warmed me where I'm a man. When Delilah spoke, I heard Ella Fitzgerald and Billie Holiday.

I said, "I knew Straight wasn't about to sell you out. But he took a shot at me outside your place yesterday."

Straight drew on his cigarette. "If I'd shot at you, man, you'd be dead."

I said, "Not if you was just aiming to send me a message. I don't know what's what between you two, but it ain't about dough. You wouldn't sell her out."

Delilah said, "Knock it off, both of you. Yeah, Muddy, I let Straight into my bed on occasion. But he knows it's for fun, is all. I like having my fun in bed." She leaned forward and lightly caressed the blonde's neck. "Ain't that right, Lacy?"

The "chauffeur" kept both hands on the wheel, her eyes dead ahead. "Yes, Miss D," was all she said in a small voice.

I said, "And what about us, you and me?" and I had trouble believing my own ears, but it was a question that came naturally since I'd been thinking on this woman so heavy even with everything that was going on.

She smiled like the picture of that lady, Mona Lisa. "You were fun too, Muddy." She leaned back into her seat and arched an eyebrow. "You *did* have fun?"

"Oh, yeah."

She had me tongue-tied, and this was a hell of a place for that to happen.

I looked up the street toward the alley where we'd left Ava and Driveabout, but there was no sign of them. I hoped they were holding steady like they said they would, staying out of sight but ready to back us up.

Delilah said, "Hell, Muddy, I run a whorehouse, and you're a road runnin' ladies' man. I know we was hot, baby, but don't fall for me, mojo man. I'm too much like you."

"Yeah, baby." I grinned. "Reckon you are."

Straight and Hank were pretending not to hear any of this. They pretended to be looking about this way and that, watching for trouble. Straight looked ready to shoot any trouble down that came his way. The lines of Hank's narrow face and his thin body were tightened up like a guitar string tuned too high.

Hank said, "Uh, Muddy. I'm nervous, standing out here in the open."

I said to Delilah, "The hillbilly's right. Fatty knows that Cantwell and Straight are fixing to catch this train. Fatty won't mind getting his hands on your books. He'd have the dirt on you then. That would come in handy, keeping you in line."

Delilah raised a compact to her face and while she studied herself in the small mirror and powdered her nose, she smiled. "Straight came to me soon as that G-man approached him."

"Sounds like Straight's a loyal cat."

"I bring that out in my men. People should be able to trust each other, don't you think?"

The train whistle cut through the morning air like a butcher's knife. We couldn't see the train beyond the depot building, but the sounds—the clatter on the tracks, a bell ringing, steam spurting—

got louder as it pulled into the station. The streamliners had taken over on the main lines, but for the most part these country lines still used old coal-burner locomotives. Black smoke sooted the air.

I said, "Delilah, you and Straight were setting Cantwell up. He thought he had Straight on his line and all the while the two of you were fixing to hi-jack this briefcase when he showed up here."

Beside me, Hank chuckled. "We beat them to it, didn't we, Muddy?"

Delilah snapped the compact shut and swung cat-like eyes on me. Even at sunrise, in public, the woman had bedroom eyes. And when our eyes met, it wasn't like the clink of steel but more like a caress.

"Muddy, I can make far better use of that ledger than any old Justice Department. One of these days soon, us coloreds are going to have more freedom in this society."

"Say what?"

"That's right. Segregation, in another ten or fifteen years it's going to be a thing of the past. Coloreds and whites will go to the same lunch counters and the same schools and drink from the same water fountain. And one fine day, a Negro will be President."

I said, "D, you best back off that hash, girl. And what's any of that got to do with this?"

Straight Johnson hadn't shifted his position from leaning against the Packard, and his fingertips stayed near the open front of his jacket.

He said to me, "You're an ignoramus, nigger."

Delilah said, "Hush that fuss, sugar. I'm explaining something to the man." She said to me, "I'm getting a jump on things, Muddy, by ten or fifteen years. I ain't got time to wait. My time is *now*. I'm going to be the first black boss of Shreveport. I've got my mind set on more than just running the rackets in darktown. Getting my hands on Fatty's ledger, all his dirty financial dealings and payoffs, that's the way for me to kick things off. I'll make his contacts into my contacts. I'll know every little secret that fat man's got."

I nodded. "That ledger is the edge you need."

"Do you have it?"

"I've got it."

"Are you going to hand it over?"

It was a question, but Straight's eyes were boring into me like the beams from a science fiction ray gun, waiting on my answer. And it had better be the one they wanted to hear.

I sent her a grin. "Hell yes, I want you to have it. Why do you think I lifted it off Cantwell? I ain't got no use for G-men. Them big changes you were talking about? They ain't happened yet and until they do, I'm keeping my distance from the government best I can."

Hank spat on the ground. "Amen to that. That son of a bitch Cantwell, he had it coming for the way—"

I said, "Cork it. Let's get this done."

Straight stepped away from the car. He came toward me with his left hand out. "I'll take the briefcase."

The fact that I was holding Cantwell's .45 was the only thing keeping him in line. I don't cotton to gunmen ordering me around. I looked at Delilah and she gave me a nod that said, *I know he's rubbing you wrong, Muddy. But let's get through this. Hand it over.*

So I did

Straight took the briefcase and stepped back.

A shot rang out.

I heard the spit of snapping glass and a small voice from inside the Packard cried, *Oh!*"

I hit a crouch and brought up the .45 and I thought, *Delilah's been hit!* My eyes whipped around, looking for where the gunfire had come from.

Delilah wasn't shot. She was reaching forward to the girl behind the steering wheel.

Lacy sat with her back straight. There was a bullet hole in the windshield, a single small hole with a spider web of cracks reaching out from it, and the same bullet had put a hole in the center of Lacy's forehead. A dribble of blood oozed from the black hole. Her eyes were wide open. When Delilah touched her, the girl in the chauffeur's uniform slumped sideways onto the front seat, below my line of view.

Delilah made a sad sound in her throat.

Hank was pressing himself close to the ground, trying to make the smallest possible target of himself, looking everywhere at once. His eyes were crazy scared, waiting for the next bullet.

Straight unholstered his .38, but that's as far as he got.

Fatty Hewitt's voice said, "Drop those guns, both of you, or you're both dead." He had to raise his voice to be heard above the commotion of the train drawing up to the platform on the other side of the depot. He emerged from behind one of the sheds.

Wiley and Macklin, who each held a pistol, flanked him to either side.

Straight considered the situation, then he dropped his pistol and raised his hands. I did the same. Wasn't much else I could do. Hank stayed where he was, close to the ground, bug-eyed.

Fatty advanced with his boys. The sun was finally showing itself from behind the depot, and the sunshine made Fatty's face seem red and sparkled off the beads of sweat at the end of his nose.

Delilah said, "Lord Lord," in a sad voice like she was crying, but there were no tears. "You didn't have to kill this poor child."

Fatty pulled out a hanky from his back pocket and dabbed at the sweat on his nose. "I'm sorry about that, Miss D, but I couldn't stand by and see you take what's rightfully mine."

His hands raised, Straight Johnson said, "You could have shot out a tire. You didn't have to smoke her."

Fatty said, "Naw, I had to make a point." He sneered at Delilah. "Mark my words well, bitch. Fatty Hewitt runs Shreveport, not some goddamn uppity nigger bitch. You best remember that from here on. If you ever fuck with me again I will snuff you out without even thinking on it, just like I did your little whore. Now do I have your attention?"

Delilah said, "More than you know."

Nobody had come running at the sound of the shot. They hadn't heard it . . . or they had, but they knew Fatty and his gunsels were about and nobody wanted trouble.

I was eyeing the .45, where I'd dropped it, but there was no way I could make a move for it with both of Fatty's gunmen watching me.

Fatty was saying, "I sure didn't want things to turn sour between us, Miss D. We've had a good relationship for some considerable time."

She said, "Sure we have. Until you sent a bunch of Ku Klux Klanners over to burn me out. That's why you sent Hank to me. You wanted to know where he was. Hank Williams was going to perish in a whorehouse fire. But that's *my* whorehouse, goddamn you. I've run the rackets in darktown and you get your cut. But I won't do business with someone who'd try to burn me out, just to kill an innocent man."

Fatty said, "That's quite a speech." He looked to Hank. "It was nothing personal, son."

Hank moaned. "Like hell it ain't personal. It's my life you tried to snuff out, you fat buzzard."

"Watch it," said Fatty. "Anyway, Miss D, I don't think I have to worry none about what Hank knows anymore, now that I've got my ledger back. I saw the way that G-man was trussed up back there like a Thanksgiving turkey. Very impressive. Who did that?"

I said, "I did."

He said, "Yes, very impressive, Muddy. I must say I'm relieved to see that you gentlemen made it out of your predicament in the bayou."

"I remember you laughing."

"You've got to admit, son, it was amusing. I mean, you and your alligator shoes and them gators." He interrupted himself with a wave of his hand. "Aw, the heck with it." His voice and his eyes grew cold. "Everybody here knows what I want." He turned to Straight. "I expect it's in that briefcase you're holding."

Hank drew himself up from the ground, as if he'd reached down deep and found some courage. "Fatty, you ain't the only one showed up here looking for something."

This made Fatty frown. "Now what the hell is that supposed to mean?"

"Someone stole his songs."

"Well, don't look at me. I'm mighty sorry to hear that, son. Yes sir, mighty sorry. You're a great artist. But Hank, you can always write new songs."

Hank made his moaning sound again. "Fatty, it don't work like that. I've got to get my songs back. If it was you who took them—"

"I don't know nothing about your damn songbook, sonny," said Fatty. "So don't get me riled. I will take my leave of you fine people and let you continue your business . . . after I get my ledger." He raised an arm and pointed at Straight as if he was picking the boy out of a lineup. "You. Bring the briefcase to me now."

Chapter 19

Hank

Fatty stood with his ham-sized hand out, and Straight Johnson approached him with the briefcase extended.

Muddy stood next to the open rear window of the Packard, thus blocking my view of Delilah.

Ever since me and Muddy escaped from that damn bayou and got away from those gators, I hadn't been able to think about anything except my songbook. That is, until Wiley and Macklin pointed their guns square at us. They stayed to either side of Fatty, just behind him.

I wished I was somewhere else. I've had guns pointed at me before and it's like this. The whole damn world freezes to a stop around you when someone's aiming a piece at you, and you can't think about anything but that these could be the final seconds of your life depending on what the asshole holding the gun decides to do.

Then hell started popping faster than a frog can snap a fly. I'm going to set down here exactly the way I remember things happening, but it's important that you bear in mind that everything happened faster than it takes you to read about.

Anyway, here's what happened.

Wiley and Macklin had their killer eyes glued on Straight Johnson, who walked up to Fatty as he'd been told. When Straight was directly in front of Fatty, he swung the briefcase up faster than Joe Louis delivering a hard right. He held the briefcase in both hands and smashed it into Fatty's face.

Fatty cried, "*Ow!*" He stumbled back, holding his face with both hands. I saw blood. His nose was bent.

Straight threw the briefcase aside and dodged around behind Fatty, reaching beneath his jacket. Wiley and Macklin were trying to angle a shot at him around Fatty, who kept getting in their way. Straight bobbed like a dancer.

Fatty stopped pawing at his beak and let the blood flow. He grabbed for hardware under his jacket. But Straight had already whipped out a matching .38 to the one he'd thrown aside earlier. Dang if he hadn't been wearing *two* guns in shoulder holsters under that Panama suit, and the gun came out blazing.

Pow!-pow! and Wiley did a funny dance like he was learning to shimmy, then his legs locked and he fell. Macklin fired and missed. A ricochet whistled. Muddy crunched low, reaching for the .45, which he'd dropped.

As for me, I decided not to bolt. With bullets flying, the safest place was pressed flat to the ground. That's what I did. But I saw everything.

Straight didn't give Macklin time for a second shot. His .38 barked once, twice, three saffron flashes that licked out from the .38's muzzle and every slug caught the hood square in the chest and punched him back one-two-three, spraddle-legged. Then Macklin folded to the ground.

Fatty let loose an angry shout that sent blood from his busted nose spraying like spittle, and he tracked his gun around toward Straight. Muddy got his fingers around the butt of the .45 and came up to a standing position in front of the open rear window of the Packard. He started to bring up the .45.

From inside the Packard, Delilah said quietly to Muddy, "Down."

Muddy turned his head and whatever he saw inside the car made him throw himself to the ground, next to me.

A shotgun blasted from inside the Packard and, from where I was, it looked like the full load caught Fatty in the face and blew his head clean off. Only it wasn't so clean. His head exploded like dynamite set off inside a pumpkin. He was lifted off his feet and dropped like a giant water buffalo.

Yes, there was a noisy locomotive a couple hundred feet away. And I'm sure there were traffic noises from the street. But the total *quiet* that descended after that was like time stopping.

There I was, bent close to the ground. There were three freshly fallen corpses, sprawled and bleeding. There was Straight Johnson, stooping down to retrieve the pistol he'd dropped. And Muddy, rising from where he'd crouched to allow Delilah a clear line of fire.

The first sound that came through to me were the flies buzzing around the heap of bloody clothes that was Fatty Hewitt's body. The flies were feeding at the strawberry jelly that had been his head. I burped bile and turned away, close to puking.

The rear door of the Packard opened and one shapely, nyloned bronze leg appeared, then the other, and Delilah emerged. Even holding the shotgun in one hand and a couple of fresh shells in the other, she looked like a queen alighting from a carriage. The black dress shimmered where it curved to her lush bosom and her hips.

A full-fledged gunfight is bound to draw onlookers soon as it's finished, no matter what the circumstance. An array of curious, nervous, excited faces of men, women and children were peering now from windows and around the corner of the depot.

Delilah broke the shotgun expertly, popped out the spent cartridges that were still smoking and reloaded. She clicked the shotgun shut with a snap and glanced my way.

"You can get up now, Mr. Williams. It's over. Are you all right?"

I said, "Jumping Jesus." My brain wasn't the only thing that was bumfuzzled. My mouth didn't seem to be working so good either.

Muddy said, "The hillbilly's okay, looks like. We're musicians. Ain't used to life in a shooting gallery."

Delilah held the sawed-off shotgun with its butt plate

balanced at her hip, and with the flicker of a sassy smile she looked like a million bucks. "You moved right when I told you to, bluesman. And I expect you'd have used that .45 if you'd had the chance."

Muddy chuckled. "Well, thanks for not blowing my head off." His eyes swept across the fallen bodies. "Looks like you just took over the rackets in this town."

"That was my intention, though I certainly never expected for harm to come to poor Lacy," and her gaze dropped into the car's interior.

As for me, my rattled brain was getting back on track.

Rising from my prone position, I said, "Look here. No matter how good a fix Fatty had with the cops, they'll be here in no time once they get word he's dead. I don't know about you, Muddy, but I aim to make myself scarce."

Muddy glanced up the street in the direction of the alley and he raised his arm as if flagging a taxicab in the big city. He said, "We're supposed to have a ride."

Right then, a quavering voice from the direction of the depot said, "Freeze!"

Talk about being blindsided!

My eyes jerked around with everybody else's at the sound of that shaky command and for a moment, I couldn't believe my eyes.

It was the cop from Crowley. He'd been in bad shape the night before at that rest area where Ava and I had faced him down and Muddy had KO-ed him in the bushes. But now he looked even worse. His uniform was dirty and disheveled and there were grass stains at his knees, most likely from his last encounter with Muddy. He'd stepped from around the far corner of the depot, shielded from us by the Packard, and he'd advanced while the shooting was in progress. Another bandage, wrapped around his head, and a badly swollen left eye that looked more purple than black now joined the bandage at the side of his head. He was balancing himself on wobbly legs and pointing his long-barreled .44 revolver at us with an arm that shook like a man with palsy. It would have been an amusing sight, I suppose, except for the gun.

Delilah stood there, bold and sassy, with one hand on one hip and her other index finger curled around the trigger of the shotgun aimed skyward, balanced at her other lush hip.

She said, "Well well well. What do we have here?"

Jerry the cop muttered, "Y'all stand where you are and let your guns drop, hear?"

From off to the side, Straight Johnson said, in an even voice, "Go fuck yourself."

The shaking gun stayed pointing in the general direction of me and Muddy, but Jerry threw an offended look at Straight.

"You shouldn't ought to talk to me like that. I'm the law."

I said, "You've seen him before, Delilah."

Muddy added, "That's right. You just don't recognize him without the hood on his head."

Delilah said, "Oh, now I remember."

Jerry was waving his gun from side to side and shouting at Muddy, "You been causing me a world of shit, nigger, ever since you done what you done to my wife and my child back in Crowley."

Muddy said, "Your child is full-growed. Put down that gun, fool."

Jerry waved his pistol at me. "And I know who you are now too, nigger lover. You assaulted me with a whiskey bottle when I was on police business."

Delilah made a rude sound. "You was on Klan business, copper. If Klan business and cop business is the same business, then that's damn well going to change now that I'm running the show."

Jerry's head started shaking back and forth as if this would clear his mind. "My head hurts. They told me them morphine pills would work 'til I got home to Crowley." He lowered his arm to his side and the pistol fell from his fingers. He said, "Oooh, I don't feel so good."

Straight holstered one of his two guns, leaned over and picked up the one Jerry had dropped.

"Dumb ass chalk. Any one of us could have burned you down three times over."

Jerry touched his head and winced. "I just come to catch this train out of here, then I seen him"—his eyes settled on Muddy—"and I knew I had me one last chance—"

The train whistle hooted. Onlookers had left the windows of the depot and we again had the vacant lot to ourselves.

I said, "Officer, what you've got is one last chance to catch that train. It's a new day, Jerry. I intend to make the most of it, and I suggest that you do the same."

His eyes seemed to focus a bit then, first on me, then over my shoulder on Muddy. "But this here blues singer got my wife in my own dang bed, and he got my daughter—"

I stepped up to Jerry and placed a hand on his shoulder. "Man, get yourself a new wife. Get your daughter to a convent. But damn, bo, guns ain't no way to settle it. You won't be doing nothing right by getting your own self killed."

His eyes caught mine and he nodded and started to speak.

Straight stepped up behind him and clubbed Jerry from behind with the butt of his pistol. Jerry's eyes rolled and he fell onto his face and did not move, but commenced making little blubbering noises. Tiny wet bubbles formed and burst on his lips.

Straight said, "I don't know which I despise more, Klansmen or cops." He holstered his second pistol, which left him still holding Jerry's .44.

We were awash in guns.

Muddy slipped his .45 back under his belt. Looking down at Jerry, he said, "There's one bad luck child," then he picked up the briefcase, which Straight had tossed aside after attacking Fatty with it, and he extended the briefcase to Delilah. "Here you are, sister. Your key to the city."

She took the briefcase from him and said, "Did you check inside?"

"It's there." But he didn't act surprised when she cracked the case open and peered inside. When she snapped the briefcase shut, Muddy said, "So what's next?"

Sirens could be heard in the distance, from several directions, closing in fast. Then came a lengthy blast of the train whistle, and the chugging and clanking of the locomotive drawing from the station.

"Right now," said Delilah, "me and Straight are going to beat that train getting out of town."

Straight reacted like that was his cue. He strode past her and snagged the shotgun from her hand, and she turned and followed him to the car.

Muddy said, "Hold on, doll. Don't leave without saying goodbye."

He caught Delilah by the waist and tugged and she came about smoothly because she wanted to, and her arms snaked around him, her tapered fingers met behind his head and she drew his face forward for a kiss while their bodies were together, and when their lips locked it was one of those kisses that's deep and the cheeks ripple because the tongues are busy. That kind of a kiss. Hot stuff.

Me, I had my own ideas. I was thinking, *Wiley and Macklin! When I found that body in the motel, these boys were johnny-on-the-spot, pretending to be FBI agents, right there in the same cabin where my songbook had been stolen from.*

I went first to Macklin's corpse, then to Wiley's and gave each as quick a frisk as I could. It wasn't very pleasant, what with the flies and messing through a dead man's pockets. I didn't find my songbook on either one of those dead dummies. But I had to check, and while I did that I kept an eye on everything going on around me. I'd had enough surprises to last me a dozen lifetimes.

Muddy and Delilah parted and she continued to the Packard, where Straight had removed the chauffeur girl's body from the front. He held her corpse as you would a sleeping child and when Delilah was settled in, Muddy assisted Straight in easing the poor girl—she looked so tiny—into the car so that Lacy was stretched across the back seat. Delilah tenderly cradled those blood-smeared blond curls. She looked at me. The morning sunlight glinted off a single tear that rolled down one of her smooth chocolate cheeks.

She said, "Mr. Williams, I apologize for any misfortune you have endured during these past several days."

I said, "Wasn't your fault, Miss Buie. You're one of the good guys, way I see it. They was messing with you as much as they were me. I blame that rascal Fatty and that klucker cop for my troubles, not to mention my Uncle Sam."

The sirens were getting closer. I've been out west where you can hear coyotes and wolves howl in the near distance. The sirens sounded like that.

Straight was behind the Packard's steering wheel. He said, "They ain't trying out those sirens for the hell of it."

Delilah said, "Hold on, baby," and she spoke to Muddy. "I've just got to know, bluesman. I know why Hank's here. He wants his songs, and I hope he finds them. But you . . . why did you risk your life by showing up here this morning?"

Muddy seemed to chuckle at himself; something he wasn't real comfortable with, I could tell.

He said, "The hillbilly here's got some crazy notion about people falling for each other. Happens to him all the time, he says. You're working some powerful mojo, woman. And you worked it on me."

She said, "You put your life on the line for me. I won't ever forget that, Muddy. If you're ever back in Shreveport—"

Muddy chuckled again. "Now I reckon that's bound to be one damn long time coming. But good luck to you, Miss D." He tapped the car roof with the palm of his hand to signal Straight, and he said to the back of that man's head, "You take good care of her, man, or the hammer falls between you and me."

Straight Johnson's only response was to feed the Packard some gas and ease the car around in a U-turn.

The Packard drove off with no one trying to stop it. There were vehicles parked at odd angles in the street. A gathering crowd of onlookers, drivers and pedestrians who were inching forward to gawk at what had just occurred, at the sprawled bodies, but so far they were keeping their distance.

Delilah's face was visible in the Packard's rear window, twisted around and looking back at Muddy.

Then the Packard was gone and it was just me and Muddy Waters standing there, surrounded by dead guys and one beat-up cop. More folks were joining the gawkers by the second and the sirens were loud, two blocks away at most.

I started to say something, and saw that Muddy was looking up the street. A Yellow cab came tearing out of the alley, taking the turn on two wheels. I saw the plume of white smoke from burnt rubber as Driveabout swerved out of the turn and raced down the street toward us, navigating around slower vehicles while picking up speed. Driveabout knew how to work the wheel.

When that Yellow glided to a stop beside us, it wasn't with a screech of tires but with the perfect smoothness of a Presidential limousine easing in for a pickup at the White House.

Driveabout's good-natured voice called, "Like I told you, boys, once the shooting stops, we've got you covered like dew on the ground." He sounded like a fella having the time of his life.

In the front passenger seat, Ava was leaning over, showing her shapely backside to the world as she thrust open the rear door for us. She couldn't pry her eyes from the human remains scattered across the lot. Her pretty face was flushed and she was breathing heavy.

"We saw everything."

Muddy said, "Good, then we don't have to talk about it."

I just wanted to get the hell out of there. The train had left the station and the crossing signal had ceased its clanging, leaving those sirens to wail like a vise squeezing my head. I felt his hand at my back and Muddy gave me a forceful push. I tripped into the cab. Muddy had flung himself in after me and the cab was speeding away before he even got the door closed. The stalled vehicles and the faces of onlookers became a blur as we were rocked back in our seats.

I glanced out through the rear window and just about peed in my pants (*and I ain't kidding!*) when I saw two police cars speeding in on the train station from one-half block behind us, their sirens and flashing lights going.

"They're on us," I cried. "We're going to be killed in a police shootout!"

"Reckon some of us are born to be bad," Ava said in a breathless voice, which she had to raise to be heard above the shifting gears and climbing engine noise. "Drive, baby!"

I muttered, "I should have run when I had the chance."

We took a corner in a skidding turn and I grabbed hold of the loop over the door to keep from being tossed into Muddy's lap. When I looked out the rear window again, the cop cars were gone and they didn't reappear.

Driveabout made a few more sharp and sudden turns to evade them. He knew the layout of the streets and alleys as only a cab driver can. "Worked on this engine myself. Hoo-doggies!"

Ava wrapped her arms around his neck and planted a kiss on the side of his face. "My daddy would have been proud to know you, darling. After him, you're the best damn wheelman I ever saw!"

We were tooling on a street that went from small businesses to residential within a few blocks. A police car came charging down the street toward us with its sirens and lights wide open. Muddy and Ava hid below window level, so that Driveabout and I looked like just an innocent cabbie hauling a lone fare. Driveabout had eased off on the speed by this time and the cop car screamed past without the men inside giving us a second glance. We continued on at the legal speed and the residences got larger and nicer, indicating that we were on the outskirts of Shreveport.

Driveabout lifted out his flask in the beaded pouch and took a healthy swig. "Reckon this blows my employment opportunities as a cab driver in these parts. Won't take long before those cops do get a description of this cab, and the company will lead them right to me. Damn, she was a good old taxi. I hate to lose her."

Ava said, "Baby, that's how I felt about my Chevy. We'll get you another taxicab, if that's what you want." The breeze rushing through the windows played with strands of her hair, which danced and shone in the morning light. She brought a pack of Luckies from the depths of her big black purse and shook loose and lighted two cigarettes, placing one of them in the corner of Driveabout's mouth. "But starting now, we've got to put these things behind us and move on."

I said, "That's what Muddy says." My heart was starting to beat right again and I was starting to relax.

Ava nodded. "Hank, I hope you understand. It's time for me to go to Nashville."

"Why sure, darling. I understand, of course. Uh, I'm still wanting to help you out any way I can." As our danger was receding, a dark despair had begun to creep over me. I said, "Reckon my songbook's gone forever. Don't know what I'm going to do about that."

Beside me, Muddy drew the .45 automatic from where it rode at his hip. He said, "I know what we can do about it." He thumbed back the hammer and placed the gun muzzle to Driveabout's right ear. "Pull off the road, cracker. That turnoff coming up will do."

Chapter 20

Muddy

Driveabout set his flask down on the seat and placed both of his hands on the steering wheel. "Uh, what's the big idea, hoss?"

The cab slowed and gently glided onto a riding path that cut across the road. I didn't take the .45 from Driveabout's ear. The pathway dipped into a ravine, and took the taxi out of sight of the road. The path narrowed and became bumpy.

I told them, "It's time you two stop acting like everyone's stupid but you. It's the other way around, fools."

Ava's eyes were full of emotion. "Muddy! You're crazy! What are you doing? We just saved your life!"

She looked like she wanted to jump me, gun or no.

Sweat oozed from under the brim of Driveabout's

cap. He braked to a stop and spoke to Ava. "Keep cool, baby. Don't get the man irritated."

"I'm already that way," I told them. "Hank, get out of the car. Take the quail with you."

"Just a sec," Hank said, and he reached blindly into her big purse, brushing aside whatever was there until his hand emerged holding a .38 revolver. He said, "Awash in guns!"

Ava wasn't so tough now. She didn't know what to think, seeing her man with a gun to his head. But she wasn't the kind to go gently.

"What are you fixing to do?" she demanded of me. "I ain't leaving Driveabout."

I took the gun muzzle from Driveabout's ear. I raised the .45 and fired a round through the roof of the taxicab. No one was looking straight at the gun or the muzzle flash would have seared their eyes. The shot sounded like a thunderclap.

I said, "When a man's got a gun, folks are supposed to do what he say."

That got their attention, and sent Hank out of the cab like he'd been kicked with a boot in the ass. He held open the front door for Ava, who emerged lugging that black purse of hers.

She was a pretty girl but you couldn't tell right then because of the way her lips were drawn tight. Her features were set hard. She didn't look at Hank, and she turned angry eyes on me.

"Now what, you . . . you kidnapper?"

I said, "I want you and Driveabout standing side by side so I can keep an eye on you. Hillybilly, bring her around the car. Driveabout, you hand me that piece you're carrying, back over your shoulder, butt first. I want to see you using just your fingertips. Understand?"

Driveabout said, "Are you going to kill us?"

I said, "Do as you're told."

Ava sneered, "Hank, Muddy's losing his mind."

Hank circled his fingers about her upper arm. "Step around the car," he told her, "like Muddy wants."

"Well ain't you the obedient one." She tugged her arm free. "Keep your paws off."

They stepped around the front of the taxi.

Driveabout made a sudden move to grab my gun arm with both his hands. I said, "Stupid," and batted him across the forehead with the barrel of the .45. Then I pushed open the door and he tumbled out onto the ground with a bright red bruise across his forehead.

Ava yelled, "Honey! Are you all right?" and she ran to his side.

With her fussing over him, Driveabout climbed to his feet, brushing away her attentions. I stepped from the cab. I left Driveabout's gun on the front seat, and held the .45. I eased the hammer back down.

Ava was defiant. Driveabout looked bleary. He'd lost his cap. His red hair was like a fright wig. Ava held her purse in front of her like a shield.

I said, "Hillbilly, do you remember at that rest stop last night, when I told you this girl had the heart of a thief?"

"Uh, yeah. I remember."

"Well, here's the proof."

I moved lightning fast, without taking the .45 off Driveabout. I sent my free hand down into Ava's big fat purse. I had to push aside a load of junk to reach the bottom.

She made a shout of half fear and half outrage, but by then I was stepping back and turning to Hank, holding his songbook in my hand. I tossed it to him.

He caught the notebook in both hands and stared down at it, then he looked up at me. He looked at Ava. He looked back down at the ringed binder and thumbed through its pages.

"Well, I'll be." Confusion and disappointment were in his voice. "Ava . . . what were you thinking?"

She still couldn't look him in the face, but the toughness had drained from her quick when the truth was revealed. Her shoulders were slumped in defeat, and her arms hung limply at her sides.

"You know what I've been thinking, Hank. I never made a secret of it."

Hank said, "You told me about your dreams and ambitions. You never told me about *this*," and he gestured with the songbook.

She said, "I just wanted to be a big country music star like you."

"Damn, girl. I got to where I am by writing my own songs, not stealing someone else's."

Driveabout looked pretty much recovered from the clout I'd given him inside the cab, and he wasn't much interested in these words between Hank and Ava. He only had eyes for the .45 in my fist, and concern that its big barrel might swing up and strike him across the head again without warning.

"What are you going to do?" he asked. He wasn't whining, but close to it. "How long have you known that she had it?"

"Not for sure until after everything went down at the train station," I said. "The other ones what could have stole it all crossed themselves off one at a time and shit, they had no reason to want a damn songbook. They was fighting over a criminal empire. Ava, though, she wanted everything those songs could bring."

Then Ava was lifting her eyes to the hillbilly. Her eyes were moist. "Oh Hank, I'm so sorry," she made a move like she wanted to step close to him, for him to console her or something.

But that would have put her directly between me and Driveabout.

I said, "Hold it right there, sister," and I said to Hank, "There's something else she said that got me thinking. She talked on how that dead guy was shot once in the head, once in the heart. But if I heard your story right, you told me that when she came to your rescue, driving her Chevy through the wall of that cabin, that stiff was lying on the floor. How'd she know how he was killed unless she done it? It took some thinking, but it fell into place for me. She's the one shot that man at the motel."

Driveabout snickered at me. "Well, ain't you the colored Charlie Chan."

Hank said to Ava, "I'd appreciate you telling me what you've been up to."

"I will," she said, in a voice that was like a small child's. "I pretended that I didn't recognize you when you checked into the motel, Hank, but truth is I *did* recognize you, and when you were at Fatty's playing your gig that night, I . . . well, I let myself into your cabin with my passkey and . . . well, I went through your stuff."

Hank said, "I'm ashamed of you. That was a bad thing to do."

"I know. I'm ashamed of myself. But when I found your songbook in that suitcase, well, I guess Muddy's right. Mama and Daddy were thieves. I reckon it's in the blood. I took your songbook and I was fixing to have Driveabout take me to Nashville and make like those songs were my own."

I said, "You killed Fatty's boy. You and Driveabout stuffed the stiff in the closet so no one walking by would see it and call the cops. You needed time to scat."

Driveabout slipped an arm around Ava's waist. "Don't tell them anything, sugar. You'll only be incriminating yourself."

Hank said, "Or is she incriminating you? Maybe it was you shot that hood."

Ava said, "No, I killed him. Once in the heart, once in the head, with your gun. Fatty's boys were lurking about the motel to get their hands on the G-man. That guy came into the cabin found me down on my hands and knees, going through Hank's suitcase. I'd just found the songbook and the gun was under some clothes in the suitcase. The guy who came in and caught me, he didn't know there was a gun. He was mean. Half-drunk. He wanted me to . . . well, he slapped me once and he told me to stay on my knees and . . . well, nobody slaps me."

Hank said, "So you gunned him down. Okay, maybe you did have to kill him." Then Hank stared knives at Driveabout. "But you, you're a different story, bub."

"Me?" said Driveabout. "Hell, I've been risking my life to save your hide just to make this little lady happy." He gave Ava a hug to make his point. "I sure ain't done nothing to put you in danger, Hank."

"I told you," said Hank, "it's back to Mr. Williams for you, you snake in the grass. You did *everything* to put me in danger. You wanted to cut out because everything you've been planning has turned to shit and now there's three dead bodies back there at the station that you don't want anything to do with. But at the start, you *wanted* me to find that body in the closet so Ava could come to my rescue like she did, and I'd be indebted to you."

Driveabout gestured with both hands. "Look, hoss, just so you know. I wanted to help out dealing with those hard boys at the motel, but Ava wouldn't let me."

I'd heard enough of these white boys' jive. I put in Muddy Waters's two cents.

I said to Driveabout, "Must have drove you crazy, rube, knowing the quail had the songbook the whole time and she was still making you shadow us and stay in it, risking your life."

Ava batted her eyes at Hank and said, in that that child's voice she was using, "Hank, you're not going to let Muddy hurt us with that gun, are you?"

Driveabout said, "Relax, kid. If they were crazy enough to kill us, they'd have done it already."

I said, "Ain't no harm going to come to either one of you, much as you deserve it."

Hank nodded. He was giving Driveabout the evil eye. "You set me up, you son of a bitch. When you picked me up from Fatty's club after my gig, you brought me to that motel and dropped me off pleasant as you please. You knew I was going to find that body and you knew it was my gun that killed him."

Driveabout sighed. "Reckon I did."

"And I'd never know that I was helping this conniving little bitch until it was too late and the contracts in Nashville were signed, and then Ava would start recording *my* songs as her own."

Ava said, "Hank, I know I made a terrible mistake, but that thug who tried to have his way with me, he had it coming."

Driveabout looked embarrassed. "I didn't mean you no harm, Hank . . . Mr. Williams. Honest injun."

Hank said, "What if it had gone down some other way? Wiley and Macklin, they fed me their cock and bull story about commie agents, but they were ready kill me in a flash if they thought it would get back Fatty's ledger. And the cops? If the police had showed up and found me with a dead man shot with my gun . . . oh yeah, you two set me up right pretty."

Ava eased herself loose of Driveabout's embrace.

"Hank, I know I've been selfish and stupid. But I've been my own worst enemy, don't you think? I did all I could to keep you safe from harm because I felt guilty and I care about you. At the motel, outside that whorehouse and down on the bayou—"

I'd heard enough.

I said, "It ain't Muddy Waters way to stand around listening when I've got something to say. Lighten it up, chick. Before the deal went down at the depot, you had a chance to hold Hank back from going into it with me. I went into it for Delilah. All Hank wanted was his songbook, and you let him walk into that showdown where he could have stopped a bullet instead of fessing up your wrong and handing him back what's rightfully his."

And just like that, Ava no longer was the apologetic little wench. She drew herself straight and sneered at me, "Thanks a lot, Muddy."

I sneered right back at her.

"Don't mention it, doll. See, I got no use for hillbillies, but I reckon this particular hillbilly has been the only partner I've had through some heavy shit. I ain't going to let you do him wrong."

Hank looked like he couldn't believe his ears. "Well I'll be. So we *are* buddies. That's right nice to hear, Muddy. I thought our association had become frayed around the edges."

"Cork it," I said, and I looked at the pair lined up before us just like I wanted them. "Strip," I told them.

Ava turned into a modest female and made a small *"Oh!"* sound and stepped back with one arm across her bosom and her hand moving down toward her front.

Driveabout said, "What kind of crazy shit do you perverts have in mind?"

I drew back the .45 like I was going to pop him again and that hushed him up right quick.

"You ain't my type and this here girl's too damn skinny. I got enough gals coming to me, I don't got to *take* nothing."

"Then what—?"

"I said, strip."

Ava said, "But why, Muddy? Why are you making us do . . . that?"

Hank snickered. "Hell, darling, even a washed up hillbilly singer like me can figure that one out. Muddy and me, we're going to skedaddle and we're traveling light. Right, Mud?"

I said, "That's right, hillbilly. Just me, you and your songbook. Ain't no room for double-crossers. Taking their clothes will keep these two off our track long enough for us to get a fresh start."

Driveabout turned his hangdog eyes on Hank. "Mr. Williams, we don't think you're washed up. Do we, hon?" he asked Ava. "Talk Muddy out of this craziness. Ava and me, we're your biggest fans. We—"

I said, "Write Hank a love letter when you get to Nashville. Now shuck 'em, both of you."

They stared at us, then they traded a look between them. Then Driveabout started loosening buttons and the chick started to slip off her dress.

She snarled at us. "You perverts just want a peek at what you couldn't get." She whisked the blue summer dress over her head like she was a stripper on a runway and tossed it through the open window of the cab. She stood there in a white slip that came down to right above those dimpled knees, showing off fine legs. And she was right, I would have liked a chance to run my hands up those milky thighs and over those firm hips. I would have had some fun with those sweet titties that lifted up under white lace with the nipples poking through like they were saying *Hey, Muddy!* I would have slipped that slip off her and—

The hissing tires of a truck passing by on the road, which we couldn't see, brought me back to my senses.

She was starting to slide the shoulder straps of her slip off her shoulders.

I said, "Stop right there, baby. That's enough. You ain't going nowhere in your undies." I looked at Driveabout. "But you drop trou or I'll drop you."

He did as I said while Ava stood there with her arms shielding her body like before, staring hate at me. It didn't take long for that boy to get bare-ass naked; bare-dick naked is more like it. That white boy's pecker had shrunk up small in his pubes like a scared little ferret peeking out from a bush. Driveabout tossed his shoes and the last of his threads into the taxi. He moved around to crouch behind Ava so Hank and me couldn't see his condition.

"There, you dirty, rotten bastards. What am I supposed to do now?"

I laughed. "What the hell do I care, chump? Find you a groundhog hole and fuck it, if you've a mind to. Whatever you do now be bound to keep you occupied, being naked and all in the broad daylight." I said to Hank, "Get in the cab, man. In the rear. That ought to look right with me wearing a taxi driver's cap."

Ava said, "You mean you're letting us go . . . after what I did?"

I shrugged. "Why the hell not? We're all outlaws here, ain't we? You two will be living high when better folks than you are starving, but it ain't my job to set that right."

Hank held up his songbook. "I've got what I want. I've got my songs back. I've got my life back. Damn, but it's been a wicked forty-eight hours. I don't want no more trouble." He climbed into the back seat of the cab.

I got behind the wheel and I put on Driveabout's cap. I copped a last look at his hangdog expression, which I could see over Ava's shoulder. He looked more like I was stealing his woman than his ride.

Ava called out, "Hank—" but you could tell her heart wasn't in it. She'd lost this hand and she knew it.

Hank didn't pay her no mind. He reached into the front and snagged up Driveabout's flask. He tipped it and took a long sip.

I steered back onto the street and drove us away from there, just an innocent Yellow cab rolling through the morning sunshine. I snapped down the sun visor and, clipped to the back, I found a packet of Dutch Masters with three cigars still in it.

"Well well," said Hank. "Things are looking up."

I handed him one of the cigars, pocketed one for later and fired the third for myself. I drove with an arm resting out the open window, enjoying the breeze and the sun. Yeah, it was a new day.

Hank finished off the flask and settled back and he took his time cupping a match to light his cigar, as if he was enjoying every second of it. He looked like a cocky hillbilly, which he was. The liquor made him that way.

He sent me a lopsided smile in the rearview and said, "Where to, Jeeves?"

"Down the road apiece until we find us a telephone. Ain't got long before this taxi gets red-hot. I sure as hell hope none of them people at the depot were fans of ours, Hank. If they recognized us, they'll tell the cops."

He made a face like he hadn't thought of that. His Adam's apple bobbed. "But we don't look like we do in our publicity photos, not after what we've been through." He was trying to sound hopeful and doing a piss-poor job of it.

I said, "Most likely folks saw nothing but the guns and them dead bodies. Yeah, that's the way of it. If that G-man keeps us out of it, we're clean. And he might do that because of feeling bad about the way he got you into it, Hank. He seemed to me like a cat who'd set things right."

Hank nodded. "We're clear of it, ain't we?"

"Looks that way. Delilah won't say nothing, and she's running Shreveport now."

Hank said, "She's a credit to her race."

I kept my eyes on the road, watching for cops.

We passed a school bus. There were delivery trucks and buses and a few cars on the road, then traffic thinned out after we left the last of the houses behind and drove through the countryside. Up ahead, the sign for a Texaco filling station came into view. Hank saw it, too.

I said, "They'll have a telephone yonder. You walk in and ask to use it. I'll stay with the car and keep it idling, case we need a fast getaway."

Hank rode with his arms stretched out along the back of the

seat, the cigar sticking out from the middle of his mouth, smoking like a chimney. "Hell yeah, a telephone. I've got to call my Billie Jean. She's most likely worried sick about me."

"The boys in my band won't be worried about me, but they'll sure enough be restless to move on and start earning money again."

"Muddy, I'll call the hotel where your band is staying."

"If they ain't there," I said, "I'm giving you Mr. Chess's number in Chicago. He'll know where they went to, and I'll put it together from there."

We cruised past the Texaco station. At the pump, a sharp young lad in a visor cap was taking money from a farmer in a pickup truck. A pair of hound dogs lazed in the shade, swiping at flies with their tails. An old cracker in dungarees sat whittling at a chunk of wood, and he didn't look up. A diner that looked like a log cabin was next to the station.

Hank said, "It's been quite an adventure, ain't it, Mud?"

"Too much of one," I said. "I don't reckon anyone's going to believe what's happened to us."

He let out a cackle. "Shoot, Billie Jean finds out half the stuff we've been up to—like that little spitfire Ava—why, she'd skin me alive."

I was patting down my do-rag, which was getting messed by the air rushing through the windows. "Sure wouldn't do no good for my image," I said, "getting treed by gators, shooting up a whorehouse. Chess would have himself a heart attack and if he lived through that he sure wouldn't have me cutting no more records."

His eyes caught mine in the rearview. "Muddy, I won't ever say nothing about it if you don't."

"Done," I said.

I drove us to a patch of shade beyond the far end of the diner. I killed the engine.

The morning air was hot and already it was sticky. The scent of magnolia was in the air and I smelled salt water from the Gulf. White clouds were like giant balls of cotton in a pale blue sky.

I took out the wallet I'd picked up at the clothing store that Driveabout had taken us to. I peeled off one of Mr. Chess's business cards, which I always carry, and handed it to Hank.

He held the card between two fingers, he read it, then he wagged it like a salute.

"Be right back," he said, and he stepped out of the cab. "And I'll run us down something to wet our whistle while we're waiting on our people to come get us."

I called after him as he was walking toward the diner. "Ask around in there, see if you can find us something with strings on it."

He tossed a look back at me and he was grinning like a happy kid. "Dog, man, down south here everyone's got themself a guitar. I'll latch onto one for a spell. Damn right. It's high time Hank Williams and Muddy Waters got together and played some music!"

And a short time later, that's what we did, sitting there in that patch of shade at a roadside diner outside Shreveport, playing for an audience of ten or twelve who wandered out from the diner and enjoyed every note. We traded off on the guitar, then we traded off singing each other's songs. I did a version of Hank's "Mind Your Own Business" that got him feeling right and damn if he didn't come right back at me with some verses of "Baby Please Don't Go" that was right in the pocket.

You should have heard us.

When we were played out, Hank returned the guitar to the folks he'd bummed it from in the diner and just after that a '52 powder blue Cad convertible with the top down roared in off the highway and sped up to us, sliding into a skidding sideways stop in a cloud of dust.

When the dust cleared, I saw a tight-bodied little blonde behind the steering wheel. She wore a white dress with big black polka dots and a plunging neckline that showed plenty. Lots of jewelry sparkled in the sunlight and red, red lipstick. Young. Real young.

I whispered to Hank, "Damn man, I'll bet you can smell her mama's milk on that baby's breath."

Now it was Hank's turn to look offended. "That there's my bride, hoss. My future wife."

The blonde reached over and pushed open the passenger door and the way she leaned into it, the neckline of her dress opened some more and gave me a good view of firm, ripe peaches that looked like they wanted to spill out.

She said, "Hank Williams, you get your skinny ass in this car this instant. Who's this colored man you're talking to?"

"Howdy, Billie Jean. This here's Muddy Waters. He—"

She said, "Pleased to meet you, I'm sure," and then she forgot I was there and she said to Hank, "You've got some tall explaining to do, mister."

He turned to me and extended his hand. "Well Muddy, I reckon this is where we say *adios*. I can't say it's been a pleasure." We shook hands and his grip was firmer than I remembered it from our first handshake. He said, "But I'm glad we're friends."

"Yeah," I said. "Me, too."

The blonde said, "Hank," and she gunned the Cad's engine.

"Coming, sweetheart."

She barely waited until he was in the car before flooring the accelerator, kicking up another storm of gravel and roaring off so fast, Hank's scrawny frame somersaulted into the back seat. He was holding onto his songbook like he would never let it go. The Cad tore off down that highway like hellhounds were on its trail.

My '51 fire engine red Cad came gliding in off the road, coming toward me smooth as a boat sailing across water. Jimmy Rogers was at the wheel. Elgin rode beside him.

When I saw Jimmy's smile and my ride easing up on me, I could feel the crazy shit already beginning to slide into the past. The world I lived in was coming to claim me.

Epilogue

Muddy

I never saw the hillbilly again.

A couple months after the events I have just related, a letter caught up with me while me and the band were working out of St. Louis. Hank had sent the letter care of the address on Mr. Chess's business card.

He wrote that he was back on the radio, playing on that *Louisiana Hayride*, and reported that things had smoothed out between him and his ex-wife, Audrey, because he was taking my advice and trying to think more on the future, and didn't I wish I was going to marry a girl as pretty as his Billie Jean. He enclosed a newspaper clipping about the daughter of a famous bank robber from the Forties, who'd been arrested during a bank heist in Texarkana. Her partner was killed in a shootout with the police. His name was Jules

LeDoux. Hank had underlined the name and written *Driveabout* next to the article. Ava Proudfoot was in custody. Her and her boyfriend's Plan B for getting to Nashville was to rob a bank for traveling money. I never did find out what happened to her.

It was good hearing from Hank but I ain't a letter-writing type of fellow, so I never did send him a reply. When he married Billie Jean it made all the newspapers because they done it twice, once in a private ceremony and again at one of Hank's shows in a packed auditorium where thousands of fans paid seventy-five cents apiece for tickets to attend. That December he had a song called "Jambalaya" riding at Number One on the charts.

Hank Williams met his maker six months after what happened to us in Shreveport. He died in the backseat of a chauffeured Cadillac traveling down a highway at midnight, hundreds of miles from his home and those who loved him, on his way to play a New Year's show up in Ohio. They say he overdosed. Booze with them goddamn pills. The boy was only twenty-nine years old.

I didn't take any more bookings in Louisiana for quite some time, just to be on the safe side. I sure as hell never heard no more from Jerry and same goes for the G-man, Cantwell, I'm glad to say.

Little Walter's career started hot that summer, but he burned out fast. I hated to see it happen. Within three years, that big fat amplified harmonica sound of his became a regular part of what they call Chicago Blues. Hundreds of harp players came after Walter, trying to copy his sound. Got so you couldn't walk into a club in Chicago without seeing some cat blowing harp in front of a band. But within five years, people got more keen on the guitar as a lead instrument in the blues, with cats like B. B. King coming up. Walter, he could always find work, but when the hits stopped coming and the money dried up, he ended his days living on the streets, hustling. I tried to get him work, but liquor and dope had sucked him dry and fucked him up. Little Walter died in 1968. He never lost that mouth of his and it got him in trouble for the last time in a back alley crap game. He was thirty-eight years old.

Elgin drifted out of the band, the way musicians do.

Jimmy Rogers got himself a good solo career.

As for Delilah Buie, it was twenty years before I saw her again.

I was opening a show for The Rolling Stones at the Astrodome in Houston. There were thousands of people in the audience, hooting and hollering for the Stones, but when my band came on they shushed themselves with respect and dug what I was putting down, and by the end of my set we had those thousands of people on their feet, hot for when the stars came out . . . the stars who had named their band after one of my songs, "Rollin' Stone Blues," which I cut back in 1950. By the 1970's, I'd even added a couple of white boys to my band. Times had changed since the days of The Boogie Woogie Inn in Shreveport. Seemed like everything Delilah had foretold about integration that day in front of the train depot had come to pass.

After we came off stage, I was in my dressing room. It was crazy. A rock 'n roll tour. All manner of frantic, wild goings-on. Musicians came by to pay their respects and other visitors and fans wanted autographs, and them skinny young white girls in feathers and bangles they were calling groupies, and everything going at high volume.

And then, there she was.

Shown in to be introduced to me with some other "leading black civic leaders," as the young man with the Afro said when he made the introductions. They were dressed for the evening and Delilah was looking classy in a floor-length black number, with her hair done up and a ruby choker at her smooth, chocolate throat. The years had been good to her.

She was introduced to me, and we exchanged polite nods and a handshake. For anyone around us, it was a VIP being granted an introduction to the star. She was Mrs. Beaumont.

Our eyes met and we traded a small smile for each other and no one else, and I could tell that inside, under that gloss of respectability, was the same she-panther I'd made wild love to once, twenty years ago. The same woman who had blown Fatty Hewitt's head off with a shotgun. But everything else about her, everything the world saw, was refined. A million years and a million miles gone from those days. I'll put it like this. That night, she wasn't smoking hash.

Then I was being introduced to the next black civic leader, and to the next, and before long they were being politely shown out.

But not before I caught the look from those cat eyes, sent in my direction over a bare brown shoulder just before she slipped from my sight.

That was the last time I saw her.

So I've told my tale.

Now, the great Muddy "Mississippi" Waters is an old man. I lay here, dying of lung cancer, a skeleton wrapped in pajamas, watching my Cubs on the television. Waiting to die.

But when I close my eyes, I can still hear days filled with the hungry whistle of tires traveling down the highway. We're living to play our music every night, rocking smoky joints with low ceilings and neon beer signs and tables full-up to the bandstand. And life has a fine, cutting edge, like it did in '52.

Photo: Sharon Holnback

About the Author

Stephen Mertz is the author of a number of highly praised mystery and suspense novels. He lives in Arizona.

CPSIA information can be obtained at www.ICGtesting.com
Printed in the USA
LVOW101338131211

259204LV00001B/27/P